DEADLY

KARISMA

An
Unfortunate
Lineage

VOLUME
V

A Novel

DEADLY KARISMA

An
Unfortunate
Lineage

VOLUME
V

A Novel

Delaine Christine

Deadly Karisma
An Unfortunate Lineage V

ISBN-13: 978-950563258

Original publication 2016 as Twisted #3 RavenCroft Series under the
pseudonym Vortigern Black. Re-published in 2018 as Trumped: The
RavenCroft Saga, Book Three with revisions under Delaine Christine

Book and Book Cover by DC Johnson
Model Pic by Volodymyr Tverdokhlib, used with permission
Scenic Cover Image by Ulf HÃ¤rstedt via 123rf.com
Interior Model Image by Badmanproduction, used with permission

Kimerah Publishing, Elkhart, IN

Printed in the United States of America.

The Prophecy

Continues...

A dove brought forth shall burst to fly
When she sends a gift through the nigh'

For during a time of memory
Its gift of peace shall set her free.

PROLOGUE

You don't want to miss
the best part
do you?

Ever heard of a love story so twisted that it made you stop dead in your tracks and stare off into oblivion with a blank expression while scratching your head going, "What the 'beep boop?'"

If you haven't before you sure are about to now.

Vortigern Black here.

That's right, I'm back with another tale of RavenCroft love, loss, and intrigue.

Or, at least, we hope.

To be honest I'm not sure this one gets entirely ironed out by the end of it. I mean it does, but it doesn't. I imagine that doesn't make much sense but then neither does this story.

Why might you be wondering?

Because…it's seriously jacked up folks!

Honestly, I just don't know where to begin with this one.

AN UNFORTUNATE LINEAGE

I suppose, to start, I should probably begin by explaining to those of you arriving late to this series about who I truly am because Vortigern Black is not really my name. It's merely an alias which allows me to maintain a certain amount of anonymity while I narrate this story for you, the reader. Officially, I am deep, deep undercover and have been for quite some time. Unofficially, I am a character within this story.

Were anyone to discover who I really am, I would likely wind up in some serious trouble, people. Why?

Because there are some who don't want the RavenCroft's story told and for good reason but we'll get into more on that later. Right now, I have the author riding my back end because she wants me to get you back up to speed on what has been going on in this here vast universal love story of the RavenCrofts since we left off with their cousins, the Blackthornes in the last one. She's being quite insistent on the matter too. So, to get her off my back, here we go.

Back in October Kahner RavenCroft, one of a set of triplets, identical twin to Kalturek, and the eldest of the RavenCroft siblings returned home with a - sort of - fiancée in tow. Along with the bride-to-be came three beautiful children, a questionable past tied up in a lot of personal and emotional baggage, and the unexpected and sudden ability to discern people's thoughts. Upon learning Sable's newfound gifts were because she was expecting RavenCroft children, both she and Kahner had some tough decisions to make. The couple soon married and settled down within the walls of the RavenCroft ranch. This pleased Bastion, the RavenCroft patriarch, for several reasons.

One, because by giving her a new identity and then marrying his son, Kahner, it doubly protected Sable from being found by her former husband, Lionel Radford who happened to be a drug lord with a vast cartel spanning many countries.

Two, because it meant Sable intended to carry the triplets she was expecting to term. Bastion would finally get to be a grandfather for the first time.

And three, because Bastion knew he wouldn't have to worry about the family secret getting out since she was staying within the family fold.

What secret do you ask?

The one where the entire RavenCroft family are gifted with unusual abilities.

That's right, Kahner, and now Sable can discern a person's thoughts. Bastion RavenCroft can do it too, although that's not widely known. Some might call that telepathy or reading minds but that's not exactly what's going on here. As this series progresses to its conclusion this will be explained in more detail.

In the case of Kahner's brother, Kalabernus, who is the second born of the RavenCroft triplets, his ability is more of a curse than a gift, but he recently has found some peace with this. Especially since his gift to see the shadowy demons aided him in thwarting a stalker who had been pursuing a gorgeous and very single woman, by the name of Ariana Davis, all the way from Massachusetts. That very same beautiful lady agreed to marry him shortly thereafter, and they are now awaiting the impending birth of their own child. Or rather … children. That's right, we sort of let that slip in that last story. They're expecting triplets as well but they don't realize that yet.

I could go through and list out everyone's ability here but, that would take too long, and we do have a story to tell. Rest assured all gets explained within. If you'd like a reference of sorts you can always check out the Character List of Suspects at the end of this story. The author of this twisted tale of weirdness has been kind enough to not only give you a listing of who I might be, but she has chosen to add what everyone is capable of as well.

Hehe. I guess the author figured we were starting to get such a plethora of characters that you might need a reference just to keep track.

Yes, indeed, there are a lot of people involved in this story of love and woe. Intended as a suspenseful mix of family drama, and intrigue with supernatural influence, it also happens to be a bit of a mystery. As you read you may notice there is more than one mystery at play here. One of which is to determine who I truly am within.

You might be wondering why all the secrecy over my identity.

Rest assured it's not because I've killed anyone or anything like that.

Shoot, I'm a Boy Scout. I've never done anything wrong. Except for maybe telling a story, I shouldn't be telling. But hey! If a certain person within this family drama had just done what I asked of them in the first place, then I would never have had to break the silence.

On that note, it's time to strap on your weird-o-meter hat and lube up that rusty dial because I guarantee you, things are about to get pretty wild.

Why might you be wondering?

I'll tell you why.

It's because Kahner's identical twin brother Kalturek and his wife Stephanie have become baby crazed. They both want one, they're determined to have one, and they're liable to do just about anything to get one.

Makes a body wonder how far exactly they're willing to go…

Chapter 1

In the last couple of books, I've started the RavenCroft story in the past but there's really no point in going back to the year two thousand this time around. Believe it or not, the author agreed with me for once. We have way too much going on in the present. If we were to go back to try and explain how this tale began then we could possibly create a dimensional time-warp that would destroy life as we know it!

Hahahaha.

Just kidding.

Whaaaaat?

A person must keep their sense of humor, after all. If you really knew who I was you'd completely understand why I said that. Besides, it would complicate the story and potentially give away too much before we get started.

Anyway, it's Thanksgiving weekend of two thousand fourteen and everyone has gathered together at the RavenCroft ranch home for the holiday weekend. As is their tradition the RavenCroft's spent the early morning hours on Black Friday attempting to maneuver around the holiday crowds.

Congregating back at the house with their present's late afternoon, they spent the evening munching on finger foods and playing poker. Bedtime rolled around for the kids forcing Sable and Kahner to break to put them to bed. At the same time, Kalturek's wife Stephanie opted out on the games declaring that they were fraught with a bunch of cheaters.

Of course, Stephanie only said that because she happened to be cheating herself and got caught. I guess she figured it was no fun anymore if they knew.

To get a head start on the next day, she took herself up to the attic in an attempt to locate the Christmas ornaments and lights that she knew everyone would be putting up in the morning. Little did she know she would wind up finding something so much more life-altering than tinsel.

- - -

This was it.

This was their chance.

Heart racing with both excitement and trepidation Stephanie RavenCroft pounded down the stairwell to the kitchen. Carrying an open box filled with paperback books in her arms, she attempted to balance her iPad on top of it as she ran.

"Kalturek," she shouted. Her foot faltered on the last few steps and she nearly fell. The iPad slid from the box and dropped to the floor. She watched as it smashed on the wooden hallway floor. "No!"

"Stephanie? Are you all right?"

Surrounded by his five siblings and their spouses, Kalturek got up from the kitchen table and made his way hastily to his wife's side.

"No, I'm not. I broke it." Swearing angrily, tears began welling in her eyes.

"Calm down, Honey. There's no need to cry or cuss for that matter. I'll replace the iPad if it's broken." Kalturek was grateful his sister-in-law's kids were already in bed. He'd never heard his wife swear like that unless they were fighting.

"No, I won't calm down," she shouted, startling everyone in the kitchen. Her eyes were wild with a mixture of excitement and fear. "I found it. I really did! The answer was right here, and it's been here all this time. She's our only chance and if we don't get to her in time it'll be too late for us."

"What are you talking about?"

"Angel Stryfe! Baby, we must find her before she gets killed. We're running out of time," she said, quickly becoming hysterical.

"You're not making any sense. Slow down and start from the beginning." Being the Sheriff of Loveland County, Kalturek was instantly on high alert after what she'd said. A woman about to be killed? How could she possibly know anything about that? His wife had been up in the attic searching for Christmas decorations for the last several hours.

"There isn't time," Stephanie exclaimed urgently. "They're going to kill her, and we'll lose our chance if we don't get to her first."

"Chance for what? More importantly, who's about to get killed?"

"Angel Stryfe. I've already told you that. Keep up already." Stephanie was becoming frustrated and cross. Her husband didn't seem to understand the urgency of the situation. She failed to realize that in her haste to tell him what she'd discovered, she hadn't fully answered his questions.

Kalturek bent down before her and patiently took her hands in his. "Stephanie, look at me." He waited until she peered up at him with her midnight blue eyes. "You're coming to us with half a story here. Who is Angel Stryfe? Who's trying to kill her? How do you know this? And what has it got to do with you and me?"

Taking a deep breath, Stephanie exhaled. She really hated it when he patronized her. "The books, Kalturek; the books in the box! It's a series called Phenomena, written by somebody called David Pearson."

Bastion RavenCroft, the head of the RavenCroft family, swiveled in his seat near the counter and stared across the kitchen at the couple on the floor.

Uh, oh.

Was it possible he'd been busted?

Kalturek gave his wife an appraising stare. "What does that have to do with this Angel Stryfe? Who is she?" Like his five siblings, Kalturek had been born with what his family believed to be supernatural powers. They each had their own unique ability. In his case, he had the ability to see a kind of aura around people, but it wasn't an emanation like what most who believed in the supernatural would imagine it would be. Instead of a range of colors, Kalturek could see a white or black auric film which often signified when people were having good or bad intentions in any given moment. As Sheriff, his power had been most advantageous in the past just as it was now, for he could see a pitch-black aura around his wife. The darkened aura hadn't been there before she'd gone up to the attic, and that worried him.

"She's an author," he heard her respond.

"I thought you said David Pearson was the author."

"I did." She swore again in exasperation. "Shut up and let me explain."

Shoving Stephanie's hands away, Kalturek stood, glaring down at her. He was losing patience with her. His wife had been getting more irritable of late and increasingly hostile with him.

"I cannot understand what it is you're trying to tell me without all the facts."

Cupping her bowed head with one hand, she snarled in frustration. "You want facts? I'll give you facts. Fact one, this David Pearson is writing about *this* family. Every deep dark secret we have, he seems to know. That includes who has what power and the real story behind how Sable got here."

Kahner's head popped up from where he'd been resting on the table, waiting to get back to their poker game. His identical features to his twin brother formed the same shocked expression that was on Kalturek's face.

"What?" Kahner exclaimed in alarm.

"You heard me." She swiped three books from the top of the box she had carried down and begun shaking them before everyone as she stood. "Fact two, book one tells of your brother Kahner and Sable meeting, getting pregnant, and married."

Sable blanched noticeably.

"Book two tells of your other brother Kalabernus and his new wife Ariana meeting and getting pregnant," Stephanie continued. "And book three … Baby! Book three is about us."

"You can't be serious." Kalturek was incredulous.

Everyone began clamoring toward the box on the floor.

"Are there more copies?" Kalturek's younger sister Mackenzie asked anxiously. Her gaze shifted toward their father Bastion. He appeared oddly subdued considering what Stephanie was telling them.

"No, it's like a continuous fictional series only in different categories or genres; for example, Phenomena for children, for youth, and for adults. These are the first three of the adult series. But Baby, book three…" Stephanie's eyes were alighting with delight. She practically danced in place as she shoved the book in his face. "Kalturek, Honey, all we have to do is find her. We find this Angel Stryfe before they kill her, and we can have what we want," she exclaimed with excitement. "Babies, Baby! We can have children of our own too, just like Kahner and Kalabernus."

Kalturek's youngest brother Drayke jumped in. "When you say just like them, do you mean…"

"Yes! The RavenCroft triplets; Kahner, Kalabernus, and you Kalturek are all meant to have triplets according to these books," Stephanie declared.

Stunned, Kalturek shook his palms before her. "Hold on a minute." He took the book from her and his eyes hastily roamed the dark cover. Opening it quickly, he tried to make sense of what his wife was saying as he scanned the pages. "I don't quite understand. Who exactly is this Angel Stryfe? How can she help us have children?" he inquired, as his brothers, Kahner and Kalabernus began removing books from the box, to investigate the validity of what she was saying.

"Book three, the one about us, it tells about her. It describes her as an author with the ability to foreshadow or see future events."

"You mean, like precognition?"

"Yes, and it also says she knows things without knowing why, kind of like your dad. But here's the real kicker. She's not just a fictional character in a book but a real-life person. I looked her up on my iPad and found her online," Stephanie continued to explain. "I figured if we were real, maybe she was too.

And she is! According to that book you're holding, she's supposedly been writing about us, kind of like this David Pearson author. When I looked her name up online I discovered it's actually true."

"Did you say she's writing about this family?" Bastion said in alarm. "She's actually published something?" Erupting hastily from his chair, the RavenCroft patriarch quickly strode across the kitchen toward them. Taking the iPad from Stephanie, he swiped his hand across the blank screen then began reading as the web page came into view. His expression was grim, his brow furrowing in concentration. He mumbled softly and glanced absentmindedly over at the book in Kalturek's hand. "I don't remember that..." his voice trailed off.

Both Synedra, the youngest of the RavenCrofts, and her husband Nathan gave Bastion an odd look.

"Yes, but it's gonna get her in trouble," Stephanie continued, seemingly distracted with her own agenda. "At least, according to that book she hasn't published her novels yet. As you can see from the iPad there, she's about to. She's been promoting her new series through the Internet and...."

"Oh, no!" Bastion's head shot up from the iPad in alarm. He stared off into space; the look on his face, one of horror.

"Exactly," Stephanie cried, her eyes widening as well, thinking he was likely having the same thought as she was. She shook her finger at Bastion, the iPad, then at Sable. "So, when drug cartel kingpins Kobi and Lionel Radford see their names pop up in conjunction with Kalysta Radford, aka Sable RavenCroft...."

Kahner gave an unflattering yelp of horror at the sound of his wife's real name being repeated from his sister-in-law's lips. No one in the family knew Sable's real name but him and his father Bastion. Her real identity had been kept secret to protect her and her children from her former husband Lionel.

"Dad," Kahner exclaimed in a panic. His wife Sable was now pregnant with his triplets, and he also had her three children to protect. This Angel Stryfe woman was going to get his whole family killed if what Stephanie said was true.

"Stop," Bastion hollered. His deep voice echoed in the kitchen, gaining everyone's attention. "Just everyone stop and calm down. Stephanie, am I to understand you've read through this novel completely?" He pointed toward book three in Kalturek's hand. "And you managed to get through the first three book descriptions on Angel Stryfe's website?" He knew full well she could speed read.

"Yes," she hedged. "I read the first two books of David Pearson's. I started the third but when he referenced what Angel Stryfe's purpose was in the story, I stopped and looked the author up to see if she was a real person. That's when I found her website. I read the first two descriptions of Angel Stryfe's first two novellas. But I only managed to get through part of book three's description before I high tailed it down here. So, all I've read is the beginning where Kalturek goes after Angel to bring her home and..."

Bastion shook his head adamantly. "No, absolutely not. He cannot go."

"But he *must* save her," Stephanie wailed. "If he doesn't then she'll get killed. Then we won't be able to have babies," she exclaimed irately.

Bastion scowled, his lips pursing in aggravation. "Well, geez, Stephanie, it's good to know your reasons for going after her are purely selfish." He continued sarcastically. "Sure, let's go after her for the sole purpose of making sure *you* can have children rather than to try and save her life, and for that matter, protect this family's secret."

Charging toward her father-in-law, Stephanie stuck her finger in his chest, not caring he was nearly a whole foot taller than her. Shooting daggers with her watering eyes, she practically spit as she spoke, her voice laced with venom.

"I've waited nearly seven years to have children with your son. Only now I find out that the only way I'm going to get them is by way of a surrogate. The surrogate in question being the woman in this book by David Pearson and the author of that online series, Angel Stryfe. I will not allow your arrogant cautious nature to destroy my chances."

Astounded, Kalturek exclaimed in surprise. He had never quite seen his wife so hysterical and angry. "What is going on with you?" He could see a black aura around her. It literally pulsed, expanding and thickening about her shoulders and head.

Overwhelmed with frustration and desperation, Stephanie yanked the iPad from Bastion, tapped the screen for the description of book three to open, and shoved it in her husband's face.

"Look! See? It's dated for this year, Kalturek, just like the other two books were, and it's eerily accurate. If this is, in fact, one woman's vision of future events then we have to move fast. Don't you see?" She pleaded with her husband, willing him to understand how serious the situation truly was. "It's dated tomorrow night. If we don't get to her first, then Kobi and Lionel Radford's men are gonna torture, rape, and kill her."

Chapter 2

Whoa! That was intense.

I tell you what, I lived through that excerpt you just read. So, when I got my hands on this story written by its original author and started reading the beginning of it, my mouth dropped to the floor. The events of that moment occurred exactly as described. That's why I told the author of this here story that she needed to keep it, as is, and not change the original writer's take on it one bit. I may not be able to speak to what everyone was thinking, but I can tell you that it's exactly what everyone said. I know this probably doesn't make a whole heck of a lot of sense just yet, but you will start to understand as this story progresses.

Something to keep in mind - and by extension to try and keep straight – is that there are two authors being discussed at this point. The first one is a little-known author by the name of David Pearson who has written a novel series entitled Phenomena. These are the books that Stephanie has found in the attic and was reading. According to what she's said so far, the stories within this adult series are loosely based on the RavenCroft family and the events which have occurred over the past couple of months. Within this Phenomena book series is the third book. This book.

That's right, I said this book. Only it's not this book.

Are you with me so far?

See, this David Pearson guy has written a novel with one version of what is currently happening within this story you're presently reading. As Stephanie just stated, Mr. Pearson tells in detail about an author by the name of Angel Stryfe who is writing about the RavenCroft family. An author who is, it turns out, not just a character within the Phenomena story but an actual person.

That's right, you heard me. A real-life flesh and blood woman by the name of Angel Stryfe. And, yes, it turns out she really is an author too. Someone who appears to have a first-hand accounting of the events which are about to transpire.

Sound familiar?

Can we say, reminiscent of Bastion RavenCroft's ability to know things without knowing why and to foresee future events?

The thing to note here is that though the family is alarmed by the books that have been found, they're even more alarmed to learn of Angel Stryfe and her stories for two reasons. First, because the woman's knowledge of Sable's real identity and her intent to post that information online could cause men from Lionel and Kobi Radford's drug cartel to eventually find their way to the RavenCroft horse ranch. The consequences of which could be life-ending for everyone. And second, because her awareness of the family secret and the eventual release of her stories with that knowledge could bring attention to their family in a way that would be most unappealing.

Unlike the David Pearson author, who was only using their first names with an alias for the last, Angel Stryfe, on the other hand, was using the RavenCroft family name. Many within the family held noteworthy positions within the community. Kalturek and Drayke in particular, as Kalturek was the Sheriff for Loveland County and Drayke was now Loveland County's Prosecuting Attorney. The media circus and ridicule alone would be impossible to overcome if it was discovered they were all characters within her book series.

None of them, however, were as distressed by the news more than Bastion. Let's just say he had his own concerns at the discovery, for he was aware of an additional danger that his children were not privy to. There was a secret organization known only by its investors as Phenom and the men who headed it would be highly interested in the discovery of a real-life family of gifted individuals. They were not openly recognized or sanctioned by the government for they were a covert group intent upon locating individuals with special abilities, retraining them with black op tactical elimination skills, and utilizing them for their own dark purposes. If the men who headed this organization found out about his family, he could lose them all forever and that was unacceptable to him. It was why he'd insisted that his children, as well as their spouses, kept their abilities secret.

How is Bastion aware of the unsanctioned secret facility?

Have patience people, you'll find out soon enough.

But that's not all he has to worry about. You see, the problem we have here is that according to Angel Stryfe's own prediction there is a decidedly small window of opportunity to do anything about what may potentially happen next.

Do you remember what Stephanie said?

They literally only had twenty-four hours.

If any of Angel's story description was true, then it meant she had inadvertently placed a target on her back and Lionel Radford's henchmen were holding the gun. The only concern both Bastion and Kahner had was whether the information could be trusted. In the back of their minds, they knew this could be a ploy to draw them out. The thought didn't make much sense to Bastion though, for if Lionel Radford already knew then why hadn't he simply shown up on their doorstep already?

In the end, Bastion came to a carefully calculated conclusion. Either way, he couldn't sit idly by and allow this author to get killed. Regardless of whether she might be able to help Kalturek and Stephanie to have children, he needed to take immediate action to secure Angel Stryfe's safety. So, he sent his son to go get her and bring her home while wondering the whole time whether she fully realized the danger she'd placed herself in. The real question here was…

-Would his son make it in time?

Oh…I almost forgot to warn you. The author sure didn't though – blasted woman. She didn't have to shoot a paper airplane across the room at my head to get my attention and remind me. Geez!

Anyway, this next bit may get a bit graphic but it's what happened and mostly how it was written originally, so consider yourself duly warned. The author apologizes for the detail, but to truly understand Angel and what she's going through as we progress, then you need to know what happens here.

- - -

Around Midnight
Saturday, November 29, 2014
Pocahontas, Iowa

Waking with a startled gasp, Angel abruptly sat up in bed. Her heart pounded frantically as she struggled to catch her breath. Eyes darting about the room in a daze she tried to adjust them to the darkness around her. The nightlight from the adjacent bathroom cast enough of a glow to allow her to view most of the room. It became clear she was back in her own bedroom, rather than trapped by the two RavenCroft men in a room at the RavenCroft Ranch.

Oddly relieved to find herself waking in the small bedroom of her mobile home, Angel couldn't help but be agitated by the incessant dream. It was nearly the same bad dream all over again, and it was extremely unsettling. Only she couldn't understand why it had changed. Always before when she would dream of the RavenCroft man, they would be pleasant dreams where he was making passionate love to her.

Recalling the sound once again of the babies crying in her ears, she shivered then rubbed her hands along her arms. She glanced at the alarm clock and could see it was just after midnight. Rolling her eyes, Angel realized she'd only been asleep for about an hour since she'd been up writing until eleven. Moaning softly from exhaustion, she peered over at her worthless husband as he slept without difficulty next to her in bed. Hearing Wilton snoring loudly, she rolled her eyes again and crept from the bed, turning to look at the bedding in frustration.

Realizing in disgust that the sheets would have to be washed again in the morning because she'd woke drenched in sweat, she groaned softly and headed towards the bathroom to relieve the pressure on her abdomen. The sweat beading along her hairline, neck, and down her back was already becoming clammy, but the shower would have to wait until morning. If she attempted to take one now she'd wake Wilton with the noise. He was a bear to deal with when awakened from a dead sleep.

Washing her hands afterwards, she was drying them on a towel when she felt the inexplicable eerie sensation that something was seriously wrong. Gasping softly as her belly clenched, her eyes darted toward the bathroom door. Naked, and feeling more exposed than usual, she threw on one of her husband's favorite t-shirts from the hamper.

Whispering loudly to Wilton, she cracked open the bathroom door.

Waking slowly, Wilton turned towards her as he rubbed his hand across his face and sat up in bed.

"What are you waking me for?" Wilton swore and glowered angrily. Seeing his wife trembling in the bathroom doorway, her eyes widening with fright, he became alarmed. His head jerked towards the bedroom door in time to see the butt of a silencer as a soft sound filled the room.

Angel watched in horror as a hole appeared on her husband's forehead. His expression of shock froze on his face and his portly body fell backwards. The sound of his arm smacking heavily against the side of the bed left her feeling sick to her stomach. Breathing deeply, Angel quickly closed the bathroom door, realizing with increasing dread that she'd known it was about to happen and had been unable to do anything to stop it.

Covering her mouth with her hands she quickly swallowed an anguished horrified cry of despair. She froze.

Was he dead?

Was her husband dead?

Wilton was supposed to be her guardian, her protector, and now he was dead?

Shot down before he even knew what was happening?

Okay, so he was a bit of a jerk at times, but she really didn't think he deserved that. Terrified, she shook violently where she stood. What in the world was she supposed to do?

Then it hit her.

She knew exactly what she had to do.

Glancing around the bathroom to the counter, she automatically grabbed the high-powered electric screw gun Wilton had placed on the charger that very morning when he'd finished working on the bathroom. The four-inch-long Phillips head screw bit was still tightly set in its mount. Dashing to the shower, trying hard to stay quiet, she opened the door and stepped inside, closing it behind her.

She could hear the door of the bathroom creak open as she shoved the screw gun behind her back with her right hand and backed up against the shower wall. Willing the hysteria she was feeling to stay buried within her, Angel stared in wide-eyed wonder and despair ahead of her. She was fully aware of her precarious position, for she knew all too well the man on the other side of the shower could see her through the frosted glass door panel. Panicking, as a tear trickled down her cheek, she prayed to God for the strength she'd need to protect her son. A startled cry escaped her lips as the dark figure swung the shower door open, training the gun on her as he stood before her. Angel's eyes were wide with fright as he stood with the silencer poised at her head.

She started to hyperventilate.

Mere hours before she'd been diligently typing on her laptop computer about this very same moment she was living through. While experiencing an overwhelming sense of déjà vu, Angel wished desperately that she'd been able to complete the chapter before heading off to bed, so she'd know if she came out of it alive.

"What you got behind your back?" the man asked in a deadly quiet tone. She'd anticipated the comment, but it was almost surreal to hear the words she'd written being spoken from his very mouth.

The man watched her face intently while stepping into the shower with her. Still holding the gun trained on her head, he stared her down as if daring her to try something - anything - to give him a reason to have a little fun with her.

"A screw gun," Angel stuttered, surprising him with her unexpectedly honest response. The surrealistic sensation of having experienced the moment already made her feel lightheaded. Her actions from then on seemed almost automatic and out of her full control. An inborn instinct and natural desire to survive took hold of her.

Taking advantage of the split second of surprise, she kneed him hard in the groin. The henchman doubled over and stumbled backwards out of the shower. Angel squealed in terror and she closed her eyes. She charged out of the shower after him, the screw gun poised high out in front of her with both hands. Ramming it as hard as she could against his chest, she depressed the button and heard the man holler in pain, as the bit of the screw gun burrowed deeper into his chest. Feeling something warm, wet, and sticky drip down her hands and spray out towards her face, she kept shoving with all her might in front of her in a blind panic. The sickening sound it was making made her nauseous.

She could hear the high-pitched whirring of the drill-gun stop suddenly as the man fell backwards into the garden tub, banging his head as he went. Opening her eyes wide Angel gasped loudly at the grotesque sight of the lifeless body in the tub. She began to shake violently, the tremors becoming increasingly spasmodic in nature. Angel stared in bewilderment and shock at the blood on her hands.

They shook.

And her hands were covered in blood.

Blood of a man she had killed. Squealing in terror, her face reddened, and her eyes bulged.

She couldn't freeze up. She didn't dare freeze up. If she did, then both she and her son was dead.

Her son.

Kal!

Something in her head finally clicked at that moment, spurring her into action. She had to get her son and get out of there fast. The nervous breakdown could wait.

Moving on trembling legs toward the bathroom door, she stepped quickly and quietly into the dark room, searching for the very items she'd used as weapons in her story. Seeing the bottle of furniture polish exactly where she'd written it would be on the dresser, Angel grabbed it up.

"Yes," she whispered. "Now where is it?"

Finding the soldering iron on the floor where she'd written the character's husband from her story had left it, she picked it up as well.

She could do this.

She had to do this.

If for no other reason, then to save her son.

She was his guardian now, his protector, just like Wilton had been for her for so many years.

Angel could hear swift footsteps coming closer from the other side of her bedroom door, drawing her attention. Taking a deep breath for courage, she threw her shoulders back in a determined stance than did exactly what she'd written her heroine had done and hid behind the bedroom door as it slowly swung open.

Waiting until Kobi Radford's man had entered her room and turned to look her way, she automatically reached out with her right arm and sprayed him in the face with the can of furniture polish. Angel could hear his screams through her sobs as she proceeded to jab the soldering iron into the henchman's forearm which held the gun. The man dropped it suddenly, as she'd expected while hollering in pain. His piercing dark eyes darted towards her and he growled angrily deep in his throat. Tears fell from Angel's eyes as she attempted to grab the gun, all the while knowing somehow she wouldn't reach it in time. Seeing her intent, the man shoved her up against the door with his other shoulder, while still holding his arm. She let out a strangled cry. His brute force slammed her hard against the door and she dropped unceremoniously to the floor.

"Stop, please stop!" Angel wailed to no avail, still holding tightly to the soldering iron. Terrified of what she was about to do, what she knew she had to do to survive, she willed the man to just leave and let her alone.

The man swore at her then shouted, staggering in pain.

Angel erupted quickly from the floor from where she'd dropped when he shoved her. He advanced on her again, just as she knew he would, and he grabbed for her. Swinging her arm around with as much might and muster as she could put into it, she stabbed him in the chest with the iron. A grunting noise escaped his lips as he stared down at the thing sticking grotesquely out of his chest. Appearing stunned, he looked back at her wide-eyed with shock. Sobbing Angel twisted the iron hard in her hand, causing him to drop to his knees.

"You gotta be kidding me," she heard him croak in a hoarse voice.

Squealing in dismay as blood poured from his wound, she tried to pull it from him for further use and protection, but it was stuck. Glancing fearfully at her bedroom door, she had merely a second to wait for the last henchman to charge through. Somehow she knew full well there was another, and he was the one she knew would terrify her the most.

The noise from their struggle had, in fact, alerted the third man still in the living room to trouble. Hearing a scuffle and his partner screaming as he was being stabbed, he ran the length of the living room through the kitchen to the bedroom. Barreling his way through the bedroom door, breaking it in the process, he was stunned to see the woman they were after standing over a bloody body crumpling to the floor.

Horrified to see the third man standing in her bedroom doorway, Angel screamed and flung the can of furniture polish at him wildly, knowing full well his intent was to shoot her.

"No!"

Ducking barely in time to escape the bullet whizzing past her head, she reached for the hardback volume of Brothers Grimm stories lying on the pile of laundry near her bed and threw it at him as well. Seeing it knock the gun out of his hand, she got the very opportunity she was looking for and darted past him through the door, just as he dove for the gun. Having difficulty finding the gun in the mess of Wilton's dirty laundry near the bed, Kobi Radford's man roared angrily.

"I'm gonna kill you with my bare hands." He tore after her, giving up on trying to find the gun.

Unable to prevent herself from slipping on the linoleum floor of the kitchen, due to the blood that had dripped on her bare feet, Angel nearly lost her balance. Letting out a terrified yelp, she felt a hand snake around her and shove her to the floor. She cried out in agony as her face smacked against the hard surface. Even knowing it was about to happen had not prepared her for the jolt of pain she experienced as it occurred.

Straddling her, the henchman turned her over and grabbed at her shirt ripping it in the process. Reeling back, he hit her hard across the face, causing blood to spurt from her nose.

Angel had to blink a couple of times to regain her senses; pain reverberated through her head. Arms flailing, she yanked at the metal leg of the dining room chair, allowing it to fall on top of him. Shoving at the chair the henchman was distracted long enough for Angel to wriggle out from beneath him. Pushing desperately up off the floor, she could hear her son screaming from his bedroom from a night fright at the same time. She knew full well what Kal was seeing in his head because the character in her book had a son just like him.

Torn between the desire to comfort her son, and the maternal instinct to protect him at all costs; her attention quickly returned to the most immediate issue.

Survival.

Angel felt the man seize her from behind as she grasped desperately for one of the knives from the cutlery block. Managing to ensnare one of the knives as he lifted her up off the floor, she kicked out with her legs in a panic. The sensation of that very movement, having felt like she'd experienced it once before, left her feeling unnaturally weightless.

Stabbing awkwardly at his right leg on an angle, she heard him roar in her ear. He dropped her roughly and gripped his leg.

Scrambling up from the floor where he left her, she watched with renewed horror as he yanked the knife from his leg then charged her. Turning to run, she felt his hand ensnare her ankle and she tripped. Catching herself as she fell, terror filled her when the thug crawled up over her, pinning her to the floor on her belly.

That had been as far as she'd gotten in her story.

Angel whimpered, unsure of what to do next. Her mind went blank. Nothing was coming to her and that terrified her.

The henchman bent low toward her head, snarling near her ear; his warm breath mere inches from her cheek. Grabbing hold of her long silver hair, he jerked her head to the side to get a better look at her bruising blood-spattered face. Glaring down at her, menace clear in his eyes, he practically spat at her as he spoke.

"I'm not gonna kill you yet," he promised harshly. "First, you're gonna answer my questions, or I slit your son's throat," he growled.

"No!" Angel screamed in horror.

He roughly shoved her, rolling her onto her back. Grappling with him briefly he easily overpowered her, pinning her once again as he hunched over her.

"Then you get to convince me not to kill you," he chuckled darkly.

Seeing the knife she'd stuck him with, in his hand Angel sobbed. Tears streamed down her cheeks. It didn't matter what he said, she knew what he intended to do to them.

To her.

"What does it matter? You're gonna kill me and my son anyway."

His lips twisted into a malicious evil grin giving truth to the words she spoke.

Angel didn't know what possessed her. Whether it was simply the despair that had taken root within her or the sheer hopelessness of her situation, but she began to scream as though the devil himself were sitting upon her.

"Help me! Someone help me, please!"

Too terrified to hear anything other than her own screams Angel almost didn't hear the front door smash open suddenly as it was being kicked in. Startled, she watched in surprise as two curious red splotches appeared on the henchman's chest. Falling forward, his weight knocked the wind out of her initially as he slumped over her - dead. Lying motionless in hushed silence, Angel was afraid to even breathe. Seeing movement out of the corner of her eye, a figure stepped over and past them, moving swiftly and quietly through to the kitchen.

Hearing two soft hollow noises near her bedroom door she whimpered softly in distress, knowing full well what it was she was hearing. She could see the silhouette of a very large man disappear into her bedroom. For a moment she heard nothing else as she stared up at the ceiling, her heart thundering wildly in her throat. Engulfed with fear she made a weak attempt to move but the heavy weight of the lifeless body pinned her to the floor. Praying that the man now in her house was there to save them, and not hurt them, she continued to lay motionless.

Chapter 3

After taking down the first thug upon entering the mobile home, Kahner RavenCroft's gaze darted around the house taking everything in. Ten years of working undercover black ops for the CIA had prepared him for just a moment like this. Aware the woman had likely been silenced by shock, he moved with stealth toward the bedroom. His priority was removing any and all additional potential threats, then he'd check on her.

Taking three more cautious steps into the kitchen, his feet barely made a sound upon the floor. He could see from his vantage another figure lying just inside the bedroom door. Hearing a soft groan coming from the thug lying there, Kahner shot two rounds in quick succession in the man's head since his chest already had a sharp implement sticking out of it. The man would have likely bled out before help could reach him anyway. Kahner was merely taking every precaution necessary.

Taking note of the body on the bed Kahner registered that a man had been shot in the head, presumably by one of the henchmen.

Had he been Angel's boyfriend?

A lover maybe?

He noted there was no ring on his left hand.

Moving further into the room he could see another body in the tub. Stepping far enough into the bathroom so he could see, he paused briefly upon seeing a screw gun sticking out of the man's chest. Realizing the guy was already dead Kahner stood erect as he stared down at the body.

"Huh, she got one." His head tilted in awe.

Turning on his heel, he walked back the way he came. Keeping his nine-millimeter gun out and ready, Kahner checked the laundry room as well. It was empty. Heading back into the living room he could see the woman still lying underneath Lionel Radford's thug on the living room floor. Coming up beside them he spoke slow and quiet.

"Don't move."

Kicking the body off her with his foot, he could see her terrified eyes, staring back up at him. He knew her age to be in her mid-forties, yet the look in her eye was that of a frightened teenage girl. Kneeling next to her Kahner was able to get a closer look. She reminded him of Stephanie. He noted she was wearing nothing but a t-shirt which had been torn down the front. He surmised it likely meant she'd come straight from bed. Seeing blood spatter across her face, all over her hands, and down her body, he knew instantly what had happened.

The woman had literally fought for her life.

Staring up at the dark figure above her, as he knelt cautiously down next to her, Angel was startled to realize she thought she knew who he was. Still trembling violently, she reached up with a shaky hand towards the man's eyes, her mouth dropping open in shock.

"Kahner RavenCroft?" Angel whispered as her breathing became erratic. "But the eyes should be crystal blue, not brown," she continued, appearing confused.

Eyeing her with both interest and suspicion he replied. "There's a lot of blood here, Angel. Any of it yours? Have you been shot or stabbed?" he asked urgently. Seeing her shake her head no, he continued. "Then let's get you out of here. You can explain how you know that later."

"Lionel Radford's men k...killed m...my husband," she stuttered her speech pattern sounding slightly odd, almost girlish. The reality of what had just happened was beginning to sink in and she wailed in despair, fresh tears dripping down her face.

Husband?

Kahner felt like he'd been punched in the gut. They hadn't realized she'd been married. This might complicate matters.

"Mommy?"

Startled by the sound of a frightened young boy calling out as a bedroom door squeaked open, Kahner flinched.

She had a son?

That complicated things even more.

Crying with joy at hearing her son alive and well, a sudden wave of relief overwhelmed Angel. Rubbing her shaking hand across her face to wipe her tears, she managed to smear the blood across her face.

"Kalturek, Baby... Mama's okay, Honey. Are you all right? St...stay where you are for a minute, okay?" Angel croaked as she came up off the floor.

Kahner tensed. She had a son and his name was Kalturek?

What was going on here?

Rarely, if ever, was he rattled, and yet at that moment, his head was spinning.

Seeing her stumble Kahner could tell her ankle had been badly injured. Reaching out he steadied her arms, holding her in place. The torn section of her shirt gaped open, exposing her belly and the pool of blood that had dripped on her from the thug's wound.

"I think it best he does not see you like this," Kahner whispered urgently, not wanting to scare the child any further. Just by touching her, he already had blood on his own hands. "Tell him a friend is coming down the hall to get him. We must go. Now."

"Am I...disappearing?" Angel asked suddenly. "Like...like you see in the movies?" Her eyes were glazed. She stared as though transfixed at the body on the floor.

He gently turned her head away, recognizing she was likely going into shock. "Yes. I'll get your son. You have one minute. Grab your computer and flash drive first, then only necessities if time allows. Can you do that?"

Nodding she understood, Angel called out to her son. She watched as Kahner strolled quickly down the hall, the hysteria building within her over what was happening.

It was real.

He was real.

And if Kahner RavenCroft was real then that meant the rest of them were all real which meant…

Shaking tremulously Angel outstretched her arms, watching her hands as though mesmerized. They trembled, the movement seemed so fast to her, she could barely see them at all. Her eyes became giant circles within her head, and she began to hyperventilate. A chaotic jumble of emotions bubbled to the surface, elation and fear creating an overwhelming mix. She'd been waiting for so long for this and hadn't even realized it was what she'd been waiting for, preparing for. For once there was a small ray of hope. Hope that she might get answers to all her questions and even find her true love.

Love.

Angel giggled; the sound akin to a teenager seeing a cute boy for the first time. The instant the noise escaped her lips she wished she could take it back. At what price was she now gaining this? She stared blankly once again at her bloody hands, not seeing them.

Consciously she could hear Kahner speaking to Kal softly from down the hall. His voice pulled her back into reality. She suddenly realized there were things she needed to remove from the house – things he'd told her to grab. She had a feeling she knew why Kahner had insisted she bring her computer and flash drives.

Still shaking visibly, Angel grabbed her son's book bag off the wall near the door. Wilton's first rule had always been to do as instructed by the one in charge and clearly Kahner was the one in charge right now.

So she did just that.

Shoving her three spiral notebooks, the contents of her purse, and her flash drive case in the bag, she hastily zipped it up.

Finding her laptop bag under her desk, she managed to trip over the body on the floor as she turned around to get her laptop, which was sitting near the recliner. Shrieking in hysterics at having touched the dead body once again, she laid a hand on her heart to help stop the frantic beating.

"It's okay. I'm okay. It's just a body," she squealed, trying desperately to regain her composure. She was supposed to be forty-five years old not a child. She needed to start acting like one, just like Wilton used to always say. Taking a deep breath, she thought to herself, what else do I need to do?

Since she was already on the floor, she ripped the cord from the surge protector and stuffed it in the bag along with the computer. By the time Kahner had returned from outside, having carried her son out to the awaiting vehicle, she was rifling through papers on her desk.

"Just leave it, Angel, it's time to go," Kahner said crossly. Hearing sirens in the distance, Kahner sensed they were running out of time fast. One of the neighbors had likely heard the ruckus from her struggle and had called the cops. Seeing her reaching for something draped with a cloth on a small table near the desk, he lost his patience.

"Just leave it, let's go!"

"I can't leave it you idiot," she snapped back while stomping her feet. She then wrapped the small mound with the swatch of fabric covering it. "If I do it'll eventually get us all killed," she insisted.

Hearing the sirens getting closer, he shouldered the duffel bag and laptop bag, then took hold of Angel's arm with the other.

"Can you walk?" he asked her urgently.

"I will run if I have to," she quipped bravely, staring at him with her wide haunted eyes. Her arms were wrapped awkwardly around the fabric encased oddly shaped item as she attempted to carry it.

Trying to ignore the pain shooting from her ankle up to her leg, Angel followed quickly after him. They fled down the steps of her home. Not taking the time to look back Angel staggered as she ran in a panic to the vehicle a few steps behind Kahner. Stepping into the open door she settled in the front passenger seat, the covered mound in her lap, while Kahner ran around to the other side. Dumping the bags on the floor behind his seat, he shut the door and took off, not even bothering with his seat belt.

"Get down as low as you can," Kahner ordered her while speeding down her street.

Managing to escape the mobile home park where she lived, he turned down one of the nearby side streets, as the first police car sped into the park. Pulling out onto the main road Kahner glared over at Angel. She'd propped the item in the seat and was now cowering on the floor of the car.

Kahner swore. "I hope that was worth nearly getting caught over," he vented angrily, pointing to the concealed item in the seat.

Head resting on the seat cushion as she faced him, Kahner could see her pulling the fabric swatch around the mound protectively. Taking a deep breath, her face scrunched up, as more tears streamed down her bloody cheeks.

"Trust me. If I'm right, and all this is real, like I think it is, then I have the feeling Bastion would have been very mad at me had it been left behind," she insisted quietly. Her voice shook.

"Why? What is it?" Kahner asked, figuring he'd play along. Her familiar usage of his father's name when she didn't even know him was unsettling.

"It's a miniature model of the RavenCroft house," she replied with a worried sob. "I made it from a picture I have in my drawing pad."

"What?" he exclaimed in surprise. "How in the world did you get...?"

"I drew it," she hiccupped softly, unable to control her emotions any longer. "I'm sorry, Kahner, I'm so sorry." Angel began crying into the seat cushion. "I had no idea, I swear. I almost put everything I know about your family on the Internet. Oh, no," she gasped, coming to a revelation. "Wilton died because of me. Because of what I wrote," she sobbed hysterically as she tried to wipe at her eyes with shaking hands. Really seeing the blood on her hands for the first time, it took a moment for her to register what it was she was looking at. Wailing loudly, she stared down at her hands in horror. "What have I done?" Hysteria bubbled forth, overwhelming her.

"You defended yourself, and you protected your son the only way you knew how," Kahner spoke calmly next to her, concerned that she was going into shock. Thinking he would need to use a tranquilizer on her for the duration of the trip as he had for the boy, Kahner was awfully glad he'd pocketed an extra one before leaving the ranch. He hadn't really anticipated he'd be bringing home more than one person.

"You have to promise me something," Angel said, sounding suddenly very calm. "I know you're going to use a tranquilizer on me," she said, trying to be brave at the thought of a shot in her arm. Her knowing statement won her a startled look from him. "It's okay, I guess, I get it. But you must promise me you won't uncover the miniature model of the ranch house and look at it," she said as she stared up at him imploringly, her mouth quivering. "I need your word, Kahner. You must trust me on this. Promise me you'll take it straight to Bastion, and not look at, or peek at it at all. Please, Kahner. Please, you have to promise me."

Kahner eyed her suspiciously while turning down a county road. He headed west toward the state line out of Iowa. It would take a few hours before they'd be crossing the border into South Dakota. Sensing the urgency in her request Kahner inhaled deeply and rubbed at his jaw. Glancing back down at her, he could see the bruises along one side of her face and the blood spatter in her hair, as well as all down her shirt and hands. Seeing the desperate look in her eye, he wondered why this model she'd made was so important to her, and why she felt it would be so significant to his dad.

"Please promise me," she begged again, choking back a sob. "I know I'm not making any sense, and I know he told you he got called away to Washington for the day, but he… he'll be back tomorrow morning so…"

"How do you know that?" Kahner inquired, staring down at her angrily, appearing stunned. "That was a last-minute call. The rest of the family doesn't even know."

Angel hesitated, her eyes shifting back and forth in front of her in a startled daze. Then suddenly she spoke. "Because that's how I was going to write it.

Heavens, it's how I wrote it," she replied in a matter-of-fact manner, smacking her hand against the seat cushion of the car. She blinked three times then closed her eyes on a wave of despair. "Please, Kahner, you have to promise me, and no one else can see it or my drawings either," she insisted, stamping her feet on the floor of the car without thinking. She yelped unexpectedly as pain shot up her leg from her injured ankle.

What she was saying wasn't making any sense and she was acting as if she were a melodramatic teenage girl. Kahner wanted and needed to interrogate her in order to find out what she knew but sensed that he wouldn't get anything out of her. She was too hysterical, and her thoughts were racing in her head, too jumbled to make any sense of, for the moment. Making a quick decision to play along with her request, Kahner nodded his head in agreement then peered out the windshield.

"I promise." He stared back down at her mesmerizing deep blue eyes. He was unsure of what was going on with her, and the role she was meant to play where his brother and sister-in-law were concerned was still hazy to him. His father had taken all the books away, hiding them so no one knew what was written other than Stephanie. She'd only managed to get through the very beginning.

Was Angel Stryfe really meant to bear his brother's children?

Kalturek was still married. Kahner couldn't imagine how that was going to work out exactly, and he cringed at the possibilities now currently running through his head.

Sighing heavily, he peered down upon the battered, broken, and bloodied woman on the floor of the car. This Angel reminded him of his father. Bastion had always had an uncanny ability to simply know things without knowing why, and Kahner couldn't help but wonder if the woman curled up on the floor of the car might well have a similar gift, as it stated in David Pearson's novel. He figured she had to, in order to know what she did, and yet at the same time, he was concerned that he might well be playing into her hand. Was she a plant by Lionel Radford, his wife Sable's former husband? Or had Ripley Braddock, the recently appointed head of WITSEC, somehow become aware of Sable and her children's location? Kahner didn't quite think so from the way she was acting, but he couldn't completely disregard that as a possibility yet.

Glancing back down at her, he could see Angel closing her eyes in distress as her lip quivered. "Now please, knock me out, Kahner, please. I keep seeing it all in my head," she sobbed quietly, her body shaking. "My God, my son, the things he must have seen."

Pulling off to the side of the road briefly, he took out the tranquilizer, reached over, and gently pushed the sleeve of her t-shirt up. Tapping her with it on her shoulder, he then smoothed out the sleeve. Seeing her eyes close almost immediately, as her body went limp, he marveled at the woman next to him on the floor. She'd managed to survive against three of

Lionel Radford's goons, having taken down two of them on her own, which was by no means an easy task. Shaking his head in frustration Kahner put the vehicle back in motion. He couldn't even imagine what Bastion was going to say when he found out he'd nearly gotten there too late to save her and the son they hadn't realized she already had.

Chapter 4

A screw gun and a soldering iron? Can you imagine?

And can I just say it?

Mankind's capacity for finding new and inventive ways to kill people appears to be unending. Especially with all the new-fangled technology that's at our disposal.

But by no means do I advocate the taking of a life.

My own personal philosophy? Do no harm…

-When able.

I've witnessed enough suffering over the years to know that no good ever comes from it. That said, I do believe when faced with a life-threatening situation, a person has the right to defend themselves and with deadly force, if warranted - just as Angel had.

The henchmen of Lionel Radford's were some pretty bad men. I'd wager their temperament was no doubt the reason why Lionel's brother, Kobi, hired that kind of man for their mercenary work. If they'd had the chance, they would have done exactly what Stephanie had read they were going to do. Angel knew it too, for she'd written about some of Lionel's men in the first book she ever wrote.

Do you remember it?

The one about Kahner and Sable? That was a pretty terrible tale as well, for Kahner had barely been able to get Sable out of Lionel and Kobi Radford's office building alive. But that was another story.

You might have also noted that Bastion sent Kahner after Angel rather than Kalturek. This may seem odd to you considering Stephanie had said Angel's book description listed that Kalturek was meant to go bring her home. What you have to understand… The RavenCroft patriarch is thinking in terms of skill rather than a random book's description of events. Were Kalturek to run into trouble, Bastion knew he could probably handle himself pretty well as he was a Sheriff and, regardless of his elected position, had gone through the same training as his deputies. But he also knew that Kahner was more skilled in dealing with unexpected developments and dangerous situations, because of his past covert undercover background within the CIA. He had also determined that a certain level of secrecy would need to be adhered to with regards to travel to and from Angel's home in Pocahontas, Iowa.

Nope, nope. Kahner was the best man for the job. Not Kalturek.

Two interesting things to note here is that prior to sending Kahner off, Bastion had explained to him that he'd received a phone call and would need to travel last minute out of town to Washington – just as Angel had said. He charged him with the responsibility of taking care of the horse ranch and household in his absence. His son was to tell anyone who asked that he was traveling on business last minute. Of course, Kahner suspected he knew what was up, as he was the only one aware that Bastion was still... Oh, how should I put this? 'In the business of secrets?' He figured his father had accepted a job and needed to fly under the radar for the next few days in order to complete it.

The other thing to keep in mind is that Bastion had done an in-depth background check on Angel Stryfe before leaving and had shared most of it with the rest of the family. What he'd found had been confusing for there had been very little on the woman. His information had not included a husband, or for that matter, a son. If the third book description of Angel's was accurate then this could complicate matters where Stephanie and Kalturek's hope of children were concerned. Angel's husband had just been killed before her very eyes and she had experienced some pretty serious trauma at the hand of Lionel Radford's henchman.

What was the likelihood she'd be willing to help them have a child by becoming a surrogate if she were in shock and grieving?

- - -

Saturday, November 29, 2015
2:45 am Mountain Time
Somewhere In Colorado

They touched down at an airport four hours out from Loveland, Colorado at nearly three in the morning. Kahner had been annoyed to find that they weren't arriving at an airport closer to home. His father had taken care of booking private transportation and hiring a pilot. Clearly, Bastion was covering all his bases in order to keep them from possibly being tracked.

Grateful, at least, that he'd had a chance to sleep for three hours, and that it was still quite dark out, he opened the door of the plane and proceeded to transfer the two bags, the model of the ranch house, as well as Angel and her son's sleeping forms. Driving away from the airport and heading out onto the highway, he happened to glance down at the miniature house sitting behind the front passenger seat not far from him. Not for the first time, Kahner wondered why she'd made him promise not to look at it. Thus far he'd managed to keep to his word, but he admitted he had a strong inclination to take a peek. If for no other reason, then to see how accurate she'd been. Deciding to remove temptation from his view he pulled off to the side of the road and placed the model in the trunk instead. He was nothing if he wasn't a man of his word.

Glancing over at Angel's sleeping form next to him, Kahner marveled once again at the similarities between her and his sister-in-law, Stephanie. They weren't exactly identical, but they were definitely similar.

Their height and shape were the same, yet Angel seemed to be more solidly built compared to Stephanie's delicate, almost petite appearance. This left Angel looking about twenty to twenty-five pounds heavier than his sister-in-law, which gave her a smoother, more rounded appearance to her figure. The curve of her hips and breasts were full leaving her with a voluptuous shape in comparison, and her legs, though short, were pleasing to the eye. Both women wore their hair long but where Stephanie's hair was blonde, Angel's was now currently an unusual silver color with golden highlights. This was contrary to the picture of her they had seen online where it had been brunette, but then everything they'd pulled up on her had been severely outdated, even her picture.

After learning of Stephanie's discovery, they had gone online and pulled everything they could find on Angel Stryfe. The statement Stephanie made when they had all first seen Angel's picture on the website still haunted him. Since the moment he found her lying on the floor of the mobile home, Kahner wondered if there was somehow significance to the resemblance. Was it possible she was right and that his brother had married the wrong woman?

He was still pondering on the notion nearly four hours later when he heard Angel stirring next to him. They were only a couple miles away from the ranch and Kahner was becoming increasingly anxious to be home. He could only imagine what his family's reaction would be to him arriving with a half-naked, blood-spattered, woman, and her son in tow. After all, they were only expecting him to bring Angel home, no children.

Knowing full well that Bastion would be furious initially over the death of the spouse, he also knew that he would, in the end, understand. The RavenCroft's made it a point to use their powers to help people as best they could. But Bastion knew that they couldn't always prevent bad things from happening to people. Even knowing this, Kahner was extremely aggravated by what had happened, tired from lack of sleep, and desperate for a shower.

Pulling onto the long drive for the house he noticed Angel's head shoot up as she stared out the window toward the house. He could hear her mumbling something under her breath and was sure she'd just said that it hadn't been a dream after all. Peering over at Kahner she shrieked suddenly, her breathing becoming erratic.

"You took out your contacts," she said finally, apologizing for shrieking at him. She seemed to regain her composure but continued to stare.

Nodding, he replied cautiously. "Yes, on the plane."

"My husband is dead," Angel spoke almost too calmly as she stared out the windshield. "Lionel and Kobi Radford's men killed him."

"How long had you been married?" Kahner inquired, seeking information. Any worries he might have had about her being distraught over the loss of her spouse disappeared with her next words.

"Ten years too long."

Kahner didn't respond. He merely watched her as he pulled up to the house. Peering over his shoulder, he was grateful to see that her son was still unconscious and probably would be for another hour. Looking back at Angel as he parked the car in front of the house, he opened his door in order to get out. Walking around the vehicle Kahner could see her watching him warily as he opened her door. Reaching in to give her a hand, she took it tentatively as her deep blue eyes darted between him and the house. The early morning light reflected upon her irises as she stepped from the vehicle, giving them almost a silvery sheen, making them appear to have changed color. The effect was startling and highly unexpected.

"This is the RavenCroft horse ranch," she said automatically when he helped her stand. "My son…"

"Is still sleeping," he responded quietly, a slight shiver running down his spine from the look in her eye. He stared back at her, trying to decipher the reaction she was having as well as his own. "I'll come back for him," he assured her, giving her a cautious look. He was definitely getting a distinct sensation from her but couldn't quite put into words what that feeling was. The sunlight caught the golden highlights in her silver hair making him wonder why she'd dyed it such an unusual color. Oddly enough it didn't seem to detract from her pleasant appearance at all.

Concerned by the expression on her face, Kahner guided her toward the house. She appeared almost jittery. Figuring he'd get one of his brothers to come out for the boy, he tried to help her along, but she hobbled in front of him as though in a daze. Trying to read her, Kahner realized her thoughts were just too jumbled to make any sense of them so he gave up.

Climbing the porch haphazardly, she reached the door then simply stood there as if unsure what to do next. Without warning the door opened, and Angel jumped, finding herself staring in awe at a large man in charcoal running pants with similar black hair and crystal-clear blue eyes to Kahner.

"Hello, Drayke," Angel said stiffly, stepping past him through the door into the entryway. Somehow she'd been able to recognize the man before her as Mackenzie's fraternal twin brother. She knew him to be the youngest of the RavenCroft brothers.

Drayke gaped at her in both surprise and alarm at the state of the woman before him. She was wearing nothing but a long white t-shirt that hung down mid-thigh, which had been torn across her front, and it was caked with dry blood. The fact that she knew who he was right away was about as unsettling as seeing dried blood smeared all over her face, hands, arms, and legs.

Angel padded through the entryway barefoot, as Drayke exclaimed in horror at the sight of her. She looked above her at the dangling light fixture hanging from the ceiling, and then around at the room as if in awe and wonder while fidgeting in place.

"Good grief, Kahner. What happened to her!"

Hearing Drayke's exclamations from the kitchen, Sable went running out in order to greet her husband.

Screaming in surprise at the sight of Angel, the rest of the family followed quickly behind her.

"Please, tell me our children aren't downstairs yet," Kahner said quickly, while anxiously staring at Kalturek who was rushing down the hall.

Skidding to a sudden halt, Kalturek took in the sight of the woman in the entryway, who looked so similar in appearance to his wife. She stared back at him, her face surrounded by unusual silver hair streaked with gold and riddled with dried blood.

"Hello, Kalturek," Angel croaked. Her eyes seemed to dull unexpectedly as if the color changed with her emotions much like a mood stone. Glancing at the rest of the household now congregating in the entryway, she peered at each one in turn. She had the look of one who wasn't quite all there. "Mackenzie, Synedra, very nice to meet you," she greeted the RavenCroft sisters who looked back at her in startled surprise as she nodded appropriately toward each of them. Her voice sounded hollow. Then her gaze cut over to Kalabernus' wife, Ariana, and Synedra's husband, Nathan, as though she were looking straight through them.

Mackenzie had gasped at first sight of Angel standing in the entryway, half-naked, and covered in blood. Placing her hand over her mouth, her eyes had grown wide. She gaped at her in fascination as the woman turned on the spot, investigating her surroundings while favoring an ankle that appeared to be badly injured. A welt the size of a golf ball had grown on the side of her foot and Mackenzie could see bruising along Angel's face and jaw. Turning as Drayke's wife Laynie strode up next to her, Mackenzie watched as she gawked at her openly as well.

"What happened?" Laynie exclaimed in horror, her eyes meeting her husband Drayke's troubled gaze.

"I was... I got there too late," Kahner's voice sounded hoarse as he spoke.

"What do you mean?" Stephanie gasped and stepped around her husband in order to get a closer look at Angel. "Is that her blood? There's so much of it. And what on earth did she do to her hair?"

"Is she bleeding?" Ariana asked with concern. She peered up at her husband Kalabernus who towered over her.

"And from where?" Kalabernus asked, his gaze narrowing on Angel with an assessing eye. There was something about her, a sort of welcoming sensation, or aura, which made him feel almost drawn to her somehow. He found he had to physically shake himself in order to regain his senses.

"Why didn't you take her to the hospital?" Mackenzie asked in annoyance, distracting Kalabernus. "My husband's on duty there today, and you know how they love to page him because of his name – Dr. Funnie ... paging Dr. Funnie. You could have requested him in the emergency room. S.T. would have happily tended to her."

"It's not her blood. At least, most of it isn't anyways, and I can't take her just anywhere right now." Kahner paused. "Because I was too late," he said again with more emphasis, his gaze shifting toward Kalturek with a meaningful look. He could see his brother was thinking through the possibilities of what might have happened.

"But, she's right here. So you got her here safely at least," Stephanie said, beaming happily.

"You don't understand, Stephanie. *He's* still sleeping in the car," Kahner replied.

"Who's sleeping in the car?"

"Her son," Kahner said quietly.

The room fell silent.

"She...she has a son?" Stephanie gasped. "How old is the child?" she asked hopefully.

Angel turned toward Stephanie, staring back at her with as much interest as Stephanie was giving her.

"He's ten. Kalturek will be traumatized when he wakes," Angel answered quietly. Tears began welling in her eyes. Stephanie could see the woman's pupils were dilated and that she was clearly in shock. The sparkling silver sheen disappeared, the color of her irises transitioning to an intense deep blue. The effect was unsettling.

Confused by her statement Stephanie inquired, "I don't understand. You said Kalturek?"

"My son – his name is Kalturek," she replied automatically, startling everyone. "Kalturek Bastion Stryfe." Angel peered self-consciously at Stephanie's husband. Sighing heavily, as she continued to glance around at her surroundings, she spoke again. "Kal often sees through my eyes. So he will have seen his father die," she declared. She began to cry. Silent tears streamed down her cheeks.

Stepping past Stephanie as she pointed to her left, Angel whispered softly in awe, completely oblivious to the shocked expressions on everyone's face at what she'd just said. The whole family peered over at Kahner in unison and he nodded his head in confirmation.

"It would appear she was married…"

"Ten dang years too long," Angel piped crossly, repeating herself as she interrupted him. Then her face suddenly contorted in anguish. "But he didn't deserve what he got. No, no. He didn't deserve to be murdered in his bed." She inhaled sharply, forcing herself to be brave and keep her emotions in check. "That would be the front living room, past that the kitchen and pantry, next to that the pool." After pointing in the direction of each room she listed, Angel's head turned towards Kalabernus who stood with his arm protectively around his wife, Ariana. She could see him watching her cautiously. "There is a pool, isn't there Kalabernus?" she asked, padding softly past Laynie and Mackenzie toward the giant man. He stood, towering over Angel, looking down at her curiously, even a bit warily. She seemed to know everyone by sight. How was that possible?

Nodding, Kalabernus replied. "There is a pool, yes."

"Thank you," Angel said politely. She nodded while tears continued to stream down her face, causing her eyes to shimmer with a silvery haze before returning to their deep blue depths of moments before. Stepping past him she hobbled down the hall peering around her as she went. Reaching the doors of the pool room she disappeared behind them.

"What in the world?" Synedra could be heard to say as she watched Angel go. "And are her eyes blue or silver?"

"I can't tell." Mackenzie shook her head as she shrugged.

"They're blue," Kahner responded. "Or, at least I think so. The light seems to affect the color."

"Or her mood maybe?" Sable inquired. Her head tilted curiously as she stared down the hallway where Angel had disappeared.

"Ten to one she's gonna jump in that pool," Nathan said suddenly as he exchanged worried glances with Kahner. The color of Angel's eyes weren't bothering him so much as the response the RavenCroft siblings seemed to be having toward her. The four men seemed drawn toward her, whereas Mackenzie and Synedra appeared anxious or uneasy in her presence.

"Uh, listen Drayke, her son is still in the car. Can you bring him in for me?" Kahner asked his brother as he headed quickly down the hallway after Angel. "I don't want him to wake up alone outside."

"I'm on it," Drayke said, exchanging looks with Kalturek and Kalabernus. Then they headed outside in order to bring the boy in, even though only one was really needed. The rest of the family walked down the hallway to see what Angel was up to.

Entering the pool room, the RavenCroft family looked on in dismay as Angel splashed her way into the pool. She was crying heavily, her body wracked with sobs as she slowly kept moving further into the water.

"My fault, my fault, all my fault," she continued repetitively. Her speech faltered as her head went under the water.

"It looks like she's having a nervous breakdown," Mackenzie stated as she witnessed the silver-headed woman bob up suddenly out of the water, spluttering as she came up.

"You would too if you'd just killed two men and watched your husband die," Kahner said evenly. He stared anxiously at the woman now wading in the pool.

"Oh God! Blood in the pool, blood in the pool! Sorry, so sorry," Angel said between sobs, her body jerking unnaturally as she attempted to wade away from all the blood. She squealed in distress at seeing the water near her turning a dirty red. Bloody red streaks ran down her arms as she struggled up the steps of the pool while holding the handrail.

Seeing her t-shirt clinging to her chest they all watched in horror as her hand snagged the torn section. The shirt ripped the rest of the way exposing the bottom half of her naked body to their view. Letting out a horrified cry of dismay Angel stared down at herself then back up at the RavenCroft family. She attempted to cover herself unsuccessfully with her hands and arms then ventured desperately back into the pool for cover.

Kahner turned away quickly as did Nathan.

"I'm thinking you and I need to leave, Kahner. Synedra, Honey, will you guys be okay getting her out the rest of the way?" Nathan asked, turning his head just enough to look at his wife. Seeing her shocked expression at learning that Angel had killed someone and at seeing the woman naked, he put his hand on her shoulder in order to gain her attention. "Synedra, I know this is a lot, Honey, but..."

"-Right, of course. Mackenzie, can you help me?" Synedra asked hopefully, nervous about being so close to the woman and so much blood.

Mackenzie nodded and they both walked bravely towards the pool attempting to coax Angel the rest of the way out.

Sable exclaimed in dismay while wiping at her eyes. "Her husband died because of my last husband, and his brother probably ordered the hit on her." More tears welled in her eyes as she turned toward Ariana in distress. "Does this mean we're no longer safe here?"

"No, Sable. Her husband died because there is evil in this world," Ariana responded quietly. "And honestly, at this point, I don't know whether any of us are safe." She stared at the silver-haired woman being helped out of the pool. The remainder of the shirt she wore clung to her full breasts. She could see long severe scar marks on either side of Angel's lower abdomen, but she couldn't tell what they were from.

"I can't even imagine what that woman just went through. With that much blood, it's a wonder she's not dead," Stephanie stated as she stared at Angel with a curious expression on her face. "I'm betting she's going to need clothes just like you did," she continued, turning toward Sable.

"I'll go get her some of mine for now," Sable offered, turning to leave. "She appears to be close to my size, maybe. Only she seems a bit shorter."

"And I'll get her shampoo and soap. She's gonna need a shower," Ariana stated, shaking her head in wonder.

"That poor woman needs medical attention," Laynie ventured, giving Mackenzie a serious look.

"As I said, S.T. is already at the hospital, but I'll call him home if I can," Mackenzie said, helping Synedra guide Angel to a lounge chair, so she could sit down.

"It's a wonder she's even able to walk on that ankle. You'd think the pain would be excruciating," Synedra exclaimed. Glancing around the pool room she searched for something to cover her with. Stepping quickly out of the pool area into the nearby bathroom, she returned with a large white towel in order to drape over her.

"Right now she's just numb all over, I'd wager," Mackenzie said knowingly. "She's in such shock that I'm sure she can't feel anything right now." Truthfully she wasn't getting a real clear read on the woman's emotional state. But Mackenzie was too self-conscious about being unable to sense anything to admit to it.

"Not true, not true. I feel everything," Angel said next to her, surprising everyone. She continued to cry while crossing her arms over herself protectively. Her face scrunched up as though in agony. "Sometimes I have to just sort of turn myself off for a while, you know? But I feel everything, absolutely everything. And as to your question, Sable, I think you're still safe. I got the feeling Lionel and Kobi's thugs intended to interrogate and torture me first before killing me. Bastion had my website pulled pretty fast before they could get anything more than the description. They don't know enough to find you yet." The words slipped out before Angel realized it. How had she known that? Then again, how had she known enough about these people to be writing about them? Clearly, her imagination was more real than fantasy.

Exchanging glances around the pool room the women stared cautiously back at her.

Watching her, as Angel eyed the pool almost longingly, Sable tapped at Ariana's arm in order to gain her attention.

"We should go get what she needs quickly. I'm hearing Kahner say her son could wake very soon," Sable stated, pointing toward her brow then the doorway. She could hear her husband's thoughts from where he stood out of sight near the pool room.

"We'll want her cleaned up before then, and before my kids come down."

"Right, of course," Ariana replied. They both turned and left quickly for their respective rooms.

"Angel, you can use the shower in the bathroom just outside the pool room," Mackenzie said quietly. "Do you need any help...?"

"No, no. I can manage. I am an adult a-after all. I just...I just. I need...I need..." Sounding much like a broken Baby Alive doll, Angel suddenly went quiet.

Synedra's gentle gaze roamed over her with an analytical stare. "You need a hot shower with soft music, lit candles, and a calming scent. Maybe even..."

"Who are you kidding?" Laynie ventured, cutting her off. "She needs a stiff drink is what *she* needs." She glanced at Stephanie as though for approval.

Wide-eyed, her sister-in-law nodded towards Laynie in agreement. "You can say that again."

Seeing the RavenCroft sisters had Angel well in order, Stephanie and Laynie left the room so they could tend to Sable's children while she ran to get clothes for Angel. Managing to discreetly help Angel to the bathroom, Mackenzie and Synedra left her there as Ariana and Sable returned with the items she would need. Handing them into her, she accepted them gratefully then closed the door behind her.

Turning and facing the shower Angel hobbled over to it and stepped inside. Taking hold of the shower head she pulled it down from where it hung. Switching it to a rain shower setting she turned the water on and simply stood under the water as it poured down over her. Angel shook violently, hopeful that the water would wash away the visions of what she was reliving in her head.

Weeping openly at the loss of her husband, she struggled to get the image of the hole in Wilton's head out of her mind. He'd been a lousy husband, no question, but he'd still been her husband. Staggering back against the shower wall, Angel rested there briefly. Then, ripping the shirt off the rest of the way, she threw it in the trash. As she trembled and sobbed, Angel began rubbing her hands and arms with such force she nearly rubbed the skin raw. Filling her entire hand with body soap, she proceeded to cleanse her body thoroughly from head to toe several times before moving on to her hair.

The whole time she continued to cry as the images of the men she had killed kept popping into her head. Desperate to get the thoughts out of her mind she grabbed her head and pressed her forehead against the shower wall. Suddenly, a thought came into her head quite unexpectedly, startling her. Standing straight as she gasped, she turned off the water frantically, not bothering to make sure she'd gotten all the conditioner out.

She had little time to waste. Grabbing a large pool towel from the rack, she quickly wrapped it around her body. Hobbling out from the bathroom, still sopping wet, she winced as she turned down the hall toward the kitchen.

Managing only a few steps down the hallway, she clutched the towel to her chest and halted where she was at when she saw Nathan step into view.

Nathan stopped abruptly at the sight of her in such a scantily clad state. Ignoring the embarrassing silence, she whispered at him urgently, even as she trembled from the cold air against her wet skin.

"Nathan...the RavenCroft children have my miniature model of this house. I made it to scale with every little detail," Angel stated quietly sounding worried. She hoped he'd catch on quickly to what it was she was trying to tell him.

Angel stared at him openly.

Sensing he hadn't put the pieces together yet when she saw him tilt his head at her in confusion, she tried again as she stuttered from the cold.

"Kalturek and Kahner are going to look at the miniature model and the pictures I drew in my drawing book of *all the rooms in this house*," she said as she enunciated each word carefully. "You have to stop them," she finished urgently.

Startled, Nathan's eyes widened in astonishment for he knew exactly what it was she was trying to tell him. It was a secret of Bastion's only he was aware of. How she knew about the secret and the fact that he was aware of it, completely flummoxed him. Swearing, he walked down the hallway past her and turned at the bathroom, heading to the study where he'd seen Kalturek and Kahner disappear to mere moments before. He recalled he'd seen Kahner carrying a bundle of something in his arms and suspected that was likely the model she was referring to.

Hoping she'd managed to stop them in time, Angel turned on the spot, in order to head back the way she came. Losing her grasp on the towel, it fell open in the front, exposing her nakedness to Drayke's view as he walked towards her from the same hallway Nathan had disappeared down. He'd removed his running jacket and wasn't wearing a t-shirt. The sight of his broad bare chest was unnerving considering her state of undress.

Shocked to see him there, Angel shrieked and grabbed her towel in order to cover herself, then tripped and fell when she dashed for the bathroom. Dazed and horrified she pushed up from the floor. Feeling Drayke's strong hands on her arms, as he easily lifted her up from the floor and plopped her back on her feet; she clutched the towel to her chest as she trembled.

Eyes twinkling, Drayke chuckled. "Nice chest." Smiling and whistling as he walked away, he shook his head, having a sudden and rather urgent need to find Laynie. She hadn't been ready anyway, so he figured they'd stay at the house today instead of going out for breakfast.

Managing to hobble back into the pool room, as her face flamed red, Angel returned to the bathroom in order to get dressed. She had just stepped inside and had returned the towel to its rack when she felt the rush of cold air against her backside. Spinning around, Angel yelped at the sight of Kalabernus's hulking frame in the bathroom doorway. Staring at him in dismay, she grabbed for the towel again.

"Oh, geez," Kalabernus exclaimed, at seeing Angel standing stark naked in the bathroom. "I'm so sorry, I didn't... I didn't know you were still..." Slamming the door shut Kalabernus turned and backed down the hallway, while avidly staring at the bathroom doors. Bumping into Nathan, he changed directions while tearing at his face with his hands.

"Oh, man, Nathan! Oh, geez!" Kalabernus choked out. Hunching over unexpectedly, he continued hastily on past Nathan down the hallway toward the front of the house. "Where's my wife? Where'd Ariana go?"

"I think I saw her go upstairs," Nathan called after him.

His gaze followed after Kalabernus, as he made a quick getaway up the stairs in the entryway. Nathan had a sneaking suspicion he knew why the man was acting the way he was. He noted the direction Kalabernus was coming from and the door he had been staring at. Sighing heavily, as his shoulders slumped, Nathan held tightly to the covered miniature model in his hand.

Originally he'd thought to hide the model on this side of the house, but it occurred to him everyone used that closet. Thinking the hall closet on the opposite side of the house was the safest place to hide it until Bastion got home; he cut through the dining room. No one ever seemed to use it anyway. Stopping suddenly, before opening the closet door, he turned slightly in the direction of the bedroom across the hall. He could clearly hear the sounds of Drayke and Laynie doing more than just making out.

"Awe, Drayke. You too?" Nathan mumbled under his breath. He shook his head in disgust, having put two and two together. Hiding the miniature model on the floor near a plethora of boxes inside the closet in one corner, he cut back through the dining room, making his way to the kitchen, in order to make a hot toddy for Angel. He had a strong feeling that poor woman, was going to need more than one before the end of the day.

Chapter 5

Good grief!

Is it my imagination or has just about everyone in the RavenCroft household seen that poor woman naked?

What are the odds of that?

And do you suppose Angel saw that coming too? Huh.

As if she hadn't been through enough already...

- - -

The charcoal sweatpants were too snug.

The white t-shirt was way too tight.

And the socks Angel had in her hand were too small.

Angel limped barefooted from the bathroom. Hands shaking, while clasping her arms across her chest, she ventured down the hall toward the kitchen anxiously. Peering around the corner into the kitchen, she noticed three children eating at a table near the patio doors. Grimacing in frustration, she was about to turn around, when she heard Nathan call out her name.

"Angel, you can come on in."

Turning abruptly, she peered back into the kitchen, looking distressed, as she held herself tightly.

"Not sure that's such a good idea," Angel said nervously, as she stood on one leg in the doorway. Seeing everyone turn toward her, she sighed heavily at the inevitable awkwardness. "The shirt is too small. I think it might be more than a bit inappropriate to wear in there considering most recent events."

Kalturek almost laughed out loud. He glanced around at his family with amusement in his eyes. Chuckling as he stood, he walked over toward Angel and pulled off the navy-blue T-shirt he was wearing.

Angel stared at Kalturek, wide-eyed, as he stood before her, shirtless, with his arm outstretched. Identical to his twin brother in every way, she marveled at his well-muscled abs, good looks, and the crystal-clear blue of his eyes. He was the complete opposite of what her husband had been in terms of condition and health; though tall and broad, Wilton had been extremely out of shape. She hadn't minded so much but it was intimidating standing next to such a virile specimen as Kalturek while he was shirtless. Peering up at him, her lip trembled slightly as she stood there unmoving.

"I heard." Kalturek shrugged as he stared down at her kindly. He gestured for her to take the shirt from his hand.

"Maybe you could just, uh..." she said in response while leaning her shoulder toward him. Getting the picture, Kalturek smiled awkwardly and draped the shirt over Angel's shoulder.

"You can use the bathroom to..."

"Yeah, I know, been there. Thanks," Angel said, limping self-consciously down the hall. Turning into the bathroom, she missed seeing, Dr. S.T. Funnie enter through the front door.

Striding down the hall towards the kitchen, S.T. ducked his head into the kitchen and dropped his case on the floor near the counter.

Catching sight of her husband, Mackenzie smiled brightly and called out to him. "Hey there, Honey!"

"You can fill me in on everything in a minute. I need to use the restroom first," Dr. S.T. said, turning toward the hallway as he called back. He continued back down the hall toward the bathroom Angel had just entered.

It didn't take but a second for what he'd said to register before Kahner shot up from his chair. "S.T., wait!" Kahner hollered. Wild-eyed, he sped toward the hallway. Skidding to a sudden stop, he could hear Angel's startled cry coming from the bathroom, and Dr. S.T. exclaiming in dismay. Everyone in the kitchen halted at what they were doing, including the three children.

Starting to realize what was going on, Sable's ten-year-old daughter Lisa stared at her mother, her eyes growing wide as she heard Angel's next words.

"Well, gee, Kalturek!" they could all here Angel yell from the bathroom as Dr. S.T. came rushing down the hall, and into the kitchen, his face flaming. "You might as well get in here. You're the only one that hasn't seen me naked yet," she hollered crossly.

Limping out of the bathroom, and down the hall toward the kitchen, Angel appeared mortified, and her face was crimson under all the bruises, as she stepped into view. Holding Sable's T-shirt and socks loosely in her hand, she peered over at Kalturek expectantly.

Kalturek leaned against the counter where he stood and peered over at Angel, brows raised. "That's quite all right, Angel," he said quietly, having a hard time keeping from laughing. The mirth in his eyes was unmistakable.

"Right, one less body scarred for life," Angel responded with a nod as she turned towards Nathan. "I think I could use that hot toddy right about now," she said in a strained voice, her throat catching, as he proceeded to place the drink in her shaking hand. Raising the glass to her lips, she was about to enjoy her first, much-needed sip, when she heard a faint voice crying out to her from the living room. Whimpering, as she stared longingly at her glass, she hobbled forward and set it gingerly on the counter.

Pointing toward the glass, she could be heard to say, as her voice trembled, "Don't...go...anywhere."

"Mama! Mommy!" Kal screamed from the front living room.

Angel hobbled out of the kitchen.

"Wait a minute. She already has a kid?" Dr. S.T. asked in surprise, turning on his wife. "You didn't tell me there was a kid involved."

"I'm here, Kalturek. I'm coming," Angel hollered, disappearing from view.

"Did she just say, Kalturek?" Dr. S.T. inquired, looking startled. Glancing toward Drayke, he saw him nod his head in assent.

"Wait until you hear what his middle name is," Kahner mumbled as he took a long shaky drink of his beer.

Noticing that Kahner was drinking already at nearly eight in the morning, Dr. S.T. had the feeling things did not go well last night. When his wife had called, told him the condition Angel had arrived in and asked him to come to the ranch, he had been surprised to learn that the woman had even been brought there. She should have been taken straight to the hospital. The fact that a child had been involved alarmed him further.

Watching closely as Angel hobbled from one room to the next, Dr. S.T. could see the huge knot on the side of her ankle. Having also seen severe scarring along with bruises on her waist, arms, and face, as well as the look of shock in her eyes, he now understood better why Mackenzie had called him home.

"Why? What's his middle name?"

"Bastion," Synedra offered.

"You've got to be kidding me," Dr. S.T. responded, sounding stunned. He always missed the good stuff. It was getting really annoying, too.

"Nope, says so on his birth certificate," Laynie said, between mouthfuls of cereal, while trying to pay attention to the sounds coming from the living room.

"Laynie, how did you find that out? Did she tell you?" Nathan asked. He stood rigid and unmoving with a spatula in hand in front of the stove as if frozen in place.

Shrugging, Laynie replied, "I was going through her bag to see if I might possibly find undergarments for her," she added. "I didn't find any, but I did find three pads of paper, a flash drive case, and his birth certificate. Incidentally, I'll run to my shop this morning and bring her some clothes from there, so you can have yours back, Sable. Angel is a completely different size than the rest of us – even Stephanie. She might have an hourglass shape like her, but her build is a bit larger, so things clearly won't fit right."

Hearing Kal's hysterical cries from the living room, Dr. S.T. strode over to the kitchen door and propped it open with his foot. He watched Angel and her son for a moment with a clinical eye. Tilting his head to one side, as he stared at her ankle, he harrumphed softly.

"That woman is in shock, so is her son. How is she even walking on that ankle without screaming in pain?" Dr. S.T. wondered aloud, crossing his arms in front of him. "I thought she was a brunette," he commented offhandedly.

"Your guess is as good as mine. I've seen grown men with knots like that on their ankle, who were incapable of moving." Kahner turned then and watched them as well through the open doorway. "As to the hair, I figure she must have dyed it recently." He could see the boy had become quite hysterical upon waking, just as Angel had predicted.

"Kal, Baby, mommy's here," Angel said, calling her son by his nickname instead. "See? I'm okay. It's okay. Everything is going to be fine now. We're safe for now." Angel hushed softly at her ten-year-old son. She held him tightly, wrapping her arms around him for comfort.

"Are you sure it's not natural?" Dr. S.T. commented, referencing her hair once again.

Kalturek scoffed. "What makes you think it's natural?"

"Take a real good look at her son there," Dr. S.T. responded while pointing. "It's mostly golden blonde but if you look close there are silver highlights in that head of hair."

"Didn't you know? It's all the rage for kids nowadays to color and highlight their hair all kinds of gosh awful colors," Stephanie said dryly, her expression one of disapproval.

Their attention was drawn back to the scene taking place in the living room. Angel held the golden-headed boy in her lap and rocked him back and forth. He appeared big for his age.

"How could you mama? How could you let Daddy die? They shot him. The man shot him, and you stood there. How could you?" Kal screamed at her.

Sobbing next to her son, Angel cried openly. "Baby, I'm sorry. I'm so sorry. I had no idea it was real. I never imagined my stories could ever be real. Kal, Honey, I'm so sorry!"

The little boy wrapped his arms around his mother then, and hugged her close, as though afraid to let go. Moaning softly, the boy stared ahead of him in shock, as he rested his head on her shoulder.

"There's a hole...there's a hole...there's a hole in my Daddy's head, Mama. There's a hole," he kept saying over and over again until his voice finally trailed off, and he stopped speaking entirely.

"Yes, Baby. There's a hole in his head. I'm so sorry you had to see that. I'm so sorry, baby boy. He's at peace now, Kal. Daddy is at peace now. He's with God in heaven," Angel said softly. She continued to cry.

Watching the scene play out before them, Drayke quietly stood and closed the kitchen door. Becoming concerned for the three children in the kitchen, he eyed Sable meaningfully, as he set down his juice glass.

"Maybe we should get the kids out of here for a while."

"Of course, you're right," Sable stood swiftly and urged the children to follow her on out of the kitchen to their rooms to get their things. The weather outside was extremely mild for November so she figured she'd take them to PlayLand for a while, if they wanted, before heading to the movies.

"He will need a sedative; her too, probably," Dr. S.T. pondered the woman's situation. "And I'll need to take a look at her…"

"Haven't you seen enough of her already?" Kalturek smirked, winning him a scowl from his sister Mackenzie.

"And you're a Sheriff? It's a wonder you were ever elected." Clearly, Mackenzie was not amused by his sense of humor.

"Yup, it's shocking really, how far good looks and a winning smile can get a man." Kalturek's response sounded irritable, causing a few raised eyebrows. It occurred to some that it was entirely possible he was getting tired of the jokes about how he'd managed to gain the role as Sheriff of Loveland County.

Rubbing at his chest in agitation, Dr. S.T. inhaled deeply. "What can I say, Kalturek? She's got bruising across her rib cage. I'm a little worried there might be cracked ribs. Or didn't any of you notice?"

"Personally, I was a little more preoccupied with those two, lovely large…"

"Drayke," Laynie hollered sharply, interrupting him before he could finish.

Grinning from ear-to-ear, Drayke simply pulled out his phone in order to shoot off a text and let his friend know they wouldn't be making it that morning. He hadn't been really keen on attending the breakfast as they'd planned, but a longtime friend and co-worker had invited them and Laynie had seemed oddly interested.

"Drayke RavenCroft, is that why you practically attacked me?" she exclaimed in irritation.

"It didn't seem like you were complaining," Drayke responded, appreciating the fact his wife had been wearing a loose skirt that morning. He winked at her and leaned over to give her a kiss as she met him halfway with a giggle and a saucy smile.

Ignoring his horny brother and sister-in-law, Kalturek set down his coffee mug and shook his head. Leaning back, he rested his hands on the counter and responded to the good doctor's inquiry.

"No, I'm the only one who hasn't seen her naked."

"Regardless, I think it's safe to say they've both been traumatized," Dr. S.T. stated, becoming miffed. "I'll need to take a look…"

"Kal, wait! Where are you going?" they heard Angel calling out. A moment later the golden-headed boy, with deep blue eyes like saucers, appeared in the hallway kitchen doorway. Upon closer inspection, Kahner noted Dr. S.T. had been right. The boy did seem to have locks of silver in his hair.

Mumbling softly, Kal could be heard to say, as he pointed, "Kitchen." Pivoting, he pointed further along. "Pantry, then pool room. The movie room is just across the…" Shuffling down the hall he disappeared, his shoulders slumping as he walked in a daze. Re-appearing in the hallway, Angel followed close behind him. Her cheeks were stained with tears and she wiped at them, appearing drawn and tired. Limping along behind him, they both soon entered the movie room. Kal crawled up on the shelving against the wall and stared at the movies. Grabbing one up, he held it out to his mother, then pointed at the giant flat screen television on the wall.

"Movie, Mamma."

"Would that help Kal, to watch a movie for a while?" Angel asked softly, noting the room appeared smaller than what she would have thought it would be. She could see Dr. S.T. peeking in at them from the other side of the room. "Can you help me, please?" she asked, not knowing where to put the DVD, or how to turn on the screen. Such things were always so complicated for her.

Taking the box from her, Dr. S.T. put the movie in for them and started it up. Kal settled into a plush chair and sat staring in awe at the giant movie screen, as he watched. Sitting down next to him, the doctor took a moment to check him over. Seeing that he appeared to be otherwise all right, he grabbed a blanket and draped it around him. Pulling it tightly about him, he tucked him in, so he was well bundled.

"Thank you, Dr. Some," the little boy said softly. He continued to watch his movie, not even bothering to look at him. "I'll be fine for now. Just the movie; need the movie."

Unsettled to hear his real first name spoken by a child he'd never met Dr. S.T. gave him an odd wide-eyed look. Did the son have a gift like what his wife Mackenzie had said his mother had? He'd never met anyone other than the RavenCroft's with such abilities.

Peering at her son, then out the movie room door, Angel was torn between sitting near her traumatized child and drinking her hot toddy. The RavenCrofts had a lot of questions for her and needed answers but she also knew she needed to be there for her son.

"It's okay Mama. Go, talk to them. I'll be all right. We're safe here after all."

"Are *we*, Kal? Are *we*...safe here?" Angel asked, catching Dr. S.T.'s curious gaze at her emphasis of 'we.'

Taking his attention off the screen for a moment, the little boy turned toward her. "Really, Mama, it's okay. *I* am safe here," he responded, their eyes locking on each other intently.

Angel bit her lip with worry.

"They have questions for you, and you really need that drink," Kal finished, his attention back on the movie, once again transfixed.

Angel watched him momentarily then suddenly realized what he needed. Hobbling back to the kitchen, she walked past Nathan and opened a cabinet. Taking down a mug, she filled it with hot water from the teapot. Opening another cabinet, she automatically grabbed a box of instant hot apple cider as if she'd known it would be there, tore the package open, and dumped it in the hot water. Mixing it thoroughly she then headed to the pantry, having gained the stunned attention of about everyone in the kitchen.

"How does she know where everything is?" Angel could hear Ariana ask in amazement from the kitchen, as she searched for the cheesy corn puffs in the pantry. Seeing a bag propped haphazardly on a shelf with a small post-it note attached, she snatched it up. Glancing at the post-it note briefly before pulling it off, she paused. Frowning initially, she then smiled brightly and left the pantry with the bag in hand, tucking the post-it in her back pocket.

Oblivious of their surprised exclamations, she carried the bag and drink in to her son, handing them off to him. Giving him a kiss on his forehead, she gave him a fierce hug and whispered to him.

"I will be back to check on you. If you need me I'll be in the kitchen or living room, okay?" Seeing him nod that he understood, while he sipped his hot apple cider contentedly, she turned to leave already feeling slightly better about being at the RavenCroft ranch.

"Mama, it's not your fault," Kal said suddenly, surprising her. Looking back at him, she could see he was still staring at the movie. "There's no way you could have known. I *do* know that. It's not your fault." Popping a corn puff kernel in his mouth, he continued to stare at the screen.

Chapter 6

Poor, poor, Dr. S.T. Funnie.

He's always missing everything.

Don't you feel sorry for that man? Being as he's an Emergency Room doctor, he's often unable to attend certain family gatherings and sometimes even gets called away in order to cover shifts at the hospital. He tries to keep up with family events, but usually, his wife Mackenzie has to update him on what's going on during his days off.

Shoot, the good doctor didn't even find out about Kalabernus's proposal to Ariana at the family's weekly Wednesday night dinner a few weeks back, until he was told he had to attend their wedding.

And on the day of the wedding at that!

I suppose in the family's defense Kalabernus and Ariana did get married pretty quickly.

Hahahaha!

Kalabernus was so afraid she'd change her mind after she said yes that he insisted they get married that Friday of the same week he proposed. Since the stalker of Ariana's was no longer a concern, Bastion had demanded that at night she go back to the cabin. The RavenCroft patriarch was simply too old school where sleepovers between couples were concerned.

Personally, I think Kalabernus just got fed up and decided the only way he was going to get any time alone with Ariana was if they married quickly. So they did. But that's a whole other trouble-filled tale.

Right now, Angel's got some explaining to do. Problem is, she's mighty tired right about now. In shock too, according to Dr. S.T.

What do you suppose is up with her son though? Is it possible little Kal's mama isn't the only one who's potentially gifted? And did he just call Dr. S.T. by the name Some?

- - -

Returning to the kitchen, Angel noted she was starting to have more and more difficulty walking. Practically dragging her leg, she hobbled toward the table. Seeing her struggling Kalabernus kicked a chair out for her as she neared, so she could sit down. Falling into the chair, she closed her eyes for a moment, wishing she'd grabbed her drink before she'd set down. Sensing someone next to her, Angel looked up and found Nathan, Synedra and Dr. S.T. standing over her.

"I'll see to the leg, and if you don't mind, Angel, we're going to check your ribs as well," the doctor said as he stared down at her.

"She needs to eat, but I don't think I'm going to be any help to her right now," Synedra commented while glancing at her husband Nathan.

"No, I think you're right, but she'll need you later tonight so it's a good thing we were planning to stay here until Monday morning," Nathan responded. "I agree, she does need to eat but not breakfast food," he said as he stood, pondering over her. Then it came to him. "Chicken quesadillas with salsa, sour cream, and Doritos, and I'll re-warm your hot toddy a bit."

"That's very interesting," Mackenzie said nearby. She stared at Angel, thinking it odd that the woman needed the same thing their father usually craved all the time. Shrugging it off, Mackenzie watched as the three figures standing before the woman disappeared.

Dr. S.T. reappeared next to Angel a second later after grabbing his medical bag from the floor near the hallway. He knelt down near her ankle and eyed it with a clinical expression. He looked up into the woman's face, noting that she'd been staring at him intently. Aside from the difference in hair, she reminded him of Stephanie which was slightly unsettling.

"We haven't officially been introduced. I'm Dr. S.T. Funnie." He shifted uncomfortably before her.

Angel chuckled at the introduction, knowing full well why he went by S.T. "I know, Dr. Some Thing Funnie. You're just as I imagined," she said with a hysterical giggle. When she'd made up the name to put in her book she had merely been trying to be funny herself. She never actually imagined someone would be cruel enough to name their child that.

The doctor grimaced. The general sound of snorts and laughter behind him grated on his nerves. The RavenCrofts had taken great amusement at his unfortunate name from the moment they'd met him years before but had, for the most part, agreed to call him Dr. S.T. or simply S.T. for short.

"May I?" the doctor inquired while gritting his teeth. He cleared his throat and reached for her leg, ignoring her usage of his full name. Seeing her nod with a grin, he pushed the pant leg up and carefully inspected her injury. "Tell me if this hurts." He pressed gently against a spot on her ankle.

Sucking air in between her teeth Angel yelped in pain then whacked his hand away with a scowl. "Of course it's going to hurt if you do that," she yelled.

Her childish response gave him a moment's pause, but he apologized nonetheless "This needs to be x-rayed."

"No, it's just sprained," Angel said.

"It should be x-rayed, as well as your ribs. There could be a break or fracture…"

"No, really. It's just sprained for now," she replied quietly, appearing distressed. "And there are no broken ribs … yet."

Nathan's head jerked toward her, giving her a suspicious look.

"There's no way to know that for sure without…"

"Dr. Some Thing Funnie, trust me. I just know." She rolled her eyes, sounding almost frustrated and awfully sure of herself.

Sitting back on his haunches, the doctor eyed her face intently. "I'd appreciate it if you would just call me Dr. S.T or simply S.T. for short. Now, how exactly did this happen?" he asked finally.

Angel's mouth pursed into an amused grin at his request, and then she anxiously glanced towards Kahner, unsure of how much she really should be saying in front of everyone. Sending out a silent query, she noted he got her message.

"Listen, I think it's time that everyone who's got somewhere they need to be should head in that general direction," Kahner insisted. "Those who were planning to stay for the day might want to just head on home now." Glancing around the room he gave all of his siblings a meaningful look. After some hesitation, each one stood and began clearing their dishes in order to depart. The sound of a cell phone beeping had everyone pausing and grabbing for their phones.

"That's mine," Nathan said, catching sight of the text message on his phone. A look of surprise stretched across his face, quickly followed by the concerned crinkle of his forehead.

"Something wrong, Nathan?" Synedra inquired, sidling up next to him.

Quickly stashing his cell phone back in his pocket he shrugged and shook his head. "It's about a job.

Nothing you need to worry about. I'll meet you down at the stables."

"You still want to go on the trail ride? Now?"

"No time like the present. Besides, I've got a client that needs something you might be able to help me find."

"All right then." Synedra began grabbing some provisions and water from the pantry. Before she and Nathan left they both peeked into the front living room where Kal had been sleeping before he woke. Noting the laptop next to Angel's bag, they both recalled Laynie's comment about sifting through Angel's things as they headed on out through the patio doors.

After clearing their dishes and food from the table everyone else filed out through the living room toward the front of the house. Several family members commented on the laptop bag lying in a chair near the sofa with a duffel bag, wondering if Angel Stryfe's stories were saved on her laptop.

Seeing Dr. S.T. still kneeling on the floor before Angel, Kahner nodded toward him then jerked his head away toward the front of the house.

"Nope, I'm not going anywhere until I know for sure she's going to be okay. I need to know how this injury was sustained. It will help me determine how severe it might be."

The room had emptied by then and the only people left in the kitchen were Kahner, Kalturek, and Dr. S.T.

"Angel, can you explain without going into too much detail?" Kahner inquired.

Taking a deep breath, she responded tremulously, "The last thug, the one you...well...We struggled, he and I. And I...well, he...he had me pinned down on the ground, so I knocked a dining chair over on him," Angel recalled, visibly flinching at the memory. "I was trying to get up and run away. But he grabbed my ankle pretty hard and I fell to the floor," she finished quietly, attempting to show the doctor the angle and motion of the incident with her hands. For some reason, the lack of noise in the kitchen was unnerving her.

Nodding in understanding, the doctor opened his bag to see if he had a wrap inside. Her theory that it was just a sprain might well be right. Not seeing a wrap in his bag, he excused himself and headed to the laundry room. Returning moments later, he proceeded to bandage Angel's leg with a small ice pack from the freezer.

"I don't want you on that ankle any more than necessary. There still could be a hairline fracture," he said while tucking the last of the bandage in place. Angel couldn't help but notice a tiny angel had been drawn in black ink on the very end of the bandage. She smiled knowingly as the doctor continued. "If your son ... Kalturek needs something, have Kahner and Sable get it for you."

Seeing he was serious, Angel acquiesced with another roll of her eyes. "All right. He's used to being called Kal, though – not Kalturek. Wilton never did like the names I'd chosen," she finished with a pout, appearing cross. "Especially Bastion for some reason, which was why Wilton wouldn't let me make it his first name." Her voice rose slightly as she spoke.

"How did you come by those names anyway?" the doctor inquired before he left. "They *are* rather unusual after all."

Angel shrugged. "Just came to me, I guess. One after the other." Breathing in a deep sigh, she allowed her shoulders to slump, as she bent over the table. She thanked him, and he left. She watched him go, her eyes narrowing when he glanced back quickly then disappeared down the hallway, passing the living room on his way toward the front of the house. Angel sighed in resignation. She wasn't looking forward to this conversation.

Clasping the mug in front of her, she finally had a chance to take the first drink of her hot toddy. Licking her lips in appreciation as she closed her eyes, Angel quickly re-opened them, at seeing the image of her husband's ashen face before her. Shaking her head, she whimpered softly.

"I might need a few more of these," Angel said, raising her head to look up at Kalturek, who had just sidled up next to her. He had the plate in hand that Nathan had made up for her before he left.

By the look on her face, Kalturek expected she wasn't kidding. Even to his own eyes, he could tell she was still clearly haunted by the events of the night before. Her hands shook slightly which gave him a moment's pause.

"For now, how about we start with this and go from there," he responded gently with a flirtatious smile. "I'm here all day, so I can get you whatever you need. You're safe here," he assured her, giving her an intense look.

Glancing down at the plate of food then back at him, she became uneasy. "I noticed your *wife* wasn't here a bit ago."

"She had somewhere to be," he responded evasively.

"I'm sure you have somewhere to be, too," she said nervously. Biting her lip, she peered up at him with a look of innocence in her eyes and took the plate from him. Her gaze shifted uncomfortably toward Kahner who was watching them closely. "You *are* the Sheriff after all."

"The nice thing about being an elected official is that I can delegate and make my own hours. You being here is more important right now."

"Right."

"Besides, as Sheriff, I feel my presence is necessary here. I figure you could use a bodyguard; you know? In order to protect *all* our interests." Kalturek leaned forward across the table as he spoke, supporting his weight on the palm of his hands.

Not missing his meaning she became agitated. "I'm sure even Stephanie would agree you have more important things to do than to babysit me." She laughed nervously.

"Angel stop." Kalturek gained her wide-eyed attention. She was acting like she felt trapped and he suspected he knew why. "I get you're feeling as though you're imposing upon my time, so allow me to assuage your guilt. Trust me when I say *both* Stephanie and I feel that I need to be here with you today." He intentionally allowed his eyes to soften before her.

"Right, because Bastion is going to be absolutely thrilled to find me here with you *and* my son when he arrives home," Angel said flatly, having trouble glancing away from his intense gaze. Then, staring down at her mug, with a look of desperation on her face, she took a long drink of her hot toddy. Giggling hysterically from the tension in the room, she wiped at her mouth.

Was she really safe at the RavenCroft ranch, she wondered? Bastion RavenCroft was presently nowhere to be seen, and she suspected she now knew what that meant because it occurred to her how she'd intended to write this story. The problem was; it wasn't just a story anymore. It was real life.

But was her real-life scenario going to follow the story in her head?

When was she finally going to get some of the answers she needed?

"I'm not stupid, Kalturek." She gave him a penetrating stare. "I'm pretty sure I know what *you* want from me." She switched her attention to his twin brother and continued. "It was never the plan to bring my husband and son here, was it Kahner? Bastion expected…"

"We didn't know you were married and had a child," Kahner admitted, halting her from speaking further. Seeing the startled look on her face he inhaled deeply. Rubbing one hand across his jaw, he noisily plunked his beer bottle on the table. His agitation over the lack of intelligence on her was obvious. "Curiously, your profile is only two to three years old. The earliest reference we could find to your name was over ten years old. What little we did find on you was limited and consisted solely of a request for copies of a birth certificate and social security number. It's as though you've only been in existence for about ten years, which makes no rational sense considering you appear to be around our age. I couldn't even find an original birth certificate."

"I expect that you wouldn't find one, now would you?" There was a mysterious glint in Angel's eye.

"Why wouldn't I find one? If I didn't know better, I'd say you had been living completely off the grid, or something, until recently." The look he threw her way was calculating.

"Or something." Her response was evasive. She had anticipated being able to talk with Bastion first before having to get into all of this and was having difficulty determining whether it was safe to speak the truth.

"You have been saying things like that since the moment I picked you up, and frankly, that concerns me." Kahner wasn't sure he trusted yet whether she was who she was claiming to be.

"What is that supposed to mean anyway – or something?" Kalturek asked. His temper flared at her evasiveness. He had the distinct feeling she was keeping something from them, and he didn't like that at all.

"Tell your father to dig deeper, and he'll figure it out." Angel's response was both loud and short. She refused to discuss the matter further until she knew for sure her son was safe first. Until then, she had no intentions of telling them everything.

Tapping his knuckles on the counter, Kalturek spoke before his brother could stop him. "From the state you were in when you arrived, it's obvious you've been through a lot. I really don't want to pressure you unless I have to, but I do think it's time the most important questions were finally asked." He looked her straight in the eye. "How exactly do you know what you do?"

Angel scoffed and rolled her eyes again. "I think we both know the answer to that."

"The power of 'Knowing' just like our father?" Kalturek asked, receiving a dirty look from his brother. Shrugging, he gave him a similar look. "It's not like she doesn't already know," he thought silently, knowing his brother alone would hear.

Angel nodded as she ate. "So it would seem. But I didn't know or understand that until recently. Honestly, I didn't," she insisted.

"And that's how you know about us, specifically the RavenCroft family," Kahner prompted.

"Yes."

"Is that also how you know what you do about my wife, me, and … you?" Kalturek inquired. His brow rose suggestively at the question. "Your book descriptions were online for anyone to view and I've read them. According to what you wrote … you're meant to give me children." The timber of his voice was low and sensual, his eyes softening on her, roaming the length of her body as if inspecting a mare for breeding.

Angel didn't respond. Her heart fluttered anxiously in her chest. Feeling slightly trapped, her gaze flitted about the kitchen ceiling once again.

"Such a coward," she said softly, barely loud enough for Kalturek to hear.

"What did you say?"

Taking a deep breath she picked up her fork from the table and proceeded to cut off a bite of the quesadilla. Adding a bit of salsa and sour cream to the bite she sat with her fork poised near her full lips before answering.

"Honestly, I don't know what you mean. Besides, are you sure you're reading that right? Or did you even bother to finish reading what you have?" she inquired sarcastically. She suspected they had more than just what she'd written, but that of another author as well.

Flabbergasted by her response Kalturek shoved away from the counter in disgust. "Are you really going to try and sit there and tell me you have no idea what's supposed to happen here?" For a brief moment, Kalturek began to wonder at the absurdity of the situation. His discussion with his wife, Stephanie, from the night before, was beginning to seem somewhat ridiculous when now faced with the woman before him. Was there something they'd missed as Angel had said? Or was she simply anxious about being in his presence just as Stephanie had predicted she'd be? Shaking his head suddenly, he shot her a steely look and took an aggressive stance, ignoring Kahner as he turned in his chair and glared.

"We agreed…" Kahner began.

"I didn't agree to anything. You kept talking. I simply never bothered responding," Kalturek argued.

"Let it go for now. She's been through enough. We wait until Dad gets home," Kahner insisted.

"Yes, let's wait until Bastion gets home," Angel mocked crossly, her gaze flitting around the kitchen.

"No. I don't think so. By then it will be too late," Kalturek said, thinking her behavior was odd. He exchanged looks with his brother, noting he wasn't the only one thinking that.

"Says who?" she asked.

"Says you … in your own book description about us. It's backed up by a reference made by another author from a similar novel series. I can believe that theory since your knowledge of this family and the events leading up to this moment has been so accurately portrayed in what you've written so far. So as surreal and absurd as this may seem I cannot discount this as being a credible, for lack of a better term, prophecy of sorts. Angel, listen, rest assured I wouldn't hurt you," Kalturek said urgently. "But we need to..."

"What you need to do, is go back home to your wife. *I* cannot help you."

"Can't or won't?"

"You're married," she said with a blush, smiling and giggling like a teenager.

Covering her hand on the table with his, Kalturek turned it over and rubbed her palm with his thumb. Stick to their plan, he thought. He had to stick to their plan.

"Your point? Many a child has been born out of wedlock," he attempted to reason.

Angel jerked her hand away, giving him a look that would kill. Her shoulder raised self-consciously as she rubbed her hand across her thigh, attempting to shake off the sensation zinging its way through her arm. Kalturek smiled knowingly at her reaction.

"Knock it off," Kahner said crossly, alarmed by his brother's behavior. He was being oddly sexually aggressive which was highly out of character for him.

Becoming miffed Angel stood, having lost her appetite. She turned to leave but Kalturek grabbed her arm.

"Let go of my arm," she said sharply, gritting her teeth.

"Angel ... you're meant to be *my* angel. Don't you see?" Kalturek crooned.

Jerking her arm from his hold she backed away. "My husband was just murdered, and you're still married. Yet you have this expectation that I'm gonna, what? Sleep with you because you and your wife want children?" Angel scoffed, angry that she was being considered a mere vessel for his seed. He clearly had no intent to leave his wife; they simply expected that since his family had brought her to safety, she'd be willing to bear his children for him. They were so desperate for a baby that they didn't seem to care about what she wanted and needed. The thought hurt, wounding her deeply.

"Are you kidding me?" She shouted in disgust, turning about the kitchen. "What exactly was it you were expecting to hear from me?" she asked the room at large then turned on Kalturek, pointing at him. "No, wait, let me guess. You, Kalturek ... you figured you'd bat those pretty blues you inherited from your father and that I would be ever so grateful to you for bringing me to so-called 'safety' that I'd jump in bed with you," she exclaimed, making a snorting sound in the back of her throat. "You weren't even the one to come save me and my son. No, it was your brother, not you. Yet here you are expecting me to carry the babies you're meant to have."

"Now we're getting to the heart of the matter. I *am* meant to have children aren't I?" Kalturek was visibly excited by the news, having picked up on what she'd said. "Triplets, like my brothers?" he asked hopefully.

"Of course you are. How is it you guys haven't figured this out already?" Angel asked scornfully, becoming thoroughly confused and cross all in one. Her brow furrowed in annoyance. Could they really not know what was happening within their own fold? Were they truly unaware that their entire family was all part of a grand universal prophecy foretold many, many years ago? Even she knew that now, and she was just a small pawn in the grand scheme of things.

"Then what's the problem here?" Kalturek asked urgently. "You want that I woo you? Be romantic? I can do that," he insisted, his expression softening on her once again. Coming toward her, he attempted to take her in his arms as he rubbed up against her.

Panicking Angel pushed at his chest, struggling to get him away. Her eyes became wild and afraid. "Stop. You have no idea what you're doing. Get away from me!"

Kahner rushed toward them. Gripping his brother's arm forcefully, he yanked it from around her waist.

"Stop it, Kalturek. That's enough! We may be a lot of things, but we do not take women by force in this house. You of all people should know that."

Kahner suddenly felt like something had shifted between them, as though he was stepping into a role with his brother that he'd never been in before. They had always considered each other equals; the three of them had, having been born triplets, regardless of the order of their birth. But for some reason now, he felt like he was being forced into a role as an older brother; the head of his siblings. The notion was overwhelming and yet felt oddly deserving somehow.

Arms wrapped around herself protectively, Angel eyed Kalturek wearily. Shaking visibly from his aggressive and amorous behavior, her gaze flitted about the kitchen nervously, wondering how many shadows were present. Instantly her eyes flashed with anger, the blue depths darkening ominously.

"What is the point to this? Why put me through this?" she cried.

"Get some space, Kalturek, I need to talk to her," Kahner demanded.

Growling in frustration Kalturek turned on his heel and left the kitchen in a huff. "I'll be back, make no mistake."

The room fell quiet in his absence.

"Come," Kahner insisted in a gentlemanly manner. "Sit down and eat, please."

Angel shook her head, still unnerved by Kalturek's amorous behavior toward her. She could see Kahner standing with his arm outstretched, attempting to placate her with softer, non-threatening behavior. Angel couldn't help but think, at that moment, that he reminded her of his father the way he was responding to her. The thought was absurd of course, as she hadn't even met Bastion yet, but that had been how she always imagined the RavenCroft patriarch to be.

"Please, you need to eat and keep up your strength. You are safe with me here," Kahner insisted gently.

Slowly moving back toward the table, Angel sat down and stared at her plate. She wasn't sure she'd be able to eat. Her hands still shook, and her heart was in her throat.

"I know you've been through a lot, but will you please tell me about last night?" he implored, needing answers of his own. He worried about pushing her too much further.

"Kahner, I woke up from one nightmare to find myself in the middle of a real-life one. If you want to know what happened last night, all you have to do is look at my laptop and you can read every gory detail," Angel said, sounding slightly exasperated in addition to being tired. She pushed the plate in front of her away.

"What do you mean?"

"I wrote out the whole bloody scene just before laying down for bed last night." Angel reached for her mug only to find it empty. Glancing imploringly toward him she lifted her mug in the air and whimpered. If she was going to go through all this she might as well be slightly tipsy. She figured it might help get her through it.

His mouth quirked up on one side with humor. "I'll get you another one." He went to work mixing another hot toddy for her. "Are you telling me you knew what was going to happen at your house before it even happened?"

"It would seem so, yes. I didn't realize that was what I was doing though, at the time. Honestly, I didn't fully understand until now, that I had this ability. I knew I was different somehow. Have ever since… Well, for the past ten to fifteen years anyway," she said, managing to catch herself before she said too much. "Sometimes I'd know a person's name before I met them or know when my son had been injured at school before they'd even call. But Wilton and I just thought I was super sensitive or something, which is what sort of gave me the idea to write the series of novels in the first place. Not that Wilton liked that at all," Angel said with a short laugh. "I had no idea any of it was real, that you all were real or even that I had any part in this." She swirled her arm in an encompassing arc about the kitchen. Noting his blank stare, she went on. "Writers add a bit of themselves to their stories all the time, right? I'm sure even David Pearson would agree," Angel said dryly. Her voice rose as she spoke. "I just figured it would be a really cool idea for a book you know? A writer writing about a family only to find out they were real and that she was writing about herself as well."

Kahner glanced her way as he was finishing her drink and gave her an odd look.

"I got that notion from a fellow author I came across on a writer's blog site," Angel said loudly. "I think her name was Ciara Biardon or some such, in case you need to know that. Who would have thought, right?" Angel's head bobbed around the room and she marveled not for the first time at finding herself sitting in the middle of the RavenCroft family kitchen. "Incidentally, Lionel Radford's men never got a chance to interrogate me. I imagine that's what you want to talk about," she said out of the blue.

Kahner frowned. Her behavior seemed slightly off somehow, and he couldn't quite figure out what it was that was bothering him about it. At times she seemed awfully loud when she didn't really need to be. He was trying to determine if that was just naturally in her nature, or if there was something else going on.

He headed towards her with her drink and Angel desperately reached for it, nearly sliding out of her chair in the process. Rushing towards her, so she didn't try and walk, he placed the mug in her trembling hand. Clasping the drink with both hands in order to steady it, Angel sipped at her hot toddy eagerly and sat gingerly back in her chair.

"Where are your bags?" Kahner stared intently at Angel. If what she was saying was true, then it was entirely possible he'd managed to prevent anything further from leaking out about his wife Sable and their kids' new location.

Angel shrugged.

Moments later Kahner disappeared into the living room then returned shortly thereafter with her book bag and laptop bag in hand. Pulling out the laptop Kahner set it on the counter, opened it up, and turned it on. She stayed silent, waiting expectantly for him to pull up the file she was referring to.

"What am I looking for here? Which file is it and where? Is it even on here?" he asked after a minute had passed.

Regaining her appetite, a bit, she had been intent on finishing her quesadilla and cheesy nacho chips.

She replied between mouthfuls. "What you're looking for is saved on the blue flash drive in the case. My other stories are saved on the other drives. Wilton bought the laptop for me second-hand so it's a piece of crap. I'm constantly losing things on it cause the screen likes to go dark on me suddenly. Which is why I got in the habit of regularly saving to both the laptop and a flash drive."

Glancing down at the bag lying next to the laptop Kahner grabbed it and dragged it closer. The bag was already open. Reaching down inside of it, he found the birth certificates Laynie had mentioned along with a folded-up marriage license.

"I don't see the flash drive case you mention. Are you sure you put it in here?" He dug further in the bag but came up with nothing.

"Uh, yeah, positive," she replied. Her eyes shifted toward the living room then back to him suspiciously.

"You didn't zip the bag closed. It probably fell out onto the floor in the living room." He shrugged as though the missing case was no big deal.

Angel sat back in her chair and stared blankly at him. He had dumped everything out on the counter, making a big show of it. Which meant her three spiral notebooks and her drawing pad were missing too. That bothered her. Why was Kahner being so blasé about the missing flash drive case? He'd been adamant at her house that she made sure to grab everything, so she did. Her mind whirred with possibilities. She tried to remember if the bag had been zipped up when she'd gone in to comfort her son when he woke. But she couldn't remember. A much more disturbing possibility was that he had snuck the flash drive case and notebooks out when she wasn't looking.

"But you said the files are saved on the laptop anyway, though, right?"

"Right." Angel stared at him, then glanced toward the kitchen door which led to the living room. Everyone had filed out in that direction when they left except Dr. S.T. Had one of the others taken the flash drive case and the three notebooks for some reason? She noticed him staring back and forth between her computer and the bag.

"What?"

"When I told you that you had a minute to pack items you needed, you spent all your time packing up this instead?" Kahner looked at her incredulously.

"Well, yeah. I mean, you did say to get the laptop and flash drives first. I figured the last thing Bastion would want was evidence of anything that had been written about any of his children left behind," Angel explained worriedly. She glanced around the kitchen then back at him, looking cross. She'd been doing that a lot - flitting her gaze about the room. Kahner was starting to wonder why. Could she also see the shadows that Kalabernus and Ariana could see?

"In my writings and in books I intended to write, I have Bastion pegged as being notorious for anonymity and...secrecy," she said, banging her hand on the table hard while scowling. "As well as having a vindictive nature," she said harshly in a raised voice as she pointed toward the books and papers. "All that might have led back to all of you. I couldn't have lived with myself knowing I'd put any of you at risk," she said, sounding genuine until she rolled her eyes, looking suddenly disgusted and temperamental. Her voice rose unexpectedly at her next words. "Heaven knows it would have killed Bastion if that had happened. I can only imagine what he would have done to *me* upon learning I was the cause of it all," she practically shouted.

Kahner's eyes grew wide. He stared at the woman before him. She was acting a bit crazy.

Sighing heavily as she drank gratefully from her mug once again, Angel began to feel a little light-headed from the liquor in it. "Lord, help me," she went on almost angrily, becoming despondent. "Knowing his background he probably wouldn't even bother killing me. No, no. That's not in his nature. No, he'd just torture me for a long, long dang while just for being the cause of your secret getting out," she fumed.

"Have you met my father or something?" Kahner inquired, becoming suspicious.

"Oh, no. I haven't had that pleasure yet," she snarled darkly. She brooded, her brow furrowing angrily as she pursed her lips in annoyance over the absolutely twisted situation she found herself in. On top of that, now her flash drives and notes were missing.

"Are you sure? Because you sure seem to know him pretty well."

"I know him all right. Yup, yup! I got that coward's number."

Chapter 7

In case you're all wondering…it was me.

Hee Hee Hee

I took them.

That's right, folks. I, Vortigern Black am the thief, the robber, the pickpocket, if you will. Shoot, I snatched the flash drive case and notebooks as soon as I realized what was likely there. I would have taken the laptop too, but that would have been too obvious.

I suppose, in the back of your minds, you're all wondering what the heck is wrong with me. Am I right? No doubt you're even asking yourselves why I would do something so despicable, so sneaky, so completely out of character. To which I respond…

Are you sure it's out of character? And…

Hello?

Are you kidding me? I'd have been an idiot not to take the opportunity when it came available. From everything that I had heard and seen up to that point, it was my understanding that this woman Angel Stryfe had been writing fairly accurate accountings of potential future events. Puhleeease! Can you imagine what a person could do with such foreknowledge?

Hehehe.

I bet you really wish you knew who I was now…

-Don't you?

And, yes, that is where the stories for this here An Unfortunate Lineage came from. The original author was, in fact, Angel Stryfe.

This explains a lot, doesn't it? I imagine you might even be having an 'aha!' moment right about now. Cause, after all, Angel Stryfe has an ability quite similar to both Bastion and his brother Rafe of the Blackthorne clan, only it's much stronger and more accurate for some reason. That's why this vast collection of stories has so many viewpoints because she's somehow able to know everyone's perspective at any given moment. Kind of eerie, if you ask me.

Anyway, once I got ahold of the stories on the flash drives, I took the first opportunity I could get and began reading everything. And I mean everything! I had to do it in stages, of course, cause, well, I do actually have a life. Plus, my spouse kept conveniently interrupting me just about every time I tried to really get into them. I swear it's like they knew I had what I had.

Sheesh! Some people are just so nosey. Do you know what I mean?

But not me. Oh, no. I'm not nosey. I'm curious. Yeah, that's it. You know, curious… like a cat.

And before you all get all riled up about how Ms. Christine is plagiarizing another author's work, well, just don't. There's no need. Because see…we have permission. Yeah, that's right. A sort of … form of consent…

-In a way.

Ah, heck. Just trust me when I tell you that no one is copying anyone's work.

Sort of.

Moving on…

While reading through everything, I made a mighty interesting discovery that sure as heck got my attention. You may recall in the very first volume you ever read how I might have mentioned I tried approaching a certain character within this story – who shall remain nameless – with a, shall we call it … proposal of sorts?

You may also recall that much to my disappointment, disgust, and irritation, they refused me.

Me. Vortigern Black, of all people.

So, I got ahold of Ms. Christine and here we are. She's writing the An Unfortunate Lineage series of stories and I'm narrating them. Phooey!

To heck with 'Nameless.'

Sorry, folks. Guess I got on a rant there. Back to the story…

Right about now, Kahner's experiencing a great deal of relief. He'd been worried at how much Angel might have shared with Lionel Radford's men and was concerned some of it had already been relayed back to him before they'd been silenced. Knowing that his wife and children were likely still safe was a pretty big weight off his shoulders. He was also starting to realize how truly self-less Angel Stryfe was for her first instinct had been to protect a family of individuals she hadn't been entirely sure were even real yet.

What was stumping him about her was her fluctuating temperament and her alarmingly accurate assessment of his father. It made him wonder just how much she really knew about him and his family.

- - -

Kahner was quiet as he stared curiously at Angel, contemplating the woman before him. His awe over the woman was twofold really. Appreciation for the efforts she'd gone to in order to protect people she didn't even know, in addition to a grudging respect for the way she responded with regard to his father. She sure didn't seem intimidated by him by any means. He wondered briefly if she'd act the same if he was present. Eyes twinkling, he began to smirk as he shook his head in wonder.

"You were protecting us," he said softly, sounding incredulous.

"Why's that so surprising?" She scowled at him.

"Because you don't even know us."

For the first time since he'd taken her from her home and brought her to the ranch, Kahner really took a good hard look at her. Her long hair was tousled and still damp from her shower. The distinctive silver coloring seemed to shimmer under the kitchen lights, the golden hues glistening as it hung in thick heavy waves around her shoulders. He imagined she was normally quite pretty like Stephanie, but the bruising along her face had become quite pronounced and the knot on the side of her leg could be seen even with the bandaging. He knew full well what Lionel's men were capable of, having seen it for himself on a few unfortunate occasions.

When he'd aided his wife Sable and her kids from running from him, Kahner had been there for her, protecting her during her harrowing escape. But in Angel's case, she'd had to defend herself and protect her son all on her own after her husband was murdered. He had renewed appreciation for what she had been through. At the same time, he felt oddly relieved, as though a weight had been lifted from his shoulders.

"Thank you, Angel," Kahner said finally.

Startled by the catch in his voice and his soft tone, she looked over at him curiously. "For what?"

"After everything you went through, your first thought when I went to pull you out wasn't for yourself or your son, but for us. I don't know that many other people would have done what you did," he finished, sounding genuinely thankful.

Becoming uncomfortable with his obvious gratitude and the odd look she was receiving, Angel stayed silent. Not really sure what to say she went back to her food and drink more for something to do with her hands than for hunger. The kitchen remained quiet until he spoke again, having recalled what else Angel had brought with her.

"The model house you dragged along. You said it was an exact replica of this house?" Kahner said as he gestured around him then peered down at the bag and laptop.

"Yes," Angel replied, grateful for the change of subject. She watched him fidget, tap nervously on the counter near the bag, and then peer in confusion from the bag to the living room then back again. Shrugging his curious behavior off, Angel gazed around the kitchen in admiration. "I drew out every room in this house as I dreamed it would be and it's as beautiful as I imagined it," she said dreamily. Glancing furtively at Kahner she looked away quickly knowing full well she couldn't allow him to pick up on the secrets that lay within the house and her mind. She realized she had to change subjects again quickly or he might pick up on what she was thinking. Setting her mug down suddenly she peered around the kitchen once again.

"You said you wrote about what happened last night," Kahner said out of the blue. "I can't find that file unless you tell me what you named it."

"Right, sorry. I do have a lot of files with story ideas. The file you want is called Twisted and it's located within the file on the desktop called RavenCroft Saga. If all you want to know right now are the events of last night at my house, then that starts at the beginning of chapter one. But if you want to see if anything else is accurate then…read from the prologue."

Kahner located the file and pulled it up on the screen. Glancing through the beginning of the novel his eyebrows rose in surprise at seeing a character list with all their names. He'd known they were all supposed to be in her story but seeing them listed out as characters was a bit unsettling.

Inhaling deeply he proceeded with the story, reading it aloud. It became apparent that what she'd written was wholly accurate. He was floored by what he was reading.

"That's exactly what Stephanie said to Dad about not letting him get in her way," he commented dryly. "Wow, she really sounded kind of hateful and self-absorbed there didn't she?"

Angel didn't comment, knowing full well what he was about to read next.

"How could you have known?" he inquired of her.

"Who knows?" Angel mumbled. Her head rested on the table. She looked forlorn, not bothering to look up in order to gauge Kahner's reaction as he read. It all seemed so surreal to her, to hear the story she'd written read back to her by one of the very characters she'd written about. "It's kind of like a movie reel in my head sometimes," she finally said. "It's hard to explain. Usually, an event or moment is very obvious to me on how it plays out. And other times..."

"Other times?" Kahner coaxed, intrigued by what she was saying.

She shrugged. "Other times I imagine several scenarios for the same thing."

"Can you give an example?"

Sitting back in her chair Angel sighed as she became thoughtful. "Like in yours and Sable's case. I always imagined the two of you making out on Anthony Margoolis's desk in order to stump Lionel's men, so you could get away. And you dumping the car in the pond in northern New Mexico just before Kalturek came and picked you up..." she stopped suddenly, her head tilting toward the ceiling as though deep in thought.

Kahner had squeezed his eyes shut in frustration as she spoke, disturbed at hearing her relay what had transpired. Realizing she'd paused he prompted her. "You were saying?"

"Right, well, as opposed to the dumping of the car, I imagined about three different scenarios for the scene in Anthony Margoolis's office. Wilton even had to help me with it. Not having ever taken men down like that by murdering them in such quick succession, I wasn't sure how something like that would play out exactly. So he ran me through how he would have done it," Angel finished. Staring down at her plate, it took a moment for her to realize what she'd just said. Wide-eyed her head shot up toward Kahner in alarm. "Kahner, I'm so sorry I didn't mean..."

"In the future, maybe use an example from someone else's story," he vented, rubbing at his jaw in frustration. He really didn't like being reminded of the men he'd had to kill. "You say your husband showed you? Was he a cop, or in the service, or something?"

"Army, as I understand it. He was listed as having been in service for four years, but he actually served for fourteen," she replied absentmindedly.

"What was his Military Occupational Specialty?"

"His initial MOS, like most entering the army, was eleven bravo ten. But he wanted to play with the 'big toys' as he put it, so he asked his commander what it would take to do that. By the end of his military career, his designation was eighteen bravo ten. Which basically means he was a…"

"Weapons specialist," Kahner said grimly, giving her an odd look.

"Yeah, he, uh, he was based out of Georgia, though he trained all over and served in eighty-second airborne with a sniper specialty. He was a jumpmaster," Angel said promptly, her gaze shifting about the room. "Yeah, I know, rather interesting coincidence there."

Confused, and sensing he'd missed something even though he'd been eavesdropping, Kalturek inquired from the hallway. "I don't understand. How is that a coincidence?"

"Let it go," Kahner said quickly, knowing full well that his brother had been listening. His siblings knew their father had been in the army at one point, but they weren't privy to the extent of Bastion's service record like he was. That knowledge had come about by pure accident.

"Why would your husband have been only listed for four years if he served for fourteen?" Kalturek asked suspiciously, coming the rest of the way into the kitchen.

"Drop it, Kalturek," Kahner said abruptly. "And I thought I told you to take a hike.

"I'm thirsty. Besides, it's not your house, yet. You only live here." Kalturek sauntered toward the fridge. He grabbed a beer from within and snapped the top off, taking a long drink for show.

Kahner harrumphed softly. "More mine than yours since I actually live here," he said under his breath. "Can you give me another more recent example, Angel?" he asked, changing subjects.

"I've never had an issue with multiple scenarios for book one or most of two," Angel said fidgeting in her seat due to Kalturek's presence so close to her. "But in book three the character…" she paused, becoming emotional. "I originally wrote that she lost her husband in a work-related accident the same day you flew out to pick her up," Angel explained, pointing towards Kahner. "But instead…" Taking a deep breath she continued. "Instead he was m-murdered by Lionel Radford's men."

"Why the change I wonder?" Kalturek asked hoping to curb the inevitable awkward silence. "Different scenario yet, essentially the same outcome."

"Like a pebble in a stream," Kahner nodded his head, contemplating the matter. He was finally starting to understand what it was that she was doing. "Because…a variable changed. Something one of us, or for that matter someone else did, changed the course of events."

Peering over at her, Kalturek looked at her in wonder. It would seem that Angel did, in fact, have the same type of power that his father had. Yet, what she was capable of seemed to be even more pronounced somehow. Marveling briefly at what she appeared to be able to do, he returned his attention to her laptop and the story she had written that he'd been eavesdropping on.

Kahner continued to read, stopping abruptly when he got to a new chapter where Kalturek and Stephanie were speaking privately on their way home Friday night in their vehicle. At this point he continued to read in silence, causing his brother to wonder at why. Kahner peered suddenly over at Kalturek with distaste, having read what had been said according to what Angel had written.

"Would you really do that?" His eyes narrowed upon his twin brother. Angel watched the by-play going on between the twins, fascinated by how they could communicate silently as they did. It was quite obvious they were having a silent conversation she couldn't hear.

"I think we both know the answer to that," Kalturek said darkly after a moment, having been silently asked the same question once again. Shoving away from the counter unexpectedly, he began pacing the kitchen in agitation as he cast an uncomfortable look toward Angel, then back at his brother. It never occurred to him that Angel would be aware of what he and Stephanie had talked about. Her hesitant and jumpy behavior toward him made a lot more sense now.

"Yes, and that's what bothers me," Kahner stared at his brother, as though seeing him for the first time.

Angel's posture became rigid and she tensed. She knew full well what their silent discussion had been about. Noticing Kalturek casting angry looks her direction Angel became anxious. Glancing back and forth between the remainder of her food and him she finally got tired of him glaring at her.

"Look, I write what comes to me, okay. It just gets dumped in my head." She gestured with her fork toward her head wildly. "How was I supposed to know that your intentions were real? Besides whom should be angry at who here?" Angel pointed her fork at him, appearing wounded and angry all at once. "You're only mad because you've been found out. Be angry at the right person, Kalturek," Angel said emphatically.

Scoffing loudly Kalturek laughed and shook his head. "Man, Lady, you got a lot of nerve."

"I've got nerve?" Angel snapped heatedly. "Would you care to tell your whole family when they arrive home today what yours and Stephanie's plans were for me?" She placed another bite of quesadilla in her mouth and glared at him impudently.

Kalturek spun on her and growled deep in his throat.

"Enough, Kalturek! What's the matter with you?" Kahner asked crossly. Something was eating at his brother and he was afraid he knew what it was; the shadows.

"What's the matter with me?" Kalturek ground out as though astounded by his brother's stupidity. "Less than twenty-four hours ago I find out Angel

119

Stryfe is the only chance my wife and I have for children and it turns out there is a deadline to boot."

"What is this deadline you keep talking about? You mentioned it before."

"Yeah! Midnight, tonight," he shouted, his response shocking his brother. "Stephanie's telling me I have only until midnight to get her pregnant. After that, I'll never get another chance. So, what do *you* think is wrong with me?" He gestured toward Angel, causing her eyes to widen and peer away as though horrified and embarrassed by the notion all in one.

"If it's any consolation, Kalturek, it could never happen anyway. I still wouldn't be able to become pregnant by you today." Angel fidgeted nervously in her seat at the look Kahner threw her way. The whole conversation seemed grossly inappropriate and sacrilegious to her mind, particularly considering her belief system. She couldn't believe they were even discussing it.

"Why not?" Kalturek gave her a disbelieving look.

Kahner looked on in dismay, seemingly offended by the very notion of his brother sleeping with a woman with the intent of getting her pregnant, while still being married to another.

"I don't have *all* the answers." With a weary sigh, she stared back at Kalturek in exasperation, smacked both hands against the table, and leaned back in her chair. "All I can tell you is how I was going to write it. And only David Pearson knows how David Pearson was going to write it," she said, becoming loud once again.

"Okay, so how were you going to write the story?" Kahner raised his hands in the air in order to silence his brother and try and instill some calm back in the room. He could see him scowling and sensed the inner turmoil he was going through. Kahner never fully realized how badly his brother wanted children until that moment.

Harrumphing softly Angel paused, appearing both irritated as well as momentarily thoughtful. She allowed her bare feet to swing beneath the table. Reaching for another chip with one hand she pushed a damp silver strand of hair back over her ear.

"You know, I had a thought," she said almost absent-mindedly then continued suddenly. "Nope, I lost it. From what I gather, Kalturek, you're basing the fact that I can help you have children off of the first three chapters of a book written by an unknown author who goes by the name David Pearson. Am I right?"

Shaking his head vigorously Kalturek argued the point. "Not just that. Your book description also says..."

"I know what it says. I did write it after all. The point is, you're still married," Angel grated out irritably while pointing towards him. "I will not agree to sleep with a married man, so you can have children. I mean, seriously, whose romance story do you think I was writing about in book three anyway? Yours, or mine?"

Perplexed, Kahner's head whirled toward her. "I thought they were one and the same."

"How could they be? He's married," Angel emphasized again.

"Your own book description says you're here in order to help me have children. Yes, or no?" Kalturek asked becoming fed up.

"Yes."

With a satisfied gleam, Kalturek banged on the counter for effect. "Then reason would dictate, I'm meant to get you pregnant today if my deadline is by midnight tonight."

"Uh, no, not necessarily, besides your assumption here, is that it's *your* deadline," Angel disagreed with him while rolling her eyes.

"You're making no sense," Kalturek hollered.

Angel gave a very unlady like snort. "Trust me. I'm making a whole lot more sense than you."

Kahner paced back and forth between the patio doors and table in frustration as Kalturek stormed angrily from the kitchen leaving the two of them alone again. The situation seemed impossible. She made it sound like the hero of her novel was some great mystery and yet even he suspected his brother and the woman sitting at the counter were meant to be together at some point. How else was she supposed to be able to help him have children? It was like one of those awful romance novels with a lover's triangle. Was there even a feasible solution, he wondered? Peering at the ceiling then back at Angel in distress, Kahner flexed his shoulders and ran his hands through his hair in aggravation as he listened to her continue

"I know it's probably little consolation, but I don't think Kalturek and Stephanie were ever really meant to have a family together." Her speech stopping abruptly Angel sat for a moment staring at the table, her expression blank.

Watching her, Kahner realized at that moment that she had had no idea what she was really saying or doing just then until she'd stopped speaking. Seeing her wise deep blue eyes peer over at him in surprise as she blinked, Kahner truly began to believe that the woman had never fully understood what her gift really was, or for that matter, that she even had an ability in the first place, until she'd arrived in their home.

"Which means, that if you are, in fact, not meant to be with him today then Kalturek will never have children," Kahner declared, stating what seemed to be obvious. "Stephanie is going to leave him. Isn't she?" He voiced the question aloud not really expecting to gain an answer. "I remember when he told her about his gift. Her eyes fairly glowed with anticipation when she learned of it. I had the feeling even then that she wanted to have children with him just so she could experience it. She's liable to leave him if she can't at least raise gifted children, I expect."

The room fell silent once again at his words.

Sitting back in her chair Angel shifted uncomfortably as she peered around the room and at the ceiling. Seeing Kahner's brooding countenance, she rolled her eyes once again. It was becoming habit forming. Realizing he was desperately in need of a consoling hand, it occurred to her, she would have to comfort him since neither Sable nor Bastion was there. Finding that ironic considering she was the one who just lost her husband and had nearly been killed, she couldn't help but wish she had someone to do that for her.

"If Bastion were here I'm sure he'd be telling you to have faith," Angel said in a tired voice, feeling quite drained all of a sudden.

"Faith?" Kahner scoffed with disgust. "In the universe, I suppose? Nah, he'd just tell us to suck it up."

Angel's lips pursed irritably. "Oh, yes of course. Because only a *supposed* father-less child, like Bastion, would be so callous, right?" she shouted. "It's probably where his name was coined from in the first place," she continued to fume. "Because Bastion is a ba…"

"Angel." Kahner stopped her before she swore. He was completely flummoxed by her sudden outburst. "What in the world?"

She banged her silverware on her plate and gave him a scathing look. Grabbing it up, she hobbled it over to the sink near where Kahner stood and dumped it in.

"First of all, it's not a bad word if it's being used in the right context rather than as an insult. And second, in lieu of Bastion, I'm telling you to *suck it up*," she said harshly, "Right?" she yelled toward the kitchen at large, flinging her arms out wide. "Because that's what I'm here for after all. Rest assured Kahner, if Kalturek's meant to have children then God will see to it that he does. But in the end, it boils down to this. Kalturek's not available right now because he's married, and Stephanie's heart isn't as open as he thinks it is, which is why they've never been able to have babies of their own in the first place."

"Right, well, you keep having faith. And Angel? I don't think I have to tell you not to leave the house. Or do I?" Kahner stated irritably, heading for the hallway. He needed a break from this woman. Her erratic behavior was confusing the crap out of him and so was the whole messed up twisted situation.

"I wouldn't dream of leaving because this courtship is so much fun after all. Every woman's dream," Angel vented loudly.

Kahner turned and stared at her, completely perplexed as he backed from the kitchen into the hallway. He was having an awful time reading her. Her emotions kept spiking causing her mind to be chaotic.

"Let's take a break. The morning is almost over, and I've still got a frisky Stallion and a skittish mare in heat to deal with down at the corrals." He paused. Groaning over the parallel of what he'd said, he quickly disappeared down the hall.

Staring after him Angel sighed sadly. Inhaling deeply, she continued talking to herself. "If it's meant to happen then He will find another way. Right?"

She'd managed to control her tears to that point but suddenly found herself unable to hold them back any longer. Overcome with emotion and the knowledge it would be a long day fending off Kalturek, she felt suddenly old beyond her years. She was only supposed to be about forty-five years old after all.

Taking her mug up in her hand, she quickly took another long drink then banged it on the counter. Out of the corner of her eye, she saw a tiny paper airplane soaring into the kitchen from the hallway near the pantry, which connected to the movie room. She tilted her head to one side at the absurdity of seeing it at that moment.

The plane came to rest on the floor near the table. Getting up she hobbled toward it and picked it up. Peeking her head down the hallway she noted her son Kal had been joined by Sable's children as he watched Batman. Apparently, they had decided to stay home rather than go with their mom. He glanced at her and waved, then went back to his movie. Catching sight of handwriting on the tiny paper airplane, she unfolded and flattened it out. The note brought her to tears.

Twisted though it be, love comes softly, you will see.

She hoped he was right.

- - -

Let me see if I've got this straight.

Kalturek and Stephanie think Angel Stryfe needs to become pregnant by him by midnight that night or he will lose his chance at ever being able to father children.

Shall I run that by you again?

The notion of the deadline alone seems awfully ridiculous to me. But you want to know what I'm really thinking right about now?

Hhhhmmm. I'm thinking…

-That is absurd!

It's one of the most wildly unreasonable, illogical, and inappropriate ideas I've ever heard. Wouldn't you say that just about sums up what's going on here?

Good grief. He's married!

I suppose you're probably wondering what Stephanie is really thinking about this, right? Could she really be so desperate to have a child that she would let her husband, a Sheriff at that, cheat on her with another woman in order to have a baby?

Hello!

How far up the dial on that weird-o-meter hat of yours, is it going right about now? Because if it's anything like mine then it's in the red.

Craziness. Just plain ridiculous!

It makes a body wonder who comes up with these far-fetched storylines anyway.

Right about here in this novel is where I had to stop reading Angel Stryfe's story cause, unfortunately, I, Vortigern Black, had 'responsibilities' which kept me from being able to continue. As I was saving Angel's files to my tablet and shutting it down, though, I made a little discovery.

What everyone else doesn't know, is that Angel had written this story once before.

That's right.

I found other files with the same titles only listed as originals. In fact, she had all their stories written, encompassing a sum total to that point of about seven novels. But apparently, when she finished writing them, she found herself going back through and re-writing some, starting with book two. It seems she'd only just started re-doing book three when her world turned upside-down because Lionel's men showed up and tried to kill her.

It might make you wonder what prompted the re-write. Personally, I believe it may have been something that happened way back when Kahner first met Sable in book one.

But, who knows?

It could have been anything or anyone, for that matter, which incited the deviation in her storyline. In the back of your mind, you're probably curious where Angel was originally going with this here twisted tale of craziness. Eh?

I know what her plan was.

I have it hidden away on my tablet.

But I'm not going to tell.

Hehehe. All I will say is that the end results appear to be the same, though how they come about is even more twisted than this version. Impossible, right? Cause nothing could be any more warped then this?

Just wait, you haven't seen anything yet.

The one question I did find myself asking as I hid my tablet and the flash drive case was this…

What was up with the little paper airplane? It had me wondering if there was significance to it. And if it was from her son, little Kal, as I suspected at the time, then what exactly was he trying to tell his mama in that note he sailed her way?

Chapter 8

For the most part, Kal was enjoying his movie. With the additional distraction of the other children in the household who'd joined him, he was having an easier time pushing the nightmares from the night before from his mind. Sable's daughter Lisa was being pretty cool with him, and they were sharing the cheesy corn puffs without argument.

Seeing his mom peering in at him out of the corner of his eye he waved, hoping she understood what he was trying to say with the gesture. It was hard, but he'd be okay. He really didn't want to think about it anyway. He knew his dad was dead now. Kal had figured that out from his night fright, but he figured he was still going to miss him pretty bad even though he hadn't been much of a dad to him. After all, he'd been the only dad he'd ever known.

His mother's screams of terror as she'd had to fight off the bad men had been frightening and occasionally they still seemed to replay in his mind when he didn't want them to. Shifting in his chair he giggled along with the rest of them, as Batman thwarted Joker once again.

He was aware of the man's presence...

-But he couldn't see him.

Thinking he was grateful to not be able to see him, he silently willed the man to go away. He wasn't ready to talk to him. Kal knew what he wanted from him, from his mother even, but was too afraid of the possible consequences.

"Not now, please. Not now," he begged silently, willing the man to go away. He wasn't sure whether he was one of the RavenCrofts who could hear his thoughts or not, for there were so many of them, but he attempted to speak to him through his mind anyway.

A few minutes passed. He could no longer sense him anymore. Had he actually moved on? If he had, would he leave his mother alone or was he liable to wind up hurting her like his father always did?

Kal sighed, worried for her. He knew he was safe, whether his mother realized it or not. Everyone wanted him, of that he was certain. But his mother, well, some only wanted her for what she might give them.

And that was what worried him.

- - -

Bastion RavenCroft was cross.

He tapped his ear lightly while listening intently to the other end of the call.

"I have an issue that requires your expertise," the hollow garbled voice informed him.

"Deliver package and transfer funds."

"Package delivered. Transferring now."

"Understood." Bastion's response was clipped. Clenching his jaw, he ended the call. The muscle in his left cheek twitched. Eyes shifting across screens of the multiple monitors along the desk, he noted with distaste which line the call had come from.

Agent Jericho Henley.

Swearing, he quickly grabbed the appropriate cell phone when he saw the payment had been dumped into his Zurich account. This wasn't a good sign.

Pickup package.

Sending the text on to his courier he rolled two feet down the long desk to the adjacent monitor. Another call was coming in. Noting which secure line it was coming from, he suspected he already knew what it was about.

"Yes?"

"Cargo dropped. Bird's away."

"Understood."

He was already aware of the delivery as they were presently secured safely within his ranch home as he spoke.

"And..." he heard the voice continue tentatively.

"Problem?" Bastion paused, wondering what more needed to be said. The job was done and payment had been made, a decidedly larger payment than what he normally gave as a result of the extremely short notice.

"Thanks for the tip," the other party responded quickly, then hung up.

That had been unprofessional.

Bastion grunted in annoyance. Sighing heavily, he realized what it likely meant. He was aware his pilot had been seeing someone. Suspecting Mack would be looking to settle down soon he scowled. Hopefully, he waited until after the holiday season to give notice. He had a bad feeling he was liable to need Mack's services again real soon.

Sliding back down to his other monitor, he picked up on a text coming in from his daughter, Mackenzie, on his personal cell.

Angel arrived. She's a mess Dad, you've no idea!
And Kahner sent us all home. What's going on?
I sense some serious vibes.

Not responding to her question Bastion posed one of his own.

Is anyone staying the night?

Mackenzie responded seconds later.

Nathan and Synedra. Kalturek and Stephanie too.

Kahner said you told him you'd be unavailable until tomorrow.

Where did you have to fly off to last minute anyway?

And you didn't answer my question.

Bastion chuckled darkly then texted back while speaking aloud. "I know." He didn't bother giving an answer to her last question.

He knew everyone was curious but until he had more answers they weren't getting any either. The situation with Angel had to be handled very carefully, especially after learning there was a child involved. That had come as a surprise even to him, particularly after learning the boy's name.

A few minutes later he noted another message coming in on yet a different line. His courier had his package. Bastion was anxious to see what the assignment was this time. He'd had multiple visions the day before Thanksgiving, warning that one would be coming, but had been getting an uneasy feeling in his gut all through the day yesterday.

The visions had been chaotic, more difficult to sift through than usual. Several of them had even been highly disturbing in nature and they involved his children. It was the first time in a long time that he'd had to worry about whether he might not have done well enough in teaching and rearing his sons. Bastion hoped his eldest would take the lead and do what needed to be done in his absence if it became necessary.

Distracted by the prompt from his courier on the secure line he tapped his forefinger lightly on the desk before him, deep in thought. Glancing over at the monitor on the opposite wall, which allowed him to view every room within the RavenCroft ranch, he caught sight of Kalturek's initial reaction to Angel as he handed her the plate Nathan had prepared for her. Trying to keep track of the conversation they were having by way of an earpiece in his left ear, he returned his attention to the secure line with the prompt from the courier.

Assignment?

He texted first, then waited impatiently for the response. Normally he didn't get this agitated, but he had a lot going on and sensed something was up within both the Phenom organization and his home.

Locate and detain until advise.

Bastion swore, then texted again. He'd been hoping it would be light work that didn't require travel.

Who?

The courier's response was swift.

Steven Adam Jameson.

In the next text, a picture of the man in question was sent even as the call from the courier rang through. Turning the voice modifier on Bastion answered the call, keeping his voice neutral as he spoke. He began pacing the room.

"Legit?"

"Yes. They want him back."

"Time-span?"

"Over ten years."

Bastion frowned. The voice had hesitated. "Why now?"

"They feel he is a threat in the open."

"You agree?"

"No. Mr. Jameson has been off the radar. Might even have a family by now."

Bastion had known the courier for nearly forty years. A spy for him within the Phenom organization in question, he knew the man would have the answers he sought regarding the current assignment. His response so far was disturbing, however. Bastion's movements slowed and his feet stopped suddenly near a carpet tack on the floor. His mind quickly sifted through the possibilities even as his eyes scanned the stark white walls of the room. The courier's responses in the past had always been short and to the point. This one was too long.

"They don't want Jameson," Bastion stated evenly.

"Affirmative."

"Progeny?"

"That's correct," the thin modified voice became momentarily silent then continued. "Locate target. Determine status. They will advise an appropriate course of action from there."

Bastion did not like that response at all. Again it was too long. His courier was being too forthcoming with answers and that never happened. The room seemed to pulse with light and air as his vision blurred slightly and he found himself staring at a frightening image. A full-figured woman with long flowing red hair and two boys of the same age were fleeing from their home, much as Angel had from hers, only somehow it was different.

No protector came for the woman with the red hair.

The red-headed lady was alone.

The vision flashed before him within a matter of seconds then it was gone. Shaking his head Bastion regained his composure quickly.

He knew what the resulting course of action would likely be. There had been a recent flurry of activity toward trying to locate and re-educate people within the Phenomena files. But he hadn't quite realized they'd moved on to creating progeny lists. Truthfully, he'd known a long time ago this step was coming but it had never occurred to him it would be happening this soon. How had he missed this? Why hadn't the Fates tipped him off as they usually did with a vision?

Once he managed to locate Steven Adam Jameson, if he found the man was already married with children, they would have him terminate the subject in question.

"Mother of progeny?"

There was a pause. It was slight, but it was there. "The chatter is, determine her power status, then they will advise."

"Understood."

The moment the courier spoke Bastion knew exactly what that meant. His own suspicions had been reaffirmed ten years ago when his daughter Synedra had met her husband Nathan; people with special abilities or 'gifts' often gravitated toward each other. He rolled his eyes in disgust and shook his head. The organization had taken fifteen years to discover what he had learned in one. And that discovery had come to him nearly forty years before, which was the only reason why he was involved with the Phenom organization now.

Distracted by shouting, then banging coming from his left ear, he yanked that earpiece out and tossed it on the desk in annoyance. He could tell Angel was upset but hadn't the time to deal with it in that instant.

"Results are both foreseen and expected."

The courier's emphasis on Phenom foreseeing and anticipating his results hadn't been lost on him. He caught the red flag the speaker was throwing his way before the speaker even realized what he'd done.

Busted.

They'd found him out.

Bastion swore internally upon hearing the alarm sensor go off on his computer program. Glancing over his shoulder he ran the length of the room, hastily gazing toward the monitor before him with the bouncing line. The web it was creating was vast but still traceable. Seeing someone had managed to get around his encryptions and had put a trace on him, he immediately double-clicked on his spike program. He knew he had less than a minute to get off before being found but was confident his spike program would crash the hacker's system before that could happen. As always, he'd used multiple host web servers which he'd looped in order to bounce his IP address all over the world, in order to make it extremely hard to track him. There was little to no chance of discovery.

Making sure to enunciate clearly, he spoke one last time, his tone a deadly rumble. "Mr. E is done...Henley." Dropping the call, he pulled the tiny gadget from his right ear and flung it across the room. Banging against the far wall, it clattered to the floor noiselessly upon landing on the plush carpeting.

Snarling, he snatched the papers from the table and flung them haphazardly in frustration, not caring about the mess he was creating. He knew full well it had been Agent Jericho Henley and not his trusted courier who was now likely dead. Bastion had noticed out of the corner of his eye a call going out on Jericho Henley's line at the same time as the one the courier made to him.

They'd known one day this moment would come. He'd seen it himself in a vision many years before, so they'd put the necessary precautions in place to prevent the discovery of his true identity and his family's location. But experiencing the sickening sensation of déjà vu and its inevitable dizzying feeling when his visions came to sudden fruition was always unsettling; especially when it involved the death of a long-time friend. Bastion was certain the man was dead, for it was the only way Henley could have possibly gotten hold of the courier's phone and his number.

He groaned outwardly at the loss, grateful for the privacy of the silent enclosed room he was currently housed in. The secret sealed location was undisclosed to all but one, and he was confident he could entrust that individual to remain silent.

Too soon.

He'd hoped for more time.

But now it had to end. With Angel's arrival at the ranch, it was just as well.

Peering back over at his laptop monitor on the opposite wall he watched the figure on its screen with renewed concern. The loud bang on the table and the shouting had forced him to remove the speaker from his other ear. Normally exceptionally good at multi-tasking, he'd been unable to concentrate on both conversations effectively with all the yelling.

The woman had clearly expected the head of the RavenCroft household to be present when she arrived. In hindsight, he acknowledged things would likely have gone smoother for her when she first got to the ranch, but it couldn't have been helped. There had been unfinished business to attend to, which he'd put off because of the Thanksgiving gathering, and frankly, he was still trying to locate information on her past.

He'd picked up on her comment about needing to dig deeper in order to find out what they needed. Bastion wished she'd felt she could have spoken more freely with them, but gathered she was likely not feeling entirely safe yet, which he supposed he understood.

Bastion had been watching the house monitor intently when Angel first arrived at the ranch. He'd been witness to her scantily clad, bloodied state, as well as her foray into the pool. Wincing at her disoriented and frightened condition, he'd promptly contacted his pool guy in order to have it cleaned. Observing her reaction to learning her surroundings were more real than imagined and seeing how she was responding to his sons now, Bastion contemplated what he knew so far about the woman. Determining he might need to go a different direction in his investigation of her, he took a seat in front of his keyboard.

He acknowledged that his absence did seem to be creating more than a little chaos, but anticipated Kahner would be capable enough to help facilitate bringing about order. Either way, he was watching the situation closely and expected things would settle down soon. If not, then he would deal with it accordingly.

Noting his son Kalturek was becoming visibly upset Bastion frowned.

"House, give me sound on speaker," he instructed his artificial intelligence system, in order to catch the remainder of the conversation. Seconds later Kalturek stormed from the kitchen leaving behind a thoroughly agitated Kahner and a woman he would hardly refer to as timid. She did appear distressed, regardless of the false bravado she was attempting to display.

Bastion pondered his next move as he paused in his Internet search on her, housing all he'd discovered so far in an encrypted file.

"House, give me sound on the mic," he said while hastily grabbing it from the floor. He placed it in his ear in order to allow him to listen and work at the same time. There was too much to do, and he almost wished there were two of him. Some things just couldn't be delegated though, he thought, recalling Kalturek's statement from earlier. That cocky display of power, Bastion was sure, hadn't helped his son's plight any. Sometimes Kalturek could be so arrogant, he mused crossly.

Making sure his notebook and pen was in his back pocket he moved quickly across the room. Bastion surmised from a brief glance at his far wall that it was safe to travel. He had another individual to track as well and it was time to get moving. He'd return to continue his research shortly. Since he was clearly never actually meant to locate the Jameson man, he now had one less obligation, which made his next chore a little easier to handle.

- - -

Wait, wait, wait…
Whaaaaat?
Bastion RavenCroft is a mercenary?
There was talk about him having been in service at one point earlier in this story. And in both books one and two, there was a brief mention of him having worked for the CIA. That said, I imagine you didn't see that one coming any more than I did when I first read that.

Or did you?
Did you think Bastion was a simple horse rancher and businessman? Or did you figure out what the author and I have been eluding to?

Either way, it sounded to me like he had some serious troubles at that point. Bastion had been working on the sly for Phenom since before he 'retired' from the CIA a few years back. I say 'retired' in that way because what he really did was stop going by the name he was using at the time. He'd been working for them under an assumed name, just like Kahner had when he'd been going by the name Toni Starck.

But of course, right? Shall I tell you what name he was using? You're gonna flip when you hear this.

Vortigern Black.

Heeheeheehee!

The question running through your head right about now is probably something like, "Does that mean the narrator Vortigern Black is actually Bastion RavenCroft?"

Maybe.

Not necessarily.

But it could be.

I'll never teeellllll!!!!

Just kidding. Eventually, I will, but not right now.

Anyway, like Kahner, Bastion returned to his real life and identity. Unlike his son, he created a dual life by becoming a mercenary for hire under another assumed name. He made the decision to do this because before he left he'd been hearing rumors about this Phenom organization and was trying to ferret them out in order to determine how dangerous they might be for him and his family. What he learned was both enlightening and frightening. His initial agenda had been to protect his own family from ever being discovered. In the end, he found himself taking jobs in order to both maintain his cover as a mercenary and to try and occasionally undermine the company's agenda while keeping tabs on what was going on within the organization.

The problem was, sometimes he had to actually bring people in, or take people out for Phenom, in order to maintain the cover he'd created. He'd become known by the heads of the organization as someone who could be counted on to get the job done. Apparently, he'd gotten too good at it, and they started realizing the mercenary they'd been hiring was one of the people they'd been trying to locate and bring in.

And that's what's happening here.

Bastion's mole was discovered, taken out, and Phenom was now hunting him. He knew that because he also knew that 'Agent' Jericho Henley was working for both sides, the CIA and Phenom. This bit of information had been his most recent discovery.

Of course, the CIA didn't know it yet. Shoot, they're always a little slow and desperate to try and catch up as far as I'm concerned.

Fortunately, Bastion had taken security measures for in the event this very situation was to occur. So, for now, his family was safe. I couldn't really tell you what those measures were as they aren't listed within any notes or documents I found of Angel's but she might not be aware of what those were. What I can tell you, is that as far as Bastion was concerned, he was no longer a mercenary and never had been. Which meant he no longer had eyes on the inside anymore.

At least … not into Phenom anyway.

No, it was time he concentrated on what was happening at home and determine what he could find out about the author Angel Stryfe who had stormed into their lives like a tornado amidst a hurricane. He knew she was there for a reason but was still trying to determine exactly what her role was, whether a surrogate or not.

Hhhhmmm, let's see where this is going, shall we?

I should warn you; you're probably not going to like what you're about to read. If you have any kind of conscience whatsoever, then you're liable to want to take a pitchfork to the people involved. It might even make you sick thinking about what is being contrived.

Try and get past it, if you can, and remember that this family, though raised with a fairly high standard of morality, did not grow up with any kind of faith-based beliefs.

Then again, being raised with faith is no guarantee of better decision making either, just look at the RavenCroft's cousins, the Blackthorne's. They'd be the perfect example of poor decision making among the faithful. This sort of thing isn't only prevalent within our times though. No Siree! After all, I do believe there are some pretty messed up and twisted tales within the Bible too, right? One even about a man named David who lusted for another woman as she was bathing, had her brought to him so he could sleep with her even though she was married to another, then sent the man to the front lines of the war in order to get killed when she wound up pregnant with his child.

Temptation, desire, want, need.

It's the driving force of many of our decisions regardless of what our faith is. I'd even go so far as to wager it's been that way since the dawn of man.

And remember, this is just a story, right?

It's not like stuff like this happens in real life after all.

Or does it?

Chapter 9

Having gone in search of his wife, Kalturek didn't have far to look. Instead of heading home as everyone else had, she'd holed up in their bedroom at the RavenCroft ranch house.

Watching Stephanie briefly as she cuddled up on the bed, attempting to read, he marveled at how beautiful she was. Angel had a similar appearance to Stephanie, but as far as he was concerned his wife was still more attractive.

Banging his head against the door jamb his heart ached at the knowledge he'd been incapable of giving her what she'd always wanted; children. Hearing the soft thudding noise behind her Stephanie turned towards the door, her troubled gaze meeting his. Overcome with emotion at the sight of her, he cleared his throat, desperate to keep from appearing weak.

"Can we talk?" he asked quietly. Moving into the room he closed the door. "I tried, Stephanie. I wasn't able to convince her and the things she's saying. They're not making sense."

Glancing at him in exasperation, Stephanie stood and faced him head-on. "It cannot be a coincidence that she's here now, on this of all days."

"Kahner did drag her here so it's really not a coincidence. Besides, from what she's saying…"

"Was it coincidence or fate that I found those books when I did?" Stephanie interrupted hastily, putting a kibosh to his attempt to wheedle out of what they'd agreed to. "She would have died along with her son if I hadn't convinced Bastion we needed to go after her. And I really don't understand why it couldn't have been you."

"Kahner is more experienced with undercover work. You know that."

"You've shot people before," she said callously. "From the sound of it, he only had to kill one person. She took care of the rest. Besides, now you lost what little leverage you could have had with her."

"How do you figure?"

"We could have played up the whole hero aspect but now we can't."

"Are you kidding me? You wanted me to guilt her into having sex and carrying my babies?"

"Whatever works."

"What's gotten into you?" Kalturek asked incredulously. It was like she wasn't the same woman anymore, and it made him uneasy.

"What's gotten into me? Kalturek, Baby! I...*we* have a chance to be able to have babies. Children gifted with powers just as you have been."

"We could end up with a kid seeing shadows, ever thought of that?"

"Not likely," she responded knowingly. He gave her a speculative look. "Bastion himself told me when we first married that it was highly rare. He only knew of one other person with it and that was his brother's son. Oh, what was his name...Drinian!" she exclaimed suddenly. "Which means it's simply hereditary."

"Exactly."

"No, I mean, as in within each family only one is born with it, if any. Do you understand what I mean?"

Kalturek nodded slowly. "Yeah, I get it. You're saying that because Ariana is seeing them right now it means we won't have to worry about that issue with one of our children. I'm just not sure..."

Stephanie suddenly exploded. "Not sure about what? Kalturek! Just get it done already."

"Get it done already? Good grief, you mean now? Don't be absurd."

"No better time than the present, I say."

"Her husband just died and she has a child!"

"All the better reason to take care of business now. Besides, we're on a deadline here."

Kalturek stared at his wife with a mixture of disgust and confusion. He'd never known her to be so cruel before.

Seeing the look, he was giving her, Stephanie inhaled deeply then exhaled in frustration. It occurred to her that pushing him too much might make him even less likely to bend to her will. Usually, he was pretty malleable but when it came to breaking the law or causing someone harm he seemed to have too much of a moral compass for her tastes. She supposed that since he was the Sheriff, she should have known he would be that way, but she hadn't realized how much of a choir boy he really was until after they'd married. Deciding to switch tactics, she knew she had to convince him this was the best way to get what they wanted.

"Honey, do you honestly think I want to hurt this woman any more than you do?" she asked, feigning a wounded look. She allowed her lip to jut out slightly and quiver as though she were about to cry, though she was far from it.

Kalturek's shoulders seemed to sag noticeably and his expression softened. Stepping away from the wall he walked toward her and took her in his arms.

"No, my love, I do understand. You just want the same thing I want – to have children."

"Exactly."

"Here's the thing, though. The way Angel is talking, I'm beginning to wonder if maybe we have this figured all wrong."

"Why? What's she saying?"

"I don't know. Something about it not being my deadline, am I sure we read everything we did right, and how it might not even be my story she was writing."

"That's nonsense. She's backpedaling is all," Stephanie assured him. "Angel is embarrassed because she was writing a love story about the two of you and she knows you're married to me. Think about it. She's been fantasizing about you all this time only to find out you're real and that she's only supposed to be a surrogate for us, rather than the love of your life. Kind of pathetic, yet, sweet."

He stared off into space, the look on his face one of indecision.

"Look, you're right, okay. Her husband did just die. But it sounds like there's not much love lost there anyway, from the way *she* talks, and it just means there's no one stopping you from having children with her," she said while batting her eyelashes at him. "You already know I fully support you in this. As to her son, he isn't an issue for me. In fact, he might just be the key to convincing her that she should do this. She's on her own now, with no job and no way of taking care of her son, right? When Bastion gets home he'll have to find a way to give her a new name like he did Sable."

Kalturek became thoughtful. He kissed her forehead lightly then tilted his head down toward her. "I get it. You think maybe she'll be willing to help us out in exchange for financial reimbursement and a new identity."

"Something like that anyway," she said evasively. One way or another she fully intended to get that woman out of the way as soon as the triplets were born. She was certain it would be three babies too, for that's what it had said it would be in what she'd read of the book description. She might even be able to get a ten-year-old son out of it if she convinced Angel to make them little Kal's Godparents. She smiled internally at the thought. It might take some time and additional sacrifice, but she knew she'd eventually get what she wanted.

Kalturek sighed heavily and closed his eyes in distress. He rested his head against hers, mumbling into her hair affectionately.

"I honestly don't know that I'm going to be able to convince Angel to agree with this but I will try again. You know I'd do anything for you." The raw emotion in his voice gave her cause to roll her eyes. She was grateful he couldn't see her face. She hated it when he'd get all mushy. It made her uncomfortable.

"You can do this. I know you can. After all, you convinced Angela and Heaton to get back together and they're about as difficult a couple of people as any."

Kalturek groaned next to her. Great! What now, she thought? "What is it Kalturek? What's wrong, Baby?" Stephanie asked in her most plaintive and soft voice.

"She's heavier than you and with really weird silver hair," he exclaimed, sounding disgusted.

"Her hair is clearly dyed. A cheap, at home job, I'm sure, which is why it looks so weird. Are you honestly telling me you can't get past that in order to have children of your own?" she asked imploringly. "How many husbands do you know who are not only being given permission to sleep with another woman but urged to? This is going to make everything better Kalturek. You'll see. It will even make our marriage stronger," she continued, sensing with irritation she still needed to fully convince him of what needed to be done. She didn't tell him that if he didn't do it, she'd likely leave him. What was the point of being married to a man with such a gift as his, if she couldn't have children with those abilities as well? She rarely was able to convince him to use his gift for the things she wanted. But children...they were more prone to being manipulated.

"Baby, I get it, all right? But Kahner's not entirely wrong. I'm a RavenCroft and a Sheriff. What we're talking about here is treading a very fine line. We can't hurt this woman just to gain what we want from her. We RavenCroft's may be a lot of things but we never take women by force. There's never been a need to."

"You act like I'm asking you to rape her or something," Stephanie accused both hurt and cross by his Boy Scout attitude.

"No, but you are asking me to manipulate her; to seduce her. Am I right?"

She had the good sense to appear genuinely uncomfortable. "Stephanie, am I right?" Kalturek prompted when he didn't get a response.

"Yes," she admitted hotly. "I'm asking you to seduce her so we can have babies. I get it okay? I'm a horrible, horrible person for even voicing such a thing, let alone asking my husband, a Sheriff," she said snidely, "to even consider such a dastardly deed." Resenting that he'd made her admit it, she became choked up. The whole situation was absurd as far as she was concerned. He was her husband, and therefore, should be getting her pregnant, not some other random woman they didn't know.

Kalturek could see the pain in her eyes and knew that he was the reason it was there. His inability to get her with child had been eating at him for some time, chipping away at his manhood. He was just as frustrated as she was.

Taking a moment to think through what he wanted to say he paused before responding. "You remember what we talked about last night, right? About what we agreed to do if she wasn't agreeable to our offer?"

"Of course," she responded quickly, knowing she needed to tread carefully. "Sometimes, all a woman needs is a little convincing in the right way."

Kalturek exhaled softly. "Are you really asking me to be intimate with another woman? To…seduce her if necessary?" He needed to hear her say it aloud.

She nodded slowly, trying not to appear too eager. "It could be good for everyone this way. We all get what we want and she gets to move on with her life in a little better class. Kahner did say she'd been living in a tiny mobile home after all."

Kalturek watched her closely wanting to be sure she was really okay with him being intimate with another woman. It bothered him more than a little that she wasn't putting up more of a fuss over that fact. But then they both realized there was no time to try and schedule an appointment with a fertility clinic. According to what she'd read in the book, they had a very short time frame of which ended tonight.

"Would you really leave me if I didn't do this? Like you said last night?"

"I'm so sorry I said that. I shouldn't have. I was upset last night and not thinking straight," she lied. "*I love you*. But when I think of how we might lose out on the chance of having and raising children together all because of a short window of opportunity and a recently widowed woman... I just... We've waited too long for this, Baby, don't you think?" she asked urgently, forcing tears to her eyes as she pretended to sob. "I wanted to experience being the mother of your children, to know what it was like to share that kind of gift. But that's already been ripped away from me by this, this woman your brother brought home and I...I...."

Kalturek wrapped his arms around her and held her close, shushing her softly in an attempt to comfort her. "It's okay. I know. I'm so sorry. You have my word. I'll do whatever I can to make this happen for us." He spoke urgently while rocking her gently.

Face buried into his chest, Stephanie RavenCroft smiled into her husband's shoulder. He was so easy to manipulate. For such a big, strong, and educated guy she would have thought he'd be a little brighter. She imagined whatever dark aura he was seeing around her right now, was being explained away in his head because of the pact they'd made. After all, as he said himself, it was treading on a thin line, morally and legally speaking.

"If we're gonna do this then you're gonna have to stay here out of the way. Because if Kahner and Sable catch you thinking about this…"

"I know, I know. You don't have to tell me twice. I'll stay in my room. Just bring me some food around dinner time and keep me apprised of what's happening. Okay?"

"Got it. Did you convince Kalabernus and Ariana to head back to the cabin?"

She bobbed her head up and down excitedly. "Kalabernus was easy," she grinned. "They just got married before Thanksgiving after all."

"I figured he'd be easy," Kalturek laughed. "Drayke and Laynie, as well as Mackenzie and S.T. left this morning."

"Good, because I was a little worried about Mackenzie," Stephanie admitted. "Her ability to sense emotions has been really ramped up lately for some reason. I wouldn't want her picking up on anything. All we have left is Synedra and Nathan, as well as Kahner and Sable because your dad's already out of town. That was a real break there," she said with a relieved sigh.

Kalturek snorted. "You're telling me. This would be hard to pull off otherwise. You do understand, I won't be able to get rid of Kahner. He and Sable live here after all. It's their place."

"I get it. I guess it's a big house, so if you keep her downstairs, maybe in the movie room then..." Stephanie stopped suddenly, seeing Kalturek shaking his head. She frowned.

"Synedra and Nathan were staying there. Remember?"

Becoming exasperated Stephanie groaned. "Then *you* have to convince Synedra to go home. Or better yet, Nathan. If he decides he wants to leave, you know Synedra will cave."

"I already tried. For some reason, Nathan seemed pretty insistent about sticking around until tomorrow morning."

"Why?" Her eyes widened suddenly in alarm. "Kalturek, do you think he's picking up on something? He tends to be pretty perceptive at times."

"No, I don't think so. I have the feeling it had more to do with wanting to go horseback riding, which is where they are now. With both their businesses, they haven't really had the chance to get out on the trails in the past few months."

"Well, shoot. Did Kahner say where he intended to put her for the night?"

Kalturek shook his head. "Not yet, though I'm guessing the bedroom downstairs next to Dad's study."

"That's perfect. You can go to her from our room by way of the shared bathroom in between. But now...what about her son?"

"I have that covered already. I was watching him a little bit ago outside the movie room from the pool area. He seemed to be getting along quite well with Sable's kids, Jordan and Adam. I figure I'll convince him to bunk in with them upstairs." Sighing contentedly against her shoulder he cringed inwardly at what he was about to do, already experiencing guilt over the deception. Kissing her gently on the forehead he took a deep breath.

"You're absolutely sure about this? I won't be with this woman without your explicit permission," he asked against her ear, unable to look at her at first.

Stephanie whispered her reply. "Yes. I wish there was another way but there isn't is there? It's the only way I can see for you to have our children."

Nodding his head Kalturek leaned into her further. "Okay. I'm gonna try and ask her again first as we talked about. But if she says no…" he trailed off meaningfully.

"I know, Baby." She pretended to cringe. Then she faced him bravely as they held each other for the longest time. After a while, her curiosity won out. "When will you ask her?"

"I'll go to her after everyone goes down for the night. I already have a…seduction plan in mind. But I won't take an unwilling participant. If she doesn't concede in the end…."

"I do understand, Baby. You're absolutely right. No force," Stephanie replied coyly, batting her lashes. Internally she was making her own little plan. One way or another she'd make sure that woman was willing, or at least had the appearance of being willing. And she already had an idea of how to accomplish it.

- - -

Unseen by Kalturek and Stephanie, the shadows cackled with glee as they floated above the couple embracing on their bed. They had spent much of the night and day tag teaming each other while working on the two human's greatest fears and desires. Dozens of shadows darted about the bedroom, gloating at their triumph at finally convincing them of their plan.

As they flitted away from the patio doors, windows and lights they continued to whisper words of encouragement for the plan that the couple had made. Three shadows swirled down from the ceiling their black inky substances coalescing into the shapes of faceless men surrounding the couple as they held each other.

"Well done." The demon called Fallen hissed next to Stephanie's ear then ran a filmy black hand down her back. Seeing her shiver, while sensing the fear and anticipation building within her, he fed off her hungrily. Grinning evilly back at the other shadows he whooped loudly, inciting the rest of the demons into a rigorous dance.

Whispering cruelly into Kalturek's ear, Zalman stopped, turning hastily toward Fallen, and hissed. "Don't get cocky," he growled angrily then went back to his crooning tone near the man's side. "That's right. Angel is ready for you, you stud. You can convince her. Then you can be the father you were always meant to be." The evil creature played upon the man's desires for children in order to ease his conscience and keep him from suspecting his wife of any foul play.

"Then you can have what you want," Fallen interjected. He intentionally sunk into Stephanie, causing her to shiver uncontrollably and cling to her husband.

"What you want is your beautiful wife," Veranke coaxed. "Not a look-a-like heifer. Do this and you'll keep her. If you don't, you'll lose her."

"Three babies of your very own, just like your brothers," Zalman chimed in as he swung around and traded places with Fallen.

At the human male's ear now, Fallen cackled with glee. "Play your cards right and you'll get the boy too. A son with your very name – named for you!"

"You're a masterful lover Kalturek," Zalman cajoled.

"You know she wants it," Fallen crooned again. "She's been dreaming of you. She needs you to ease her pain, her loss."

"It's not cheating when you have permission," Veranke continued the incessant badgering happily. If things went as planned, then they'd have their own reward around midnight.

Cackling together evilly they watched as Kalturek eased away from his wife, tucked a small pad of paper and a pen in his back pocket and left the bedroom.

"Follow him. Make sure he sticks to the plan," Zalman ordered. Sailing through the door after him, the shadows Fallen and Veranke stayed close to the human male while Zalman continued to watch the woman. She stared after Kalturek, a look of satisfaction on her face.

"Good girl, Stephanie. Soon you'll have everything you want," Zalman crowed, pleased with their plan. "Now, what do you need to do to make sure Angel is a willing participant?"

- - -

Whoa! Hold the phone! Where the heck did that come from?

Seems sort of out of the blue to see this excerpt on the shadowy demonic trio but Ms. Christine was pretty insistent it needed to be here for two very important reasons.

One, because we found this excerpt in Angel Stryfe's original story. That led the author of this here twisted tale to believe that these demons, or fallen angels as some might call them, had been messing with Kalturek and especially Stephanie something fierce. According to Angel's notes and her original story, the 'troublesome three' were intent upon making sure this happened between Angel and Kalturek.

Makes a body wonder why doesn't it?

What possible purpose does it serve for them other than to cause chaos? Or is that their only intent?

The 'troublesome three' didn't seem to want Sable or Ariana to follow through with their pregnancy's, so why were they so insistent upon Kalturek and Angel coupling for that purpose?

All very good questions to which I presently have no answers to.

The second reason we've left this excerpt in, is that Ms. Christine seemed to think you need to know that there are outside forces which can't be seen that were taunting, tempting, and pushing this couple into making this plan. They were toying with them and playing upon their greatest desires. The real question was, did that make Stephanie and Kalturek bad people?

Reading this, one might say Kalturek wasn't so bad, he's just being led astray by both his wife and these creatures. But now, Stephanie?

Hhhhmmm.

After learning all that, I'd say a person should wonder about her because it sounds more like a woman with an ulterior motive then it does bad judgement. Apparently, she'd a plan for quite some time too. That seems more like extremely bad character to me. Wouldn't you say?

Then again, I guess I can't blame her for wanting to know what it's like to have a heads up on the good versus the evil front. Imagine what one might be able to do were they to be gifted in such a way. It might be mighty handy. The RavenCrofts have chosen to use their abilities to try and help people, but…

I wonder…

So far our stories have revolved around people who are inherently good but imperfect who sometimes make some really bad choices.

What if the individual was inherently evil?

If such an ability were real and it fell into the wrong hands...

-What do you suppose would happen?

Poor, poor, Angel.

Chapter 10

After checking on her son Angel debated on what to do next. Kahner had left her laptop open on the counter in the kitchen so she went back to it and looked at the screen. Forwarding through to the end of what she'd written, she pushed the laptop toward the opposite side of the counter, limped around to one of the bar stools, and sat down. She felt like she should be writing but wasn't sure where to begin. And she really didn't know if she wanted to go back and finish writing what had happened so far.

Tapping her fingers on the counter, she bit her lip, struggling desperately to keep from recalling the violent memories from the night before.

Her hands began to shake.

Shivering as tears threatened to spill forth, Angel's gaze darted once again around the kitchen.

She needed a hug.

She needed a distraction.

Heck, she needed another drink.

For some reason, her gaze flitted to the Internet icon on her screen. Angel had a wireless card on her laptop. Would it be safe to jump online, she wondered? That could be a good distraction. Kahner wasn't around at the moment to ask. Carefully weighing her options, she gulped down her tears and decided to risk it, because for some reason she was getting an urgent, overwhelming feeling that she might have an e-mail. Whatever she was sensing was there might be extremely important, she thought. Double-clicking on the icon she logged into her e-mail account.

Initially, all she saw was junk mail until she refreshed her page and an e-mail appeared from someone listed simply as "Conundrum." A thrill of excitement ran through her as she imagined who it might be. Furtively glancing in the direction Kahner had left moments before, a secretive smile played across her lips and her eyes danced. Could it be him, the one she thought it was? And was this how it was all supposed to start? With e-mails? Things weren't following exactly how she'd imagined, but variables had changed after all. Curious, the anticipation of what she might find overtaking her, she opened the e-mail and read:

Get off the Internet.

That was it?
That was all the person wrote?

Oh, good grief!

Completely deflated, Angel groaned loudly in disgust while rolling her eyes. She exited the site and shut down her computer.

Angel had long ago given up on romance. Her husband Wilton had been inept with such things. But when she had discovered her fantasy was really real, she had apparently allowed herself to mistakenly hope for something more this time around. She knew she was meant to be here for one of the RavenCroft men, and she was pretty certain she knew who it was but was less than thrilled with how she suspected it was likely to transpire.

Sighing heavily, she got up from the bar stool and, for some reason, found herself limping and half hopping toward the entrance. She felt out of sorts and a bit dazed. Hearing a soft scraping noise behind her near the stairwell, she peered down the opposite hallway but didn't see anyone. Glancing curiously at the closet, it occurred to her that that was where Nathan had likely put her miniature model of the ranch house. She hobbled toward it. Opening the closet door, she looked inside.

There was nothing.

Nothing but coats, hats and boxes.

Gingerly dropping to her knees on the floor she rooted around to see if Nathan had put the model underneath something else but he hadn't. It was missing from the closet.

Angel leaned back and stared within.

What did this mean?

She had intended to write that Nathan had placed it in the closet in order to hide it from the RavenCroft children until Bastion could take control of it. She assumed that it would be in the closet now, but it wasn't. Had someone found it? And if so, then who? Or, had Nathan not hidden it here as she'd thought?

Placing her hands in her lap Angel became thoughtful, her head tilting to one side as she stared into the cluttered closet. The missing model made her nervous. If the wrong person got their hands on it, then she could be in real trouble.

Grabbing hold of the closet door handles she used them to help pull herself up from the floor. She was about to close it when she noticed a piece of paper from a notepad tacked to the back of the door. It caught her attention because a tiny figure of an angel, like the one on the wrap on her ankle, had been drawn on the top of the small paper. Pulling it from the back of the door she read what was written.

Angels shouldn't be snooping.

She became cross.

"What the…? Now what the heck is that supposed to mean?" she said in a loud whisper.

Noting a blackbird drawn at the bottom of the page she suspected the individual who wrote it was trying to draw a raven, thinking they were being cute. Snorting loudly with disgust she folded the small paper and tucked it in her back pocket with the last one.

Closing the closet door, she gasped suddenly at the unexpected sight of Kalturek standing just behind the door. She hadn't heard him come up on her from the hallway. Laying a hand on the wildly beating heart within her chest she caught her breath and stared back at him, wild-eyed.

"Find what you were looking for?" He gave her a curious almost knowing look.

Angel tensed, unsure what to say and whether he'd seen her reading the note she'd found. Had he found the model of the ranch and had he left the note? Was he messing with her?

"No, actually, I didn't," she replied finally.

"What did you expect to find?"

"I was just looking for a sweatshirt or something," she replied, trying to keep from fidgeting. "I'm a bit chilled."

His brow rose.

Angel felt stupid and anxious. She knew full well her aura had likely turned black, giving away her attempt at deceit.

"You couldn't find a sweatshirt in the coat closet?" he asked, hinting at mild humor in his tone. She didn't respond, just stared at him, giving him what he perceived to be innocent doe eyes. It occurred to Kalturek that she might be too self-conscious about randomly borrowing someone else's stuff without permission. "You can borrow mine," he offered, opening the door. He reached in and grabbed the spare sweatshirt he kept within, handing it off to her.

"I couldn't possibly," Angel stammered. The sweatshirt dangled in her hand.

"Sure you can. You're wearing my shirt, why not my sweatshirt too?"

"Right."

He took it from her and began helping her into it awkwardly. Zipping it up for her as if she were a child, he patted it down across her front and around her waist, tucking his fingers loosely into the edge of the pocket on either side.

"How did you get out here anyway?" he asked, practically holding her hostage where she stood precariously.

"I do have two legs."

Kalturek frowned at her. "And a badly sprained ankle. S.T. said you shouldn't be moving around."

"What? And miss a chance at seeing the house of my dreams?" Realizing how that must have sounded Angel blushed, wanting to kick herself. "I just meant…"

"I get it. You've probably imagined this place many times over as you've written your stories," Kalturek said, as an idea popped into his head. "I'll give you a tour," he offered, thinking it might be a good way to get her to become more comfortable with him. "I'll show you its many bedrooms and hidden secrets," he teased.

Taken aback by his offer and mention of secrets and bedrooms Angel stammered. "That's awfully nice of you to offer but as you pointed out I shouldn't really be on my feet so…"

"I can fix that." Without warning, Kalturek bent down and picked her up in his arms.

Startled at unexpectedly being hauled off her feet and against his chest, she gave a yelp of surprise. "What do you think you're doing?"

"What? Never been carried in a man's arms before, have you?" Kalturek asked giving her a mischievous grin. Her face radiated with heat and turned pink.

"Just once that I can remember, and it's a vague memory at that," Angel supplied dryly.

"Well then...now you have a moment to remember." Their gazes locked as he searched her face. He could see her breathing was becoming heavy and he was trying to determine whether it was attraction or anxiety she was experiencing. Was it possible he was starting to reach her? Her next words confirmed that he wasn't even close.

"Put me down. I'm more than capable of managing on my own."

Deflated, he debated briefly on whether to do as she asked but the memory of Stephanie's threats to leave him during Friday night's discussion haunted him. Deciding he had to see this through he shook his head.

"Nonsense. You've been here nearly half the day and not had a chance to see your dream home." Ignoring her request Kalturek spun around and headed toward the first room off the entryway. Without thinking, he kicked the door open and stepped into the bedroom where he and his wife had been moments before. Thankfully, Stephanie wasn't there or the presence of him carrying Angel into their bedroom might have been really awkward. But then he suddenly wondered where his wife *had* gone off to. They agreed she'd stay in the bedroom for the day.

"Kalturek…" Angel ground out in a warning.

"This is the first of two bedrooms on our main level. They were part of the original house before the renovation," he proceeded to explain, ignoring her protests. "The back portion of the house where the study, movie room, and pool room are, was added on later." He turned where he stood, giving her a full vantage of the room.

Distracted by the view before her she secretly had to admit to a love for the walls of oak logs as she gazed dreamily at the fireplace built into the exterior wall. She suspected it shared the same flue with the upstairs bedroom and wondered briefly at the extra upkeep required. But as her gaze shifted around the room Angel's eyes became the size of saucers at the sight of the queen-size bed nestled between the windows of the front of the house. Instantly she was back on alert, her moment of reverie crushed by the bed looming both ominously and yet oddly propitiously, before her.

"Right, good enough," she said quickly, kicking out with her legs, forcing him to have to put her down on the bed. She hastily jumped up, almost falling to the floor, having nearly put too much weight on her sprained ankle. Kalturek reached out in order to steady her, his large hands firmly holding her up and in place. Insisting she was more than capable of hopping from room to room on her own, she anxiously pushed his hands away.

Kalturek grudgingly led the way, a sheepish grin playing at the corners of his lips. He kept his pace slow so she could walk with a lame gait not far behind.

She had seen most of the main level already but was fascinated by the vast book collection in Bastion's study and somewhat envious of the movie room. Waving at her son and the children in greeting, they wandered back to the front of the house, stopping off in the laundry and dining rooms. Then they took the stairs to the second floor. Her pace slowed measurably as they ascended.

"Dad's room is the first at the top of the stairs and generally it's off limits to everyone. There are two entrances to his room."

Angel nodded as she hopped up the steps on one leg, already aware of that fact. "There are five bedrooms and three bathrooms upstairs, right?" she asked in a ragged breath, hoping he'd confirm her curiosity.

He turned toward her in astonishment. "Yes, that's correct."

After showing her each room he came back to his father's bedroom door off the hallway. For some reason, he stopped near the keypad lock on the door. She watched as Kalturek punched in the key code with a mixture of alarm and anxiety at what he was doing. Hadn't he just said a little bit ago that his father's room was off limits to everyone? A second later he opened the door and gestured for her to peer inside. Initially, she was adamantly against intruding upon his father's room, but her own curious nature soon won out at his promptings.

"You know the key code to your father's room?" She tentatively stepped into the room, in order to get a better view. It was the largest of all the bedrooms and like all the rest had a fireplace in it as well. Her brief glimpse to her immediate right confirmed he had a walk-in closet which connected to the bedroom next door. Bastion's own personal bathroom was next to the closet. The door was ajar, allowing her a brief glimpse of its inner contents. Few pictures hung on the walls but she imagined that had more to do with the exterior and interior walls having been constructed with logs rather than drywall. Hanging things would be more of a challenge and would take away from the beauty of the sanded and stained wooden finish.

"It wasn't hard to figure it out. Like most people, Dad made the mistake of making the code a birth date of a family member." He grinned, then shrugged.

"Oh? And who's would that be?"

"Mom's birthdate, of course."

"Right, and does everyone know this?" She tried to sound blasé. Kalturek didn't need to know she was very much aware of what Inara RavenCroft's birth date was.

"No, it's supposed to be a secret," he admitted sheepishly while scratching at his forehead, wondering why he'd told her. "So, uh, don't tell anyone I told you," he said in a conspiratorial whisper. It was odd, he thought, he'd never even told Stephanie that he'd figured it out. "Every house has secrets after all. You of all people should know that." Kalturek gave her a meaningful look as he winked.

Perplexed by his statement Angel worried at what he might mean. Did he know its true secrets? Had he seen her model or her drawing pad? Angel had noticed the drawing pad wasn't with her bag anymore.

Closing the bedroom door behind them as they left, Kalturek made sure the lock registered before moving on. His hand slid into hers, and he held it while assisting her down the stairs. She could hear him sigh next to her so she peered up at him curiously. His crystal-clear blue eyes met hers, mesmerizing her by their intensity.

"I really wish you'd just let me carry you down. You're liable to fall even with my help," he said next to her ear, sending a little shiver down her spine.

For some inexplicable reason, she found herself wondering how much he and Kahner actually looked like their father and began imagining what he might look like twenty years older. Would he one day have salt and pepper coloring above his ears and near his temple? Such a feature would give him a distinguished appearance with an even sexier quality about him then what he already had. She thought the RavenCroft men were most definitely not lacking for good looks. Glancing away suddenly, Angel held her breath and attempted to quicken her pace as they neared the bottom of the stairs.

"Thanks for the tour," she said hastily. There was an urgency in her manner and tone that betrayed the genial false smile she sent his way.

Stepping down from the last step, anxious to gain distance from him, she swung around too quickly in her attempt to turn toward the hallway leading to the kitchen. The awkward movement placed pressure on her swollen ankle. Crying out in pain she fell toward the floor. Kalturek's arm reached out to grab her, as he hastened down the last few steps after her, but he wasn't quick enough. The loud thump of her left hip, and the resounding smacking noise of her left arm and hand against the hardwood floor carried into the kitchen and down the hallway. Dazed, Angel rolled to her back as she exhaled and groaned from the pain now reverberating along her hip, up her torso, and along her arm into the palm of her hand.

"Angel, are you all right?" Kalturek asked with concern, bending down next to her.

"I'm on the floor in pain. Do I look all right to you?" Angel snapped.

Cross at being so clumsy and embarrassed to be lying on the floor in a heap before him, she attempted to sit up too quickly. The sudden movement made her dizzy, forcing her to slump back to the floor. She stared up at the ceiling, marveling briefly at the architecture of the entryway with the log beams crisscrossing in order to create the high ceiling required for the stairwell.

"Huh, from this vantage the entryway is really quite beautiful," she commented offhandedly with a comical smile, the stress of the moment getting to her. The absurdity of the statement made her laugh, then groan suddenly at the jarring motion of her body shaking with mirth.

Kahner quickly joined Kalturek at her side, having heard the incident from the kitchen as he was coming in from outdoors. Batting his brother's hands out of the way, while giving him a dark look, Kahner attempted to help her up from the floor. At the same time, Angel could hear the soft patter of sock-clad feet running down the hallway from the movie room.

"Mama?" Kal called upon seeing his mother being helped up from her sprawled state on the floor. Sable's children, Lisa, Jordan, and Adam stood next to him, their curious gazes taking everything in.

The young boy gave his mother a woeful searching look as if asking her with his eyes if he could do anything for her. Shaking her head Angel responded.

"I'm okay," she insisted, not wanting to worry him any more than necessary.

"I got her, Kal. Don't you worry I'll take good care of your mama. She'll be just fine," Kahner assured him. He lifted her off the floor in one fell swoop and carried her back into the kitchen, leaving the children to scamper back to the movie room.

"That was for Kal's sake. Now tell me seriously, are you hurt?" Kahner asked.

"Yes and no. Just put me down."

His movements halted halfway to the counter, his clear blue eyes piercing into hers. "Be honest. Did you hurt yourself in that fall?" He spoke with a warning tone.

She huffed indignantly. "No, I just hurt my pride is all. Just dump me back in a chair somewhere, please."

"I'll set you back at the counter. It's time for lunch shortly anyway."

"Lunch? I just got done with breakfast," Angel exclaimed, becoming flustered. "Would you put me down already? I'm not an invalid."

"You could have fooled me."

He was holding her close against his toned, well-muscled body. Angel found she was liking it a bit more than she cared to. It was so similar to the feel of his brother's yet somehow slightly different.

"That was more like brunch for you. You took a long time to eat it," Kahner stated next to her ear, causing her to shiver noticeably in his arms. Angel's vision blurred slightly as she stared at him. She had the impression of another man's face hovering before his. Wizened with age its eyes seemingly laughed at her when he turned toward her and gave her an easy smile. He set her down on a bar stool, then patted at her left side forcing her back to reality.

What in the world was wrong with her, she wondered? So what? Now she was seeing things?

Adjusting the stool next to her, Kahner carefully lifted her injured right leg so it rested on the stool.

Thanking him softly, she noted Kalturek watching them like a hawk from the hallway. "I'm not really hungry," she stated.

"The rest of us probably are, kids included," Kahner replied. "Kalturek and I will rustle up some food while you take it easy after that fall. Then maybe we can pick up on that conversation again afterwards."

Tucking her hands into the pockets of the sweatshirt Kalturek had loaned her, Angel nodded. Feeling a small piece of paper in the left pocket, she pulled it out and peered down at it curiously.

It read:

Enjoy the tour, did we?

Angel blinked, her eyes shifting suspiciously toward the men on the other side of the counter. As before, the little angel drawing began the missive, and it was signed with the drawing of a small black raven. Her gaze shifted about the kitchen then back at the two men pulling food and condiments from the fridge and cupboards. She wondered if the messages were from whom she thought they were as a little thrill, filled her with hope? This could be a little romantic if it was.

Her eyes flitted between Kahner and Kalturek. Their backs were facing her as they worked. Standing side by side, they were preparing Panini sandwiches for them and the kids. If she hadn't so recently finished eating she might have been enticed by the sounds of the sizzling butter against the grill and the smell of the herbed bread toasting. They were piled high with ingredients like roast beef and Swiss or chicken and provolone with peppers and onions. She could see them lightly crushing the sandwiches between the griddles of the sandwich maker, as it pressed them together into a gooey grilled mess of meat and cheese.

Watching Kahner intently and then Kalturek, it occurred to her then, that she hadn't seen either Stephanie or Sable since earlier in the day. A pinprick of anxiety made her belly uneasy. Was she alone with these men, she thought suddenly? She could understand Stephanie's absence but wondered at Sable's.

"Where did Sable disappear to? I haven't seen her in a while," Angel asked slyly while filching the pen from the backpack on the counter next to her without them seeing. Scrawling a response at the bottom of the note, she then folded it back up and hid it in the palm of her hand.

Yes. I especially liked your room.

Not bothering to add the recipient's name or signature drawing to it in case she was wrong, Angel did, however, sign the note with a tiny drawing of her own. She hoped the one receiving it would get the meaning in her message and signature drawing. Glancing up, Angel noticed Kahner cast a subtle, yet unreadable look toward his brother for some reason. He then responded without peering back at her.

"She went with Stephanie to the movies. They were gonna stop off at a store on the way home. Something about chocolate cravings. They probably won't be home until closer to dinner time."

"Right. Makes sense, being pregnant and…well…a woman." Thinking quickly Angel carefully and quietly lifted her leg from the bar stool and hopped on one foot toward the pantry. It made more noise than she had intended.

"Where are you going?" Kalturek called both hearing and catching sight of her movements.

"I have a craving of my own. Got a problem with that?" she shouted back, disappearing into the pantry. The instant she was alone inside the small room, filled to the top shelf with all manner of edible goodies, she wondered at where she should leave the note. It was lunchtime, but she suspected he would come in here to get something crunchy to eat with whatever else he had. Her gaze roamed the pantry. Seeing a pile of barbecue potato chip bags on a lower shelf near the floor she smiled brightly. Those were his favorite; she was sure of it. Snatching a bag, she attempted to prop the note on the pile. It wasn't too obvious but would still be visible. She nervously hoped the party it was intended for would get her message.

Hopping back to the kitchen, she retook her seat at the counter, hefting her leg onto the stool next to her. Heaving a sigh of relief, she noisily opened her potato chip bag.

"Thought you said you weren't hungry. And I could have gotten that for you, you know?" Kahner pointed toward the bag in her hand with his spatula. Then, lifting a sandwich off the Panini grill he set it on a plate.

"Those look good," Kalturek commented, his eyes squinting across the counter at her hungrily.

"I guess I just have the munchies. Besides, you're busy."

"Does your son like chicken and provolone cheese?" Kalturek inquired while flipping another Panini.

"He eats just about anything, except onions."

"Seriously?" Kahner's brow arched in surprise, his gaze darting toward Kalturek.

"Yeah, why?"

Both men shared a bemused look.

"I cannot stand onions. Especially on sandwiches," Kalturek answered, making a face.

"Happy coincidence, I guess." She harrumphed softly.

"That's the last one, Kahner. I'll go get the kids. You want to pull it off the sandwich maker for me when it's done?" Catching his brother's nod, Kalturek disappeared down the hall.

Everyone was quiet as Angel watched Kahner cut the Paninis. Staring down at the plates afterwards, he pursed his lips in thought as if contemplating over the food before him. Clapping his hands together suddenly, causing her to jump, he peered over at her and her bag.

"I know what's missing," he said, as he left the kitchen the same way Kalturek had.

Angel nervously sat poised with a chip in hand near her mouth, as both men came wandering back in moments later, with identical bags of barbecue chips in hand and four kids in tow. Eyes widening in alarm, she gaped open-mouthed at the men as the kids settled in with their food.

Had they found her note? And if so, which one got there first? Kahner or Kalturek? Oh, good Lord what had she done? Dropping the chip into her lap accidentally, she palmed her forehead into her hand, groaning internally.

Dumping chips from the bags onto the plates for the kids Kalturek then rested his hands against the counter. Fixing her with what appeared to be an almost mischievous grin, he spoke.

"Angel, you sure you're not hungry for a nice hot one?" he asked, wiggling his eyebrows at her meaningfully.

He beamed at her as she choked on the chip she'd shoved in her mouth in horror. At the same time, Kahner's gaze narrowed on his brother. He slammed the spatula into the sink violently while gesturing toward the children seated at the tables.

Even through her watering eyes, Angel could see Kalturek's shrugging stance. She could also see Kahner's protective posture and almost accusatory look her way. Oh, to have the ability to read minds right now, she thought, wishing desperately she'd never left the note.

Chapter 11

Angel was finally alone with him in the kitchen.

Lunch was over and Kahner was cleaning up after the kids had eaten. Kalturek had offered to take Kal and his children outside to the stables in order to see the horses so they had a few minutes to talk privately without prying ears. This suited him just fine. Clearing his throat, he cast a cautious look toward Angel.

"How are you holding up?"

"About as well as one might think. Especially with Kalturek trying to suck up to my son by plying him with horses."

Kahner suspected he knew why his brother was attempting to spend time with Angel's son and wasn't sure how he felt about that. It wasn't sitting right with him.

"No, really. I'm worried about your state of mind right now," he insisted, appearing genuine. "You're dealing with the loss of a spouse along with a lot of sudden changes, and it's all happening all at once."

Angel propped her elbow up against the smooth counter surface. Her chin rested against the palm of her right hand as she gazed at him languidly. Recalling the note that she found in the bathroom but moments before, on the toilet paper roll of all places, she still wasn't sure if the right party had found her note. There was only one way to find out for sure.

"Hhhmmm, yes. I am dealing with a lot. I imagine things will become easier to swallow as the day progresses into the evening. You know, when things become clearer to everyone. Don't you think?" Her eyes glinted unexpectedly with mischief and her lips curved into a sly secretive smile as she gazed at Kahner with an intense expression.

"Is there something you're not telling me that I need to know?" He was taken aback by the dreamy, almost wistful look she had on her face as she stared at him. If he didn't know better he'd have thought she was acting like a love-struck teenager the way she was looking at him.

Thinking she was finally acclimating to her imagination being a reality, he figured she was probably investigating her subject matter for accuracy. Two could play at this game. Returning the favor, his gaze flitted over her from head to foot. He really noticed her eyes this time. They were the color of dark sapphires and seemed to sparkle with silver flecks of light. As he gazed into her eyes he found he was unexpectedly drawn to her at that moment and he didn't know why. Physically shaking himself free of the ridiculous thought, he had to remind himself that he was married and that he loved his wife.

Whether she was aware of it or not, Angel was like one of the Sirens of Greek mythology, a temptress who had the ability to draw a man into their traps with the mere sound of their voice. He now understood better what his brother was going through.

Chuckling, Angel's voice became mellow as she spoke. "Would it be safe to say that everyone expects I've been brought here to bear the children of a RavenCroft?" she asked boldly, leaning over her mug as if in an attempt to get a better look at him. Then she sipped at the hot brew, all the while peering over the rim of her mug in his direction. Her eyes fluttered lazily. It was the third hot toddy for the day that he'd made for her, and it was helping to keep her otherwise shaky exterior calm.

Kahner was taken aback. Was she attempting, in some warped way, to flirt with him? What in the world was going on here? Mulling over the question, he took an extra moment before answering, wanting to be careful how he responded.

"The general consensus is…yes," he answered honestly. "Some concern has been expressed through texts back and forth amongst us over your age and whether you'd be able to conceive at all at this point, let alone triplets. But Dr. S.T. did point out that women between the age of forty and fifty are actually much more likely to have a multiple birth pregnancy." He figured it was best to be upfront with her. From the moment Stephanie had found and shared what she had of David Pearson's novels, he suspected most were anticipating this was how events were meant to unfold.

"What made you bring me here? I mean, I know your father Bastion told you to come to get me. But why? Why is it so all-fired important that *I* conceive these three children?"

"So, you definitely think it'll be triplets?" Kahner probed her, trying to figure out exactly what she knew. He'd long since determined the woman before him had nothing to do with Lionel and Kobi Radford other than the fact that she'd been writing about individuals she thought had been fictional.

"Yes, it'll be triplets. With the right woman, at the right time, triplets will always beget triplets in the Blackthorne line." She clearly had a full grasp of how the family heritage worked. "And Bastion RavenCroft, whether he likes it or not, originated from the Blackthorne line. The same line that stems from the Weir-deVere's of Scotland. But here's the thing. Kalturek is not entirely wrong. There is a deadline with this - a window of opportunity as they say - or at least, that's how I was going to write this story."

Exasperated, Kahner vented. "But why? Why did you have to create such a short deadline for this? With a little more time…"

Angel waved her hand in front of her in order to gain his attention and silence him. "My dear Kahner, *I* didn't create this time frame. This goes beyond any realm of control we, as humans have. Don't you understand?"

"So you're saying Fate has deigned for this to happen?"

"Fate, or God. Whichever or whatever you believe," Angel said blandly, staying neutral on that score. That conversation, she knew, was for another time for she was well aware of their disbelieving nature where God was concerned.

"Okay, so what? The conception and…and birth of these three children is meant to affect some outcome or purpose?"

"Exactly."

"So what is it?"

"What is what?"

"The purpose of this set of triplets?"

"You're gonna hate this part."

"Why?"

"Because you always hate it when it turns out your brother, Drayke, is right about something. He lords it over you and never lets you forget it."

Kahner stood there, his mind momentarily drawing a blank. Seeing he was struggling Angel prompted him gently with a simple question.

"The first Wednesday of this month you had a guest come to dinner and you all discovered she was pregnant. How did you all determine this and who was the father?"

"You're talking about Ariana, Kalabernus's new wife. She was seeing shadows that night."

"Oh? Is that all she was seeing?"

Kahner's eyes lit up. "Drayke realized she was also seeing the Light. He said that..." Kahner's voice trailed off as understanding hit him. The pieces of a vast puzzle seemed to be finally falling into place within his mind. Gripping the counter for support he stared at Angel, a mixture of emotion swirling within his chest.

"In every instance, with every gift, or power, or whatever you want to call it, there's always a balance," Angel stated calmly. "Wouldn't you say? So tell me Kahner, what's out of balance?"

"What's out of balance?"

"Yes, what or who doesn't make sense?"

Kahner's head tilted forward toward the counter deep in thought, his mind racing through what it was she was saying.

"Kalturek sees both good and bad auras," he said finally, tapping one finger on the counter

"Yes."

"Mackenzie senses good and bad emotions," he continued, extending another finger.

"You're getting there."

"Synedra knows when someone is healthy or sick, Drayke knows truth from a lie and also sees the light, but Kalabernus..."

"Only sees shadows."

He groaned. "Drayke *was* right that night! He was never meant to see the light, was he?"

Angel shook her head stoically. "No, Drayke wasn't meant to."

Kahner was conflicted. The knowledge that his brother Kalabernus had been tormented all these years by the shadows and hadn't had the light to protect him as it was meant to, tore at him.

"Something happened. I don't know what," she said quickly, knowing full well that would be his next question. "But I think his ability or power was split somehow. He was always meant to see both, like Ariana."

"You believe the conception and birth of these triplets are going to help him somehow, don't you?" he asked suddenly. Her head jerked toward him as if surprised he'd come to that revelation so quickly. "You said it yourself, something is out of balance. And like anything set out of balance something must occur to set things right."

Angel fidgeted, becoming slightly uncomfortable under his intense scrutiny.

Kahner began pacing back and forth in front of her, his gaze repeatedly falling on her as his feet shuffled back and forth.

"Triplets," he mumbled, his forehead creasing slightly while deep in thought. Angel imagined he looked a lot like his father when he'd get that way.

"Threes. Everything in threes. And why now I wonder?" his head jerked her direction and he stopped pacing. "Everything seems to be happening in threes!" he exclaimed. Extending his arm toward her he ticked off what he said with his first three fingers. "There's three of us. And until now, none of us has been able to have kids. But then a month ago I met Sable and got her pregnant with triplets."

"Oh? You're having triplets are you?" Angel inquired with a smug, almost satisfied look on her face. She seemed almost amused for some reason.

"Yes! Then Ariana showed up and meets Kalabernus and now she's expecting triplets."

"Yes, *she* is, isn't she?" Angel replied, sensing Kahner missed her inflection. He was way too distracted with what was currently running through his head and he was clearly excited by his new discoveries.

"And now…" he paused, staring at her avidly. "Now you're here. It would stand to reason that it's Kalturek's turn." His arm dropped as he looked at her curiously.

"Is it now?" Angel said, fidgeting once again. She looked away.

"Why can't it be Kalturek and Stephanie?"

"Because such abilities should never be in the hands of those who would manipulate it for their own dark purposes."

Kahner interrupted her. "Are you saying that Kalturek would do that?"

"I never said that, and would you let me finish?" she practically shouted as she banged her hand on the table loudly, annoyance and impatience laced in her tone. "They're being provoked, Kahner!"

"What do you mean?"

"You saw Kalturek with me just now during lunch, didn't you?"

Kahner thought back over the way his brother had been acting each time he had been in the kitchen. Every time he'd been aggressive and amorous with her, trying to convince her along with his thinking like a horny teenager would. Even during lunch Kalturek repeatedly dropped one innuendo-laced comment after another, to the point of becoming verbally badgering. Understanding what she was getting at, he sighed heavily.

Angel could see him connecting the dots in his head. "The shadows *want* this to happen with me and him. At least, that's how I was going to write it. But why? If it was going to correct the balance, then they'd be trying to keep us apart, but instead, I think... I think they're being manipulated, Kalturek and Stephanie because they're trying to bring us together and we're not meant to be."

"But you are here now because you're definitely meant to have RavenCroft children. Have I at least got that part right?"

"I believe so, yes," she said quietly. Her eyes darted about the kitchen anxiously.

Kahner was becoming frustrated and he even looked tired. It had already been a long day for him. Running his hands through his hair in aggravation he began pacing again as he periodically glanced her way.

"Okay," he said slowly. "If it's not meant to be Kalturek...then who?"

"Who indeed?" Angel said softly, either unable or unwilling to look at him.

"Angel?" Kahner prompted her. "Do you know?"

She frowned. Biting her lip, she leaned back in her seat and stretched. Gaze shifting around the room worriedly, her eyes eventually found their way back to him. He shrugged at her, arms wide expectantly as if awaiting her response with bated breath.

Angel started to speak all the while shifting nervously in her seat. She knew she had to say this right or he might misconstrue her meaning.

"Kahner, if it really came down to it, if you knew it could help ease your brother's torment," she paused, taking a deep breath while gauging her words so far. "And if you knew there was no other way to prevent a serious wrong to another, what would you be willing to do in order to affect the right outcome? Would you be willing to go against your own twin brother?" She lifted her gaze to him, imploring him to understand what she was trying to say. She could tell his mind was trying hard to work its way around what she was saying. A thought popped suddenly in her head and before she knew it her next words came out in a rush. "Is a person really legally married if they're using an assumed name when they get married?"

He froze.

The silence within the kitchen was deafening.

It put her instantly on edge.

Where in the world had the last question come from? And had she said what she'd needed to correctly? Did he understand what she was trying to tell him? The agonizingly horrifying sound that escaped his throat led her to believe otherwise.

Oh, good grief, she thought. Her fifteen-year-old mind in her forty-five-year-old body had screwed her again. As humiliating as it would have been, maybe she should have just laid it all out for him. Kahner was now staring at her as though he was standing before an oncoming Mac truck.

He exclaimed in horror. "No, no, no! You mean, like…take his place?" he cried, sounding more than a little thunderstruck. "Six babies?" The incredulity in his voice made Angel cringe and she watched as his face became ashen. Pivoting where he stood he moved to leave the room then halted abruptly. His head dropped and he smacked his forehead with the palm of his hand.

"Oh, geez! Sable's gonna kill me," he declared, then hastily disappeared, not once looking back.

Angel instantly began to hyperventilate, unsure whether she should be offended by his revolted look or not. Tears welled in her eyes as she sat up in her chair, wanting nothing more than to run yet knowing that she couldn't.

Twisted.

That's what this was.

Horribly, terribly, and morbidly twisted.

The whole situation could have easily been avoided, she thought. But no, Bastion had to disappear for the day and not be here when she arrived. He was supposed to have answers for her, after all, and he could have helped smooth things over for the necessary transition.

She groaned, flinging her hands across her face. "It's your fault you know?" she said aloud to the empty kitchen. "All your fault," she said even louder, then swore irately. "Bastion, you jerk! You should have been here, you little pervert," she vented crossly, all the while knowing full well the man was likely listening. She, as opposed to the RavenCroft children, knew he had the place bugged, and that he was likely watching them as they spoke, for there were cameras everywhere.

"And we both know who you *really* are, don't we Bastion?" she said contemptuously. A dull ache was beginning at her temple. Her irises bore into the mug cupped within her taut fingers, threatening to break it with her vice-like grip.

This was it, right here in her hands, she thought. The words on the side of the black cup mocked her even as she read and re-read them over and over again. The image of a raven on the side of the cup was etched in white, as was the quote it displayed.

"For every man, there is only one…" She read aloud, turning the mug so she could finish reading it. "-Woman," she croaked, choking back a sob at feeling tears threatening to spill forth. Somehow she knew this lousy mug was gonna be her downfall. Shoving her empty mug roughly away she got up from her chair.

"That's just great! And now I have to get up and walk on this blasted leg because I have to pee again."

Chapter 12

I bet you thought this story was messed up enough already, eh?

And no … you didn't hear that wrong. It turns out Angel was, in fact, meant to bear children for one of the RavenCroft men. The question right now was, which one?

According to Angel, she didn't believe it could be the Sheriff.

Kahner was panicking because he now thought it was supposed to be him. The problem was, he was already happily married and expecting a set of triplets of his own. Or is he? Kahner may have reverted back to his legal name when he arrived in Loveland but Sable had taken up an assumed name when she'd married him. The way Angel was talking, she'd sure made it sound like it could be him.

Didn't she?

All I can say … is uh, oh.

What do you suppose Kahner's wife, Sable, is going to say when she finds out about all this? Man, I sure wouldn't want to be in on that conversation.

I'm telling you, it's like some jacked up love triangle on crack.

Does anyone want to take odds on who it's gonna wind up being?

One thing for sure, the RavenCrofts certainly had themselves a pretty big dilemma and Angel appeared to be smack dab in the middle of it. Whether by prophecy or natural design, it would seem that the only way for the balance to be corrected, and for Kalabernus to begin seeing the light as he was always meant to, was if Angel, like Sable and Ariana before her, were to conceive and bear RavenCroft triplets.

It kind of made me wonder what the whole purpose of any of this was in the long run. Because wouldn't it just correct itself once Kalabernus passed away one day? After all, it's been that way for forty years now. Why the sudden and urgent need to fix this? And even if this swayed balance didn't need to be corrected why the need for three sets of triplets in order to accomplish it?

Good grief! That's sure a lot of babies.

Bastion did always say that he wanted grandchildren. I guess he's about to get his wish granted and almost literally ten-fold.

Oh, and then there's this whole thing with the note passing that was going on. I had originally thought the little airplane had been from Angel's son Kal. It's sort of sweet really and yet disturbing at the same time because it would seem Angel had an admirer of sorts. From the sounds of it, at that point, not even she was entirely sure who the individual was signing the black raven, for originally there had been no passing of notes within her story. Angel does seem awfully hopeful as to who it might be which could lead one to believe that she had a crush on one of the RavenCroft's.

The question was, which one?

And who was passing her the notes?

- - -

The vise-like hold Angel had on her mug was nothing compared to the suffocating grip which had taken hold of Bastion's chest. The news Angel was relaying would have been like a bombshell of epic proportions had he not already had a similar vision that very morning when he was traveling to, what he fondly referred to, as his war room. The things she said simply confirmed his own suspicions. The weight upon his shoulders increased exponentially. Closing his eyes briefly he placed his forefinger and thumb against the pressure point between his eyes and nose. He couldn't afford a headache today. There was still clearly too much to do, and he was quickly running out of time

Bastion had, as Angel suspected, been listening in on the conversation she had with Kahner even as he was returning with his lunch. Normally he didn't run out for his meals for his small kitchenette was usually stocked with, at the very least, microwaveable dinners. But with the holidays nearing he'd been lax about restocking the cabinets.

Originally poised before the microwave as he waited for the blasted machine to nuke his Sarsaparilla tea, he'd wandered back toward the monitor screen which housed the feed from the RavenCroft kitchen. The silver-haired beauty was not only yelling at him again but swearing at him.

His temper flared.

She was liable to give him away if she kept this up.

Shocked initially by her final outburst at needing to relieve herself, he then chortled out loud unexpectedly. The few crinkles near his eyes became more pronounced as he watched with both amusement and bated breath as she stumbled from the bar stool and landed in a heap on the floor. Her blustering and swearing gave him cause to laugh again when she found her foot again and began hopping from the kitchen down the hall.

"House, kitchen corridor please," Bastion said aloud, prompting his A.I. system to change the view. From this vantage, he could see Angel practically staggering to the bathroom door across from the movie room. She tried the doorknob only to be halted by another party calling from the other side.

"I know, Mama! I'm hurrying," Kal could be heard calling out to her, from the other side.

Angel scowled, clearly in a mood. "*This* is your fault too you know?" she continued to vent irately.

Bastion gaped at the woman on the screen, all the while shaking his head in wonder. "How is, you're having to pee my fault?" he said aloud, knowing full well he was talking to himself but not caring. "You're the one drinking the hot toddies."

"Yeah, that's right. You heard me, this is all your fault," she said again, as though she'd heard him and was responding to his query. Her head swiveled about the hallway and toward the ceiling, her long silver hair swinging around her shoulders. The golden hues caught the lights casting down from the ceiling, illuminating the hallway and its sleek wooden floors.

"How do you figure that? It's your danged body," Bastion growled, becoming slightly irritated with the woman, regardless of the current distance between them.

"If you'd just put more than one lousy bathroom on the main floor…." Angel complained as she swore, her voice echoing through the speakers of the monitor. She continued to hop in place anxiously as she waited impatiently.

Bastion swore in unison with her and then scowled. The same old argument his children used to give him when they'd have people over to show movies raged in his head. It wasn't like there wasn't another bathroom on the main level. He'd put one in between the two bedrooms on the main floor when he renovated the house many years ago. But between his six children, their respective friends, and their boyfriends or girlfriends and now spouses, apparently, none of them could ever remember that fact, including Angel. He knew she was well aware of the layout of his home between the eerily accurate drawings and miniature model she'd built. But he'd also watched his son give her a tour of it not but an hour ago, including his own bedroom, much to Bastion's irritation. As an afterthought, he realized he'd have to promptly change that code too, or it could become a problem, even as soon as this evening.

"And I'm well aware there is another one," she huffed suddenly. "I'm just not going to make it that far!" Angel wailed plaintively. She was becoming visibly winded from her constant movement and had a pained expression on her face.

"For heaven sakes woman. Stop jumping and cross your legs already," Bastion ranted.

The door to the bathroom opened suddenly, clearly startling her. She gave a very un-ladylike yelp of surprise as her foot slipped and she wound up sprawled on the floor. Her bottom smacked first and the look on her face was priceless, almost comical.

Bastion flinched, stepping forward as he saw her fall as if to assist her, yet knowing there was nothing he could do from where he was. He sighed heavily, brow furrowing in consternation.

"Woman, I swear it's like you're…accident prone," Bastion grumbled, his lips curling into a wide grin. No sooner had the words slipped out when he overheard her next comment.

"Accident prone for sure. You can say that again."

Bastion cocked his head to one side thoughtfully as he watched her. How was she doing that? Was it truly a mere coincidence or did she have another power he wasn't aware of yet?

"I'm so sorry, Mama. I was trying to hurry. Are you okay?" Kal exclaimed, wincing at his mother's distressed state.

"I'm fine, I'm fine, I'm fine," she grumbled crossly. She was definitely irritated.

Laughing out loud, Bastion watched her scoot on her bottom into the bathroom, the door slamming behind her in her wake. The poor boy just stared after her then lifted his head toward the ceiling.

"Try not to hold it against her. In terms of memory, she's only aged fifteen years."

The boy's words range in Bastion's ears even as he heard the microwave ding from the kitchenette. His mouth moved silently, repeating what Angel's son had said.

"In terms of memory... Fifteen years... I wonder..."

Forgetting about his food and tea, he jerked the chair out from the long desk, sat down, and wheeled it toward his main tower. That's where the search needed to begin, he was sure of it. Typing in the parameters he began investigating articles from fifteen years prior. The difficulty now was determining the location to start at. She'd been found and brought to his home from Pocahontas, Iowa but had she come from somewhere else originally?

"Where did you come from, Angel?" he murmured softly.

As he worked, Bastion paid little attention to the song the boy had begun to sing as he stood outside the bathroom door, seemingly waiting on his mother. After a moment, something in what he heard the boy crooning caught his attention.

The song was vaguely familiar but Kal was singing off key which was why Bastion hadn't picked up on it before, and he was sure the boy had also changed the words a bit. He turned toward the monitor as Kal sang softly. His eyes were staring off into space as if he wasn't fully there. He sang of a woman walking along a mountainside, presumably near a forest and stream. Then he continued on about a mountain lake with clear blue waters. When he hit the refrain of the song Bastion couldn't help but be astounded by what he was hearing and seeing.

"You little devil," Bastion murmured as the boy continued singing. "You're trying to give me a message aren't you?"

Kal belted the refrain once more, his voice cracking, the tune disastrously ruined by his inability to stay on key.

"All right, all right. I got it," Bastion said finally, waving a hand in the air as he shook his head. "I can both see and hear you."

The boy stopped singing suddenly but continued to hum softly as he turned back toward the movie room where Bastion's new grand-daughter, Lisa, now stood looking at him.

"Watcha doing?" Lisa gave the boy an odd look.

"Just remembering a tune. Thought it might be relevant," Kal replied with a noncommittal shrug.

"Okay..."

Bastion's new granddaughter was obviously confused but chose to ignore the curious behavior.

"Batman is chasing Joker through the city. Want to see?" she asked brightly.

"Oh, yeah! I love it when he does that."

The boy's excitement over viewing a chase on the big screen spurred his return to the movie room. Though the children seemed to enjoy the short jaunt out to see the horses with Kalturek, clearly their favored past time was watching superhero movies.

Whistling softly in awe, Bastion chuckled. Discovering new powers in people was always interesting, he thought, but he could honestly say he'd never known anyone to do what the boy and his mother were doing. He wasn't even sure what to call this particular ability. It was as if they could hear people talking from a distance and yet somehow Bastion suspected that wasn't quite what they were doing.

Returning his attention back to the monitor before him, Bastion added Colorado and the Rocky Mountains to his designation parameters, which was the clue Kal had been attempting to pass on to him. Was it possible she'd been in Colorado before, but had moved away for some reason?

His eyes shifted swiftly across the monitor as he leafed through one old news report after another from fifteen years before. He had a feeling this was still going to take a while even with the hint but suspected the boy had saved him hours of endless searching through irrelevant articles. Fortunately, he was a speed reader just as his daughter-in-law Stephanie was.

An hour and a half later he finally found what he was looking for, and about time too. A local newspaper from Grand Lake, Colorado, a small town with barely 450 people, had submitted an article dated July fifth of two thousand which covered unusual activity off the shore of Grand Lake adjacent to the Rocky Mountain National Park. Topping the front page of the news was a small headshot of a woman, dressed in a hospital gown, who looked a lot like Angel, only her hair was longer. Next to the picture, its header read 'Woman Found Wandering Mountains.'

Bastion's cheek twitched as he read the article, his consternation over her situation increasing with every new word imprinted upon his brain. The woman listed simply as Jane Doe in the article had been found by an unnamed male camper as he was hiking toward the lake in order to see the fireworks display. Lacking clothing and any identifying information, the man had promptly covered her in his own hunting jacket and turned her over to a local hospital. Authorities were asking for anyone to come forward who might know the woman in question.

Upon finishing the article Bastion's head bent forward and rested upon the cupped hands before him. He had not foreseen this at all, and it complicated matters greatly. He now appreciated better why Angel had been so upset by his absence when she arrived. After nearly fifteen years of waiting, she had hoped he would already have some answers for her, or at the very least, would be able to find out what she needed to know. Bastion wondered how much she was aware of the events of that morning. His discovery by Agent Henley and the now confirmed deceased state of his courier meant he no longer had eyes within the Phenom organization. That meant he no longer had a way of finding out what she needed to know, at least, no way that was easy. Most government officials weren't even aware Phenom existed.

Troubled, Bastion leaned back in his chair then erupted from it without warning. The desk chair bounced in place then swiveled around in his absence. He began to pace.

Even throughout his searching, Bastion had still been able to track, for the most part, where and what everyone was doing at his ranch home. Normally he would not be so concerned with the whereabouts of his adult children and their spouses or, for that matter, what they were doing. The cameras and sound he'd installed in his home had only ever been meant for security purposes. But today was an especially different day than most. If Bastion wasn't careful, the wrong person would find his way to her tonight. For Kalabernus's sake, he needed for that to not happen. It was why he was keeping a close eye on his sons and, in particular, Stephanie. He just didn't trust that woman right now.

He knew Kalturek had been hovering around Angel most of the day, finding not so innocuous reasons for seeking her out, and it was clearly rattling her. He was also aware Kahner had been avoiding her completely since after his talk with her at lunchtime. From the looks of things, his daughter Synedra and her husband Nathan had yet to return from the trails. Hopefully, they were finding what they had been desperately looking for most of the day and would be returning soon. According to David Pearson's novel, what Nathan was trying to locate could still wind up playing a crucial role this evening.

Bastion was still pacing the room, contemplating on the terrible, troubling, and twisted situation within his home when the air around him pulsed unexpectedly, then froze in place, giving a feeling of unreality to the room. The vision being relayed to him was disjointed but he could clearly see a very confused Sable following after Stephanie, who appeared quite pleased with herself, as they exited the Asian market in town. The air pulsed once again and another vision took its place, one that upset him a great deal. Locked within his vision he couldn't even react as the tall figure lifted an unconscious Angel from the couch in the living room. His favorite mug lay empty next to her on the floor. The room was dark and the man's back was to him, so it was unclear who specifically the individual was and what his intent might be.

The air shifted once more and he found himself watching Angel as she padded gracefully through a forest laden with trees in the dark. He could tell she was naked, though all he could see was her curvaceous backside as she was walking away. In the near distance, a spray of fireworks erupted in the sky above a cool blue mountain lake, the sight of which startled her, forcing her to halt in her progression and look up. Her face was flushed and appeared younger, her sapphire eyes sparkling with a silver light enhanced by the silver hair dangling haphazardly to her waist. She seemed in awe of her surroundings as well as the lights in the sky, and yet, unconcerned by her lack of clothing. Her mannerism and demeanor were almost childlike, though her body was clearly that of a young woman about thirty years of age. It gave him pause to wonder what exactly had happened to her.

The next vision came with no warning. The blackness enshrouding this one prevented him from being able to see anything. But he could hear. The soft sounds of a woman's sobs echoed in his ears. At first, they were tolerable to a point, but then the crescendo of the wails erupted into an unbearable cacophony. Desperate to wrench away Bastion forced his eyes closed, gulping in air as he stumbled forward, finally free of the disturbing noise and vision. Sweat beaded upon his brow and his body shook, the tremors forcing him to a sitting position on the floor.

Carefully graduating his breathing in order to gain control he physically shook his head and wiped a hand across his forehead. Finally managing to calm himself, he began to wade through his memory of the visions, hoping to recall everything accurately.

There had been four of them this time.

That wasn't as unusual as was the increasing length of each vision as he had them. Typically, when he'd have multiple visions in a row they were short and decreased in length. It was the opposite this time, which was why he'd had such difficulty breaking free from the trance-like state. It was also why it had affected him more this time then what they usually did.

Mouth parched, as it always was after a vision for some reason, he came up from the floor and moved swiftly toward the microwave. Seeing his cup of Sarsaparilla tea still sitting inside on the tray awaiting its removal, he pulled it out and greedily drank it down, not bothering to re-warm it. Filling the mug again with water he added more tea, set it back in the microwave, and punched the button to heat.

Bastion's mind raced over everything he'd learned so far, formulating a plan as he awaited the heated brew's completion. Either way, Angel was going to need a new identity, so that had to take precedence for the moment, or he'd never be able to get the appropriate papers drawn up by tonight. His first step was to find an available name for her and her son, then begin getting documents in order. After that, he'd need to take a little trip. It was time to visit an old friend. The man still owed him a favor, and he figured it was about time he claimed his due.

Chapter 13

Notes.

Angel had found several in the last few hours.

She'd been finding them in the most innocuous of places too, like the cabinet in the kitchen when she was grabbing for a pouch of hot apple cider. The one she found on the light switch in the study was the one she thought had been particularly ingenious. She'd discovered that one after announcing she was heading to the study to see if she could find a book to read. The missive had a recommendation for her, and it both amused and annoyed her, so she had responded by saying she preferred the classics, like Wuthering Heights.

She was having an awful lot of fun answering the messages too and looked forward to each new one she received. Angel had been making the habit of returning the notes to the locations where she'd found them instead of trying to find new places to put them. She figured it was easier that way.

The notes were coming from the man she thought they were. She was sure of it now; at least, as sure as she could be. The last one she'd discovered by chance on the dining room table as she'd crossed through to get to the kitchen for a snack. Glancing at it briefly upon finding it, she'd been pleasantly surprised. It had her thinking about what the individual was trying to learn about her, and the notion tickled her, making her feel unexpectedly light-hearted. It seemed he actually was attempting to discreetly woo her in the only way he knew how under the circumstances. Prying eyes were everywhere after all, and she knew he was aware of that more than most.

Wandering into the movie room where the children were playing games, having finally turned off the movie screen, Angel took up a seat near the fireplace. Unfolding the half sheet of white paper, she perused the contents of the page carefully. It was covered in nearly a half dozen small pictures, each one with a tiny box next to it. Angel suspected she was meant to select which items she liked the best.

She smiled nostalgically.

When the nurses at the hospital first told her about love and romance they'd had difficulty getting her to understand what was meant to happen between men and women. So they'd given her a couple of romance novels which had been pretty graphic. Chuckling softly at the memory she immediately checked off the picture of the roaring fireplace. In the first book she'd read, the man in it had started a fire in the hearth, and it had crackled and popped as the lovers had coupled before it. Since reading that excerpt she'd always imagined such a moment like that with a man might be quite nice.

Tapping the pen against her bottom lip she glanced over at her son, who was avidly playing card games on the floor with Lisa, Jordan, and Adam. She became introspective as she watched them play together and was grateful her son had someone to spend time with.

Would she like candlelight, she wondered?

She supposed she would.

Her husband Wilton had never used them to woo her. When he'd returned to her as he'd said he would, three years later than what he'd originally told her, there hadn't been much of a courtship. The basis for her knowledge of love and romance had been from cheesy romance novels. Because of that, she'd had starry eyes over a vague memory of her rescuer, and at the time he had been kind, in good shape, and quite handsome. If she'd known then what she knew now, she might never have married Wilton, but then she wouldn't have had Kal. Angel couldn't imagine not having her son in her life. So, in the end, she had been grateful to Wilton, even if he had been lacking in romantic skills. Real life had not played out as the fictional romance novels always did, that was for sure.

Placing the pen against the paper she opted to check off the candles as well. If she'd like a roaring fire, then she figured she might like a few lighted candles too. Becoming increasingly excited Angel tucked her good leg underneath her and bent over the paper in her lap, thoroughly engrossed in the selection process. The next picture was flowers, specifically Alabaster Roses. She definitely liked those so she marked the tiny box next to that picture right away. Further down was another picture that made her blush and giggle. Crossing the picture out, she made a note next to it.

Why bother? You're going to take it off me anyway, right?

A soft fanciful smile played at her lips as her gaze flitted down to the last picture on the page.

Chocolates.

Hello?

Of course chocolates! She *was* a woman after all.

Her task complete, Angel signed the paper with her little drawing then re-folded it along its creased seems. Feeling uncharacteristically elated for some reason, she struggled to her feet and made her way out of the room.

"I'll be back in a minute, Kal."

"Okay, Mama." The way he spoke, Angel could tell by his response that he was distracted by the game.

Hobbling slowly down the hallway she passed the bathroom and turned left into the formal dining room. Using the carefully polished and varnished table and chairs to assist her, she limped her way to the middle of the room near the wall shared by the stairwell closets. The paper was tucked in the palm of her hand and she was about to lay it on the table when her senses came to full attention.

From the hallway she'd just come from, Kahner entered the room and stopped abruptly at the sight of her. Mere seconds later, he was joined on the opposite side of the room by Kalturek, who entered the room from the other entrance. Both men peered at her questioningly as she stood leaning against the table for support, looking more than a little guilty. Heat surged up her neck, shoulders, and into her face at their careful scrutiny.

"What are you doing?"

"Nothing."

Kahner doubted it was nothing. She looked anything but innocent, and he could see something tucked in her hand. His eyes flashed with recognition, and he glared at his brother who returned the steely look.

"What do you have in your hand?" Kalturek asked, his brow lifting in question. He pointed at her hand with the note. His head turned back toward his identical twin brother almost expectantly.

"Just paper. It's nothing important," she said dismissively, tucking her hand closer to her side.

Kahner frowned. "Not important, huh?"

"Where'd it come from?" Kalturek asked.

"My son."

Kahner chuckled. His eyes darted cautiously toward his brother. "Right, your son. Why is it I can't read either one of you right now?"

Both men moved toward her.

Her eyes shifted back and forth uneasily between the two men the closer they came to her. If she could have run, she would have.

Kalturek was skeptical. His brother rarely had difficulty reading anyone. "I couldn't say for sure why that would be. Let's see what your son gave you, Angel." Kalturek gripped a corner of the paper and tugged it from her hand. Kahner snatched it away from him.

"Give it back. That's not yours."

"It's not yours either," Kahner challenged. "I'd say this here belongs to Angel. And, oh look, it's a note. How sweet," Kahner said, winking at her. "Don't you think its sweet, Angel?" His gaze roamed the contents of the page, the muscle in his neck twitching anxiously.

Kalturek yanked the paper from Kahner's hand. "It's not a note."

"Sure it is."

"Notes have words, idiot. This has pictures."

"Clearly. I'm just amazed you even know what a word is."

"Like you ever got past picture books."

Kahner scoffed in response.

"I just saw you yesterday reading a comic book," Kalturek accused.

"I was reading to Adam and Jordan, you dolt. That's what fathers do," Kahner shot back as Kalturek perused the paper curiously then looked down at Angel. In order to gain a better view of the page, Kahner leaned closer to her. So close they nearly touched.

"Let's see what Kal wants to know about his mother," Kahner said, tongue in cheek. They all knew full well it wasn't from her son. Taking hold of the other side of the paper, he pulled it closer so both he and his brother could see it better under the lights.

"Why, it looks like Angel enjoys a roaring fire…"

"-And candlelight."

"Yes, and flowers too. Good to know."

Both men stopped suddenly, turning to look at her upon seeing the note she'd written and the items she'd crossed off. Angel would have covered her face in humiliation but she refused to give them the satisfaction. Instead, she met their gaze, daring either one to speak it aloud.

"I'm not sure Kal needs to know that," Kahner said finally on an exhale, breaking the silence. His head, like his brother's, was spinning over the imagery her carefully handwritten words were producing in his mind.

"Agreed. Yet, still noteworthy."

"Chocolates," Kahner continued quickly, his eyes growing softer as he took in her flushed pallor. "Angel likes chocolates."

"Why, Angel. I'd say this means…"

"What? What does it mean?" she challenged, feeling trapped and angry for it. "That I'm a pathetic hopeless romantic because of a bunch of nurses who couldn't have the decency to teach me the reality of the ways of men?" Angel practically shouted at them. She'd become choked up and hated herself for appearing weak. She had to be strong. She had to be. Wilton had taught her it was the only way to survive.

Taken aback by her outburst, both men appeared startled. Then Kahner's eyes narrowed upon her.

"Angel…why did you learn from nurses about…"

"You know what, just forget about it," she snapped, thoroughly flustered and wounded. "It's not like any of this ever mattered anyway. Wilton never bothered with any of that stuff, so why would a RavenCroft care? All you all want from me are a bunch of babies anyway." She'd been stupid. Clearly, the person who'd left the note for her had meant to be cruel, not romantic. Snatching the paperback she ripped it in half. Hastily stacking the torn page, she tore it again, her fingers trembling as she repeated the process several more times, rendering the note into tiny bits of paper.

"Angel, wait!" Kahner called after her. She had tossed the bits of paper on the floor near the wall and was attempting to limp quickly from the room.

"Just forget it."

Left with silence the identical brothers stared after her than met each other's heated gaze. Kahner spoke first.

"What's the matter with you?"

"You know full well…"

"Let it go!"

"No."

"Why?"

"Are you kidding me? I won't lose her, Kahner! That woman, Angel, is my chance for…"

"For what? For happiness? For children? For keeping your wife?"

"For everything!" Kalturek shouted sounding utterly desperate. His voice thundered within the dining room and reverberated down the hall.

"Don't do this," Kahner urged, knowing he sounded just as desperate as his brother. "Don't make me have to choose."

Kalturek grunted with disgust. "Stay out of this. It has nothing to do with you."

"More than you think. There's more going on here than what you know."

"Whatever." Kalturek moved to leave.

"I won't let you hurt her."

"I never said I was going to hurt her. Besides, she said it herself, she's going to take it off anyway." Kalturek disappeared, heading toward the front of the house to his bedroom.

Kahner watched him go. It was really bothering him that he hadn't been able to read Angel or his brother's thoughts just then.

Inhaling a troubled breath, he scowled, his eyes shifting to the floor where Angel had tossed the torn-up note. Her comment about the nurses bothered

Kahner a great deal too and led him to believe there was so much more she wasn't telling him. At least now he knew a lot more than what he did. He'd found the novels written by David Pearson within his father's study along with his book collection. He didn't know why he'd never noticed them there before and wondered if his father had realized the significance of them at the time he purchased them. There were about a dozen books in total of the Phenomena adult series, but he'd only pulled out the third one since he knew it was the one relevant to what was happening now. Aspects of the story were slightly different from reality but it was the same premise for the most part. Leafing through the story, he'd skimmed the pages, attempting to gain the knowledge he sought and needed the most.

He wondered, not for the first time, who the author of the book series was, and how his father had come by the copies he had. At some point, they would have to investigate who this David Pearson really was, but Kahner figured they could get into that more when Bastion returned home.

What was significant was that she might be right. According to what he'd gleaned from the book, if she were to conceive triplets by the end of this evening then the continuation of a prophecy of sorts would correct the balance left uneven and one day set Kalabernus free from his tormentors. He'd begin to see the light which would protect him from the shadows incessant assault. Kalabernus had already gone forty years having been tormented by the blasted shadowy figures and Kahner figured he was more than due for a reprieve from them. If the wrong RavenCroft begets her with children, however, then it would screw everything up for the unbalance would grow, potentially setting off a horrendous chain of events in time.

Shaking his head, he realized he couldn't let that happen. The shadows were clearly trying to sway Kalturek and Stephanie into believing that what they were attempting to convince Angel of doing was not only justifiable but morally okay. That had become painfully obvious. His brother would never even consider such a thing if they weren't.

Kahner knew he had a decision to make where Angel was concerned and soon, but he just didn't want to have to make it. He truly did love his wife Sable and didn't want to ruin what they had together. The conflict within him grew for he couldn't help but wonder how taking his brother's place was any better, yet somehow, he argued it was. The dilemma he faced was impossible. How could things have become so twisted?

One brother wanted to get Angel pregnant in order to have children and supposedly save his marriage, and yet, another *needed* her to have RavenCroft triplets in order to find peace. In Kahner's mind, Kalabernus had more of a need then Kalturek did because he wasn't so sure anymore that his twin brother's marriage was meant to be saved. For what woman would be okay with their spouse of eight years sleeping with another woman?

- - -

That's a very good point wouldn't you agree?

Then again, a woman barely married for a month wouldn't be any more okay with such behavior either. Unless…

No. No way.

Sorry folks, I'm having too much trouble getting past the notion of justifiable cheating. How do you suppose this is going to get ironed out anyway? Angel is clearly sweet on someone and becoming angry for it. Her fanciful dreams of at least a little romance have been dashed. I imagine she's feeling extremely vulnerable right about now and starting to worry that she'll end up with the wrong RavenCroft.

Any thoughts yet on who's passing her the notes?

Hhhhmmm. I imagine you have a lot of questions running through your head right about now. One of which might be, what exactly is going on with Angel? It sounds like at one point a long time back she was found wandering naked in the Colorado Rocky Mountains and taken to a hospital for … what exactly?

Memory issues?

Why else do you suppose a nurse would have to explain to Angel about what transpired between a man and a woman in love?

This wouldn't be a mystery if it wasn't mysterious but no worries, you'll start getting some answers soon.

Hahahaha.

Not likely before finding yourself asking more questions, though.

Chapter 14

Angel was brooding...

She had been for quite a while.

Returning to the movie room after the confrontation in the dining room, she had hoped the presence of the children would dissuade the RavenCroft men from seeking her out. She needed a break from them so she could think without them influencing her. After the debacle in the dining room, her first instinct was to leave and get as far away from them all as possible. But there was still a small part of her that wanted desperately for her story to end as she had always hoped, dreamed, and intended to write that it would. God, however, had a funny and somewhat sick sense of humor, she'd come to discover. The rippling effect of a decision, much like that of a rock in a stream, often caused even more troubles, or in her case, heartache.

All fanciful notions of love and romance had been squelched from her brain at that point. None of the RavenCrofts really wanted her there. That much was obvious. They just wanted what she could give them. Whether their desire was for peace, children, or absolution, that depended on the individual. But only one could truly love her, of that she was sure, and he was the one she wanted. He was the hero, the lover, the guardian and protector of her story, and yet, in some ways the villain as well because he was liable to end up hurting someone in order to be with her.

Sighing, she rested her head on the plush cushy arm of the chair within which she sat. Her injured leg was propped up on the matching step stool. She was trying to ignore the discomfort but the pain in the ankle was admittedly becoming worse as the hour progressed.

"Mama, can I go up to Jordan and Adam's room? Adam says they have video games upstairs," Kal pleaded.

She smiled slowly for his benefit and ruffled his hair. "Sure, have fun! And you know what? Maybe if they let you, and their parents say it's okay, you could sleep in their room tonight?"

"Yeah! That'd be cool." Jordan cheered.

Adam shouted, "Sleepover! All right! I'll ask mom."

The three boys tore out of the room leaving Lisa behind.

Lisa shook her head in wonder. "Boys," she said simply then continued. "I think I'm going to go read until dinner is ready." She sauntered out.

Glancing out the window next to her, Angel realized it probably was getting close to dinner. The sky was already showing signs of the rich golden and pink hues of an oncoming sunset. Her belly was rumbling too, but then she hadn't bothered with lunch since she'd finished eating breakfast so late. Trying to take her mind off of food she reached for the remote, thinking to watch some television for a while. She hadn't received any more notes recently, but then she'd opted to stay stationary since her ankle had started bothering her more.

The messages had kept her entertained and excited for the evening to arrive when she knew he would come for her.

The lack of them made her nervous.

Though, she supposed there wasn't much chance of finding one if she wasn't wandering the house.

Managing to finally figure out how to turn the screen on Angel gaped quite unexpectedly at a giant visual of, of all things, a white raven in flight. The soft melodic strains of a piano with accompanying music filled the room from the moment the imagery came to view on the screen. It sounded familiar but she couldn't presently place it.

"Huh, aren't white ravens pretty rare?" she said aloud, not realizing she was talking to herself.

The sight of the bird brought her to tears, though she had no idea why. Its wings were spread wide, reflecting the sun's rays as it soared through the air.

"It's so beautiful," she breathed. "It's like the angel of the Ravens, all sleek and white."

The screen flickered and a flourish of words flitted across her view underneath the white raven as it continued to soar.

White ravens are the rarest of breeds.

She was punching at buttons on the remote, unable to get it to switch channels when she saw the words. She sat forward in the chair arching one eyebrow, her mouth dropping in amazement. It was as though the television was answering her question. The same image seemed to replay over and over again of the bird. Was this a message? Was the individual who had been leaving her notes attempting to pass on a message of some sort? If they were, she didn't understand it this time.

The sounds of voices and movement in the kitchen carried down the hallway, gaining her attention. Hastily, she turned the television off, just in case it actually had been meant as a message. Moments later she could see a figure walking slowly down the hallway to the pantry. Catching sight of Angel watching her, Synedra changed directions and came to the movie room doorway instead.

"Did you get the message?" Synedra asked.

Angel looked at her. Had that been from Synedra for some reason and not the man passing her notes?

"Yeah, I got the message. I couldn't say I understood it, though."

Synedra gave her a funny look. "What part of 'ice your ankle' is hard to figure out?"

"Oh, wait. Sorry, I was thinking of... Oh, never mind. What message?" she stammered. Internally she kicked herself for being an idiot. Of course, it hadn't been from Synedra. She was suddenly in a mood. It had probably been a Discovery channel special that someone had recorded and it had gotten stuck in the machine or something.

Synedra pursed her lips in aggravation. "Kahner; he was supposed to tell you to stay immobile, keep the ankle iced, and to take some ibuprofen." Her eyes narrowed upon Angel's ankle.

"Nope. I can honestly say, I didn't get that one."

Stepping into the room, Synedra moved toward her and leaned down. Pulling the pant leg back she revealed the grisly knot on the side of Angel's ankle. The knot was the size of a softball now and the whole ankle had a large purplish-blue ring around it.

"This looks horribly painful, Angel. By the looks of it, even worse than this morning," Synedra commented, poking gingerly at the swollen mound.

Angel inhaled sharply at her touch and winced. "Yup, yup. It is."

"That's it, stay put. No more moving around without help. I'll be back."

Disappearing down the hallway, then to the pantry again, Synedra returned shortly with water, Ibuprofen, and an ice pack. Giving orders to take the pills and keep the ice pack on, she left once again, assuring her she'd send Nathan in for her when dinner was ready.

Angel did as she was told, not particularly caring to get up anyway. She could hear the sounds of people bustling around in the kitchen and thought to offer her help but knew they wouldn't accept it. It was probably just as well. She never had been much of a cook, much to Wilton's annoyance, and had the bad habit of burning things. There was only one thing she was good at making in a kitchen, and she hadn't made those in a long time.

A few minutes after Synedra left, Kahner appeared in the doorway with a bundle of wood in hand. Her eyes grew wide at the sight of him. He looked like he'd just come from a shower, for his short black hair was wet and curling about his ears. The effect was somehow alluring to her, the sight of it making her shiver with the notion of running her hands through it, which made her feel silly.

"It's, uh, getting chilly in here and the woodpile is low." Not looking at her, Kahner quickly went to work building a fire. Striking a long match to kindling he carefully set it within. She watched him gaze at the fire as it slowly came to blaze. The soft flames flickering with blue and golden light reflected in his shimmering crystal blue eyes.

"There. That should make it better." Standing, Kahner glanced at her, his hands now in his jean pockets. He peered around the room. "Until then…"

Grabbing an afghan from the nearest couch he tossed it across her legs, reset the ice pack on her ankle, and tucked the blanket around her more snugly. Then he took a seat on the footrest next to her legs.

"There's something I was hoping to discuss with you," he began, folding his hands together before him. "About earlier today, you said something…"

"Kahner, what are you doing?" Nathan asked suddenly from the doorway.

"Just, uh, making her more comfortable," Kahner said, losing his nerve at the sight of his brother-in-law. Hastily getting up, he stepped away from her. Promptly leaving the room, he walked past Nathan as he went.

Nathan's eyes searched her face with an appraising worried look. "Are you okay, Angel?"

The softness in his tone just about undid her. She struggled to keep him from seeing her so vulnerable. Her emotions were all over the place; anxiety, fear and the need to feel wanted and loved had become so overwhelming as Kahner had tended to her. Not sure she could speak without croaking she simply nodded and turned away.

"All right then. Let me know if you need anything. We're back for the night," Nathan explained and headed back to the kitchen.

She had the feeling he was trying to reassure her somehow but it wasn't working. Once again alone in the movie room, Angel became restless and after a while finally decided to try to reach the bathroom. She'd made the mistake of drinking the entire glass of water Synedra had given her and the need to go was becoming urgent.

Returning from the bathroom a few minutes later, she found a red rose in the chair she'd vacated, along with a small box of chocolates, and a book entitled, A Wrinkle In Time. She laughed and cried at the same time, both excited and relieved by the gesture. There was a note on the cover.

I didn't mean to upset you.

She frowned. The handwriting was different this time, and it wasn't addressed with the little angel picture or signed with the black raven. What did that mean? She'd gotten used to seeing the small angel figure heading the notes. She found she missed the little raven too. Folding the note, she tucked it in the opposite back pocket from the one she'd been using for the messages since it was starting to fill up. The red rose was a nice touch, she supposed, and the box of candy looked good. They were chocolate with caramel and pecans which weren't really her favorite, but she still liked them.

Opening the box, she popped a chocolate in her mouth just as Synedra padded softly to the door and leaned in.

"Dinner's ready if you'd like to join us."

Angel glanced at her ankle. It was really sore. Getting back and forth from the bathroom had been an awful lot of trouble. She wasn't sure she wanted to attempt the trek to the kitchen. Then she imagined the awkwardness of eating at the same table with Kahner, Kalturek, and their wives.

She chewed at the sweet and salty treat then covered her mouth as she spoke. "No thanks, I'm good."

Synedra hesitated. "Are you sure?"

Angel nodded and she left.

Bending her head down to investigate the chocolate box, she had just selected her next chocolate and was taking a bite from it as Nathan appeared in the room. She looked up and caught his gaze.

Taking in the sight of the roaring fire as well as the rose, book, and chocolates in her lap Nathan frowned.

"I understand you never actually had lunch today," Nathan said, registering her forlorn expression and sad eyes. "You really need to eat dinner tonight."

"I know. The ankle – it's just really bothering me bad. I guess I should have stayed off of it more but I didn't get Synedra's message. I have these, though, so I'm good."

Nathan chuckled. "You need more than chocolate."

"They have caramel and nuts too. See?" Thrusting her hand out to him so he could see, she waved it in front of him then took a big bite.

Shaking his head, Nathan walked over and scooped her up before she could argue with him. Squealing in surprise, her mouth full of chocolate, nuts, and gooey caramel, she was unable to voice her opposition to his manhandling.

"Bastion would never forgive me if I allowed a recently widowed and injured woman to wallow away alone in a room without being properly fed and tended to."

Nathan carried her down the hallway and to the kitchen as she chewed and finally managed to swallow her treat. "No doubt I'm at the very bottom of that man's list of things to worry about right now," Angel muttered as he put her down in one of the stools at the counter. "Gee, I've had more men carrying me around today than I have in my entire life! At least...that I can remember."

Picking up on what she said Synedra asked, "That you can remember? What do you mean?"

"She's been saying stuff like that all day today," Kahner responded, glancing in the direction where Angel now sat at the counter. Grabbing the milk from the fridge he began pouring glasses for everyone then set one in front of Angel too. Her face noticeably blanched at the sight of it.

"No, thank you," she croaked, becoming instantly worked up. "I don't want it. Take it away from me."

Setting the second casserole pan he'd just taken from the oven onto the stove, Nathan turned toward her suddenly and gave her a curious look.

"You need to drink milk. It's good for you," Kahner urged.

Placing plates filled with enchiladas, rice, lettuce salad and fruit in front of the kids, Synedra turned around then stopped. She could see Nathan staring peculiarly at Angel as Kahner continued to urge her to take the milk glass.

"I said I don't want it." Angel's voice rose as Kahner shoved the milk glass toward her on the counter. Her fearful response gained everyone's attention.

"All you had today were hot toddies."

"That's not true. I had water every time I went to the bathroom," Angel said weakly. She couldn't take her fear filled eyes off the white liquid within the glass.

"You need something healthy," Kalturek insisted in agreement. Reaching past Kahner, he picked up the glass and attempted to hand it to her. Angel gasped and shrank away.

"Wait. Stop!" Nathan said shortly, taking hold of Kalturek's wrist. He pulled the offending glass away from her as little Kal ran over to them from the table. Taking the glass from Kalturek's hand, he noted the confusion in his expression.

"Mama's afraid of milk. You can't let it get that close to her," he said quietly. Giving his mother a sympathetic look he sipped at the glass. Catching the grateful smile, she threw his way, he carried it away and sat back down.

"You're afraid of milk?" Kalturek asked quietly, instantly feeling like a cad, yet wondering at such an odd fear.

Angel nodded, her cheeks flushing in embarrassment. For some reason, tears were trying to form near her eyes again. The instantaneous fear she'd experienced at the sight of the milk so close to her had been overwhelming.

"I know." Angel gave a small weak laugh. "It probably seems silly."

"Not at all. Everyone has a phobia of one form or another," Synedra offered, trying to put Angel at ease. "Now me? I'm afraid of mice."

"Yeah, but that actually makes sense. They're small, dirty, and creepy with their beady little eyes," Sable countered. "How does one become afraid of milk?" she asked curiously.

"I don't know. I just have been. That is, for as far back as I can remember."

Nathan stopped dishing food on the plates in front of him and looked over at her. "Angel, how far back do you remember?"

"About fifteen years." The response had been automatic and without thought. Angel appeared momentarily stunned by her own frank candor. She could almost feel everyone's eyes upon her. Needing a distraction, she took a bite of the chicken enchilada on her plate. The unwanted attention was making her nervous and jittery.

"What does that mean?" Kalturek asked

"Are you saying you have no memory of anything from the time you were born until fifteen years ago?" Kahner inquired. It occurred to him that, that bit of knowledge might explain why there was so little information to be found on her.

Angel didn't respond. Fidgeting with her napkin, she cast a wary gaze about the kitchen. For some reason, she felt like she was getting all worked up. Between the milk and their questions, she was starting to feel trapped. She'd never liked that feeling.

"You know what? I'm not really hungry," Angel said finally, making it a point to raise her voice a bit, so it sounded at least stronger than what it was. Dropping her napkin and fork on the counter, she tried to scoot back in her bar stool so it would be easier to get up. Putting too much force into her shove, her stool tipped backwards instead. Her arms flung out wildly as she lost her balance within her seat and the stool descended to the floor, taking her with it. Before she hit, Nathan managed to get behind her. Grabbing hold of the wooden seat back with one arm, he snaked his other out around her waist, pinning her in place within her seat.

"I got you, Angel. I won't let you fall," he said against her ear.

For some reason, his words and close proximity evoked a latent memory and a very brief image flashed before Angel's eyes. The moment was surreal. The sensation of Nathan setting her chair legs back down on the wooden floor reminded her of a moment long ago when she'd been held safely and securely in place by another man's arms.

"Wilton," she breathed. Her voice was shaky.

"Angel? Are you all right?" Synedra asked. The woman was shaking, her gaze fixed on a spot before her that Synedra suspected they couldn't see. The look on her face didn't seem frightened so much as disoriented and confused.

"Y...yes, I'm fine. Sorry," Angel whispered finally, swallowing hard. There was a tremor in her voice. "But I think I'm done with dinner. Thanks anyway."

"You've barely eaten," Nathan said with real concern. He suspected she was having a flashback of sorts and wondered at what had brought it on. Had it been the milk, the conversation, or him catching her as she fell? For all he knew it could have been a combination of those events.

"Nathan, please, I just... I really need to be left alone right now."

Her behavior and tone were somewhat reminiscent of that morning when she first arrived. Nathan had the strong sense that she wasn't normally the jittery sort, but she'd had a lot happen to her in a short amount of time. Not sure he wanted a repeat of that morning he gave his wife a questioning glance. Synedra promptly responded with an agreeable bob of her head, likely having a similar thought.

"All right. I'll help you back to the movie room," Nathan offered, assisting her from the chair. Her pant leg rose on her injured leg as he aided her, and he caught sight of the knot on her ankle. "How recently did she have that Ibuprofen?" he asked his wife.

"Just before we put the enchiladas in the oven. Why?"

He didn't respond but glanced worriedly toward Kalturek then Kahner for some reason. "I think we're gonna put heat on that next."

Angel nodded her head in ascent but didn't say another word. The blank, almost lost expression left her appearing fragile. Where moments before she had a brightness about her, now the light, in her eyes especially, had dulled. She silently allowed him to carry her back and settle her into her chair near the fireplace. They brought her dinner into her and left her in peace. Before Synedra left she gave Angel an appraising stare.

"I'll bring you some tea, all right? It'll help with your nerves."

Angel's eyes opened wide with alarm. "As long as *you* make it."

"Of course."

"That's fine then," Angel said. "Just as long as it's you making it and no one else. And Synedra?"

"Yes?"

"Is Stephanie joining you all for dinner?"

"I don't know. I don't think so, why?"

"No reason, just … do me a favor. Please don't let anyone else touch the mug."

Thinking her request was odd Synedra frowned but nodded her head in agreement.

- - -

Is it just me, or does Angel seem awfully edgy about that cup of tea she's about to get? Makes a body wonder what she knows that we don't. But then, she appears to know a lot about all the stuff we don't know. I also get the feeling like there are more questions than there are answers.

There's definitely a lot going on in this twisted tale, wouldn't you say? Would it help if I broke it down some for you?

All right, all right!

Sorry. The author's nagging at me again and telling me that I should, so here's what we have so far...

A series of books by an unknown author named David Pearson hinting at Angel's purpose at being a surrogate for Kalturek and Stephanie.

An author and her son being brought to the ranch by Kahner after physically being assaulted and narrowly escaping the clutches of Lionel Radford's henchmen.

An accurately written accounting of the events which have transpired so far, written by Angel Stryfe, the same author mentioned in David Pearson's book.

A confirmation, of sorts, in Angel's own words that her purpose is to bear triplets for a RavenCroft triplet – possibly Kahner? – in order to continue a prophecy meant to correct an imbalance of good versus evil for Kalabernus.

A woman with lost time and memory for a period of about thirty years who just lost her husband of ten years and happens to be afraid of milk – of all things.

A bunch of flirtatious notes being passed back and forth between Angel and a mysterious individual who's been signing the missives with a little black raven.

A son of Angel's with the name Kalturek.

A bunch of shadowy demonic creatures pulling out all the stops to convince Kalturek and Stephanie of a detestable and loathsome plan in order to get the children they want so badly.

And a Sheriff's wife who is determined to have the chance to raise a gifted RavenCroft child, regardless of the cost.

Hhhhmmm.

I don't know about you, but if it were me, I think my head would be about to explode in confusion from all that information if I didn't already know what the outcome was.

See, being the gracious, kind, and generous individual that I am, I figured I better list this all out for you, the reader because Ms. Christine sure knows how to write a story and make it confusing. Then again, in her defense, I suppose there is a lot of chaos going on here and, believe it or not, it's about to get worse.

That's right, things are about to pick up big time from here on out. So you likely won't be hearing from me for a bit unless an interruption is required or a pivotal piece of information needs to be passed on to you. Because I sure wouldn't want to take your head out of the story at this point.

Once again, I should warn you, some of this might be a bit hard to swallow. Especially on around about chapter fifteen or so, I'd say. But if you stick with it, you might be pleasantly surprised at what you find out.

Hahahaha.

Then again, pretty soon you might just be saying...

-Whaaaaat?

Chapter 15

"What are you doing out here?"

"You said you were going to bring me some dinner."

"We're not done eating yet."

"You're making me wait till everyone is done?" Stephanie huffed. "By then the food will be cold! Just forget it. I'll get it myself."

Nathan couldn't get past Stephanie and Kalturek's short exchange before she'd returned to her bedroom. Their behavior was highly suspicious, as far as he was concerned, and it had set him on edge. He'd watched Stephanie stomp to the cupboard and grab a plate as his wife had pulled the teapot from the stove and moved to the counter. The mug Angel had been using all day was now next to Synedra on the counter waiting to be filled.

Nathan recalled glancing over at Kalturek then, who had been watching Kahner and Sable closely, looking worried.

Why had Kalturek been worried, Nathan wondered?

When he looked back at the counter and stove, Synedra had left to get something from the pantry and Stephanie had set her plate on the counter. She placed sour cream, salsa, cheese and lettuce on her plate first, rather than her food. Nathan remembered thinking it was especially odd at the time because he didn't think Stephanie even liked sour cream.

Unfortunately, Jordan bumped Adam at that moment, causing him to spill his milk all over Nathan's shirt sleeve. By the time he glanced back Stephanie was making a hasty retreat from the kitchen back to her room, and she was passing Synedra who had returned from the pantry with honey in hand. Nathan had gotten up and joined his wife at the counter. He noted she'd already placed the hot water in with the tea bag in the mug.

"What tea are you giving Angel?"

"Chamomile, it'll help settle her nerves and her belly. She really needs it," Synedra replied sympathetically.

"Agreed," he responded. Nathan's narrowed suspicious gaze followed the direction Stephanie had disappeared down the hall. "Tell you what, why don't you make her a new cup?"

"Why?" Synedra asked just as suspiciously.

Nathan shrugged. "No reason. I just have the feeling she might like a different flavor better."

"I know, not everyone likes chamomile. But it's all I have left here that helps with what's ailing her, and this bag is the last one."

"I see." Nathan's expression was pinched and Synedra managed to pick up on it.

"Nathan, is something wrong?"

"I don't know," Nathan stared down at the mug. "I'm sure it's nothing. Just a feeling is all. You know me." He patted his wife's side and smiled, giving her a chaste kiss on the forehead.

"Yeah...I know you," Synedra responded with a concerned look.

"I bet the clover honey would taste better than the one you have there."

"You think so? Hmmm. You know what you might be right. I'll go get it." Taking the jar with her, she headed back to the pantry. Before she returned Nathan slipped something in the drink and stirred. It had taken him forever to find the root while trekking through the woods, but he was awfully glad now that they'd stayed out on the trails till he'd found some. He hoped, in the end, he was wrong, and that it wasn't necessary, but he'd been assured either way that it was harmless on its own. His only concern now was that he'd correctly measured the powdered substance he'd made from it. He could have consulted his wife's council on that, but he didn't want to worry her, and Angel really needed the tea.

- - -

Bastion fumed.

Blasted air traffic controllers and their rules.

They'd been hovering over the airfield for some time now and he was becoming impatient. The flight itself only took an hour and a half. Locating and getting his contact to do what he wanted and needed had been an entirely different matter. The man had been quite drunk by the time he found him and had been in the middle of a shouting match with a Romanian poker player who had accused him of cheating at cards. Not one to take kindly to insults, whether justified or not, Judge Harold Lumas had become extremely belligerent. The ensuing fight had been inevitable and had required Bastion to have to step in when he arrived.

Adjusting in his seat at the memory of Sorin Radu's sucker punch in the gut, Bastion grunted softly. It still ached even now, and he'd received the barrel-chested brute's unanticipated slam to the stomach almost three hours ago.

Checking his watch Bastion grimaced, becoming antsy. If they didn't set down soon he wouldn't make it in time. He punched at the console again.

"Pilot, any word?"

"They're saying right now it could be another half hour, Sir, before a runway will be ready. A storm near Denver bumped several flights that could make it their way and..."

"I don't care what you have to do. You get me down now! They've already had us up here nearly a half hour. I don't have another half hour to wait."

"I'm trying, Sir. The controller is insisting..."

"Tell you what. You give him this message. You tell that poor excuse for a human being that if he doesn't want pictures of him and Savanna finding their way to her daddy then he better get us down." Bastion growled darkly, knowing full well which controller he was likely dealing with.

There was a slight pause on the other end. Bastion waited impatiently for a response. A moment later it came.

"Sir, please sit back and make sure your seat belt is on as we make our descent. We'll be landing near hanger eight momentarily. The temperature is currently seventeen degrees and there's a storm front quickly moving in. Time of arrival, nine fifty-eight."

Even as the pilot finished speaking they were already making their decent. "See now, it helps to have a little stashed in your pocket for a rainy day," Bastion grumbled, not bothering to buckle up.

"Sir, uh, controller three wants to know when he might get those pictures back." The pilot's voice range back over the speaker.

Bastion chuckled darkly, his blackened mood not entirely diminished yet. "Tell the little freak that we're gonna hang on to them a while longer," Bastion responded. He wasn't in the mood to placate the sick prick today. Besides, he fully intended to pass them on to the appropriate authorities. Child molesters, as far as he was concerned, didn't deserve second chances.

Moments later he felt the wheels of the plane touching down and they soon pulled up near the hangar. Taking a moment to check his house feed before logging off, he noted with satisfaction that everything appeared quiet for the moment. Angel was sleeping peacefully in the movie room and everyone else had headed off to bed for the night. Bastion tucked his laptop in his satchel, switched over to his android, and placed an earbud in his left ear. Stepping down out of the plane he gave the pilot a thumbs up while hefting his small satchel over his shoulder.

As he neared the car waiting for him outside the hangar, however, he heard a sound through his earbuds that he'd been hoping all day he wouldn't hear.

The sounds of voices then moments later, two men struggling in a darkened hallway, had his blood boiling and his heart racing.

"No...no, no! I'm not there yet." He'd spent all day racing against time, desperate to prevent this very situation from occurring. Yanking the car door open, Bastion leaped in, torqued the key, starting the engine, and tore out of the hangar parking lot. Bastion had run out of time and was already too late.

- - -

Rolling over in his sleep, Nathan reached for his cell phone from the nightstand and dialed Kalabernus. There was no answer. Disconnecting the call, he dialed again. No answer. Mumbling incoherently, he continued to dial his phone and disconnect each time Kalabernus failed to pick up within three rings. Next to him, his wife Synedra came awake from the noise he was making.

"Honey, what are you doing?"

"He won't answer."

"Who?"

"Your brother."

"Which one, I have four," she asked groggily, irritated to have been awakened

"Kalabernus, he won't answer."

"Honey, can't it wait till morning? It's almost ten o'clock at night. You know I have to be up early."

"No. He needs to know. It's about to happen and I can't stop him."

"Nathan? Honey…are you even awake?" Synedra noticed her husband's eyes were open. He acted like he was awake, and he was talking to her, but he didn't seem to be fully there somehow.

Nathan looked past her then back at his phone. He tried to call Kalabernus once more and again there was no answer. Canceling the call, he rang him all over again. It looked as if he was going to continue dialing until he finally reached him.

Worried about what he'd said and how he was acting, she realized he was sleep-walking and wouldn't let it go anytime soon. Wide awake now, she grabbed her cell phone and selected Ariana's number. If Kalabernus wasn't answering there was likely only one reason why. Cross now, and ready to pulverize her brother, she pursed her lips in frustration as she waited impatiently for Ariana to answer. She was certain Ariana would pick up when she saw her trying to call them as well. Three more rings later she heard a click on the other end. Not even waiting for Ariana to greet her she hollered into the phone.

"Tell my brother to give his horny body a rest and answer his dang phone!" She knew she sounded irate but she didn't care. She was tired from riding trails all day, and it was the Sunday night before Cyber week. Her shop would be extra busy this week, and she had to be in early to stock.

"Synedra? What's wrong…?"

"Nathan is sleep-walking. He's trying to call Kalabernus in his sleep and he won't stop until my brother picks up," she yelled. Noting the determined and worried set to his facial features, she added as an afterthought, "I think something might be wrong."

Synedra could hear Ariana talking to Kalabernus in the background. A second later she could hear her brother's deep voice echoing through Nathan's phone.

"Nathan, you can stop calling me now…"

"He's gonna get her, Shadowman."

There was a pause on the other end. What in the world was going on? She hadn't heard anyone call Kalabernus Shadowman since they were kids. How did her husband even know about that nickname?

"Who's gonna get who, Nathan?"

Something in her brother's tone worried her. Where before Kalabernus had been humoring him, now he sounded fully alert and concerned.

"It'll happen soon. Kalturek will go after her, and Kahner will try and take his place because of you."

"Nathan, you're not making any sense."

"You were always meant to see both. Three more will save you."

"Wait, Nathan, I can't hear you. Three more what will save me?"

"Babies."

Stunned, Synedra gaped openly at her husband.

"It's gonna happen soon and I can't stop him. He'll take me down. I can't stop him. I can't stop him. I can't stop him." Nathan kept repeating himself over and over again then disconnected from Kalabernus and fixed Synedra with a blank stare. There was an eerie look in his eyes that made her shiver uneasily.

"Synedra, what in the world is going on?" Ariana's voice piped through her phone, gaining her attention.

"I don't know but I better get off. I have a really bad feeling about all this."

"Wait, don't hang up. Kalabernus wants to talk to you."

A second later she could hear her brother speak through her phone. "Why do you have a bad feeling?"

She didn't answer right away. No one in the family knew the true story about how she and Nathan had met.

"Synedra, what are you not telling me?" Kalabernus's deep voice ground out.

She took a deep breath. "The last time he did this was seven years ago when he and I first met. That night…"

"It was the night your store was burglarized and you nearly got shot wasn't it?"

"How did you know?"

"I'm on my way."

And he was gone.

She stared down at her phone then back over at her husband who sat ramrod straight in bed, gazing diligently toward the bedroom door as if waiting for something.

"Nathan?"

He was no longer repeating himself, just watching the door. A tremor of fear ran through her, filling her with a sense of dread.

"Nathan, Honey?" she probed gently, worried about disturbing him too much. She knew it could be dangerous to disrupt someone when they were in such a trance-like dream walking state. "Nathan, you said three babies will save my brother. Save him from what?"

"Three by three will set him free. Only through Angel may he be set free."

"Three by three… Angel?" Synedra was confused. She wondered if this had something to do with the Phenomena books Stephanie found but she didn't get a chance to query him further. The sound of a door creeping open from down the hallway gave her cause for additional concern, particularly when she saw her husband's reaction to it.

Body jerking, he leaped out of bed and sped for the door, not bothering to throw on a shirt or slippers. "Stay here and lock the door. Do *not* come out no matter what," he whispered harshly back at her. There was a crazed, almost desperate look in his eye.

"Nathan?"

"Shadowman will knock three times and bring me back to you."

It was the last thing he said to her before he disappeared through the bedroom door.

Chapter 16

The house was quiet.

No sound could be heard even among the shadows creeping along the corridors. Beams of moonlight illuminated a niche here and there as it peaked through the cracks between the shades in the living room, kitchen, and movie room. The stillness of the hour of ten was curiously ominous as she slept without a care in the chair, unaware of the two figures moving with stealth toward her. Angel lay with her silver hair glistening in moonbeams, while her face, cast in shadows, rested against her shoulder and the arm cushion of the chair. The empty black mug dangled precariously within her fingertips as the arm holding it laid limply across her other forearm.

Kalturek found her first.

He stood momentarily watching her.

The fire in the hearth was dying, but the rose still lay nearby, as did the chocolates. He truly hoped she'd enjoyed them.

Hearing a noise coming from the opposite hallway from where he came, he shifted quickly out of the doorway. Kalturek knew full well who it was and was determined to alter the other's plan for her.

Hiding out of sight, he watched with trepidation as the other man entered the room. Would he really do it, Kalturek wondered? Would he really attempt to thwart his destiny?

Kahner entered the room.

He too gazed upon the woman before him, wondering why the Fates could be so cruel. The heavy burden he felt weighed at his heart. Could he go through with this? Could he truly make this woman his for one night simply to gain what was needed from her?

Kahner's mind shifted to his family, and he wondered what they would think of him in the morning if he did this. Then he worried about what they'd think of him if he didn't.

Inhaling deeply, his hand tightened at his side and his posture suddenly changed from a relaxed pose to a military stance. He spoke then, his voice barely above a whisper, yet it held a wealth of menace within.

"I know you're there."

The figure in the corner of the room tensed, his eyes flashing with reproach. "If you know that, then you know I cannot let you stop me."

"And you know you can't win."

Their eyes found each other in the dark. The crystal blue depths of their irises smoldered with the same determination, though Kalturek's eyes were slightly less sure of them self.

"What will you do *if* you win?" Kalturek whispered, his voice carrying across the room.

"What I must," Kahner replied with regret, his gaze returning to the woman lying peacefully on the chair. In that instant, the moonlight shifted, casting Angel's face from shadows into the light. The silver hair fairly gleamed about her face as it fell down her shoulders in loose waves.

"You're no match for me. You never were."

"No, *you* are no match for *me*. I am not the man I once was."

"Clearly, for you intend to steal what is mine."

"What is yours? Don't be stupid. This is not a game!"

"No. It most definitely isn't."

The first punch came without warning.

Identical in thought and in mind, they both struck in unison, though later they would debate who really threw the first punch. They warred with each other, punching, kicking, fighting fiercely, and both with purpose. Each had their own agenda, and they both thought they were right. Oblivious to the third man waiting patiently outside the doorway, they continued to battle ferociously. Though equal in size, stature, and build they were not equally trained to fight. In the end, only one prevailed.

The man outside the doorway heard it.

The loud thwack of the last punch which brought Kalturek down.

Panting, his breaths labored, Kahner stumbled and wiped at his face. He had to give Kalturek credit, for he had truly fought with all his might. It just wasn't enough and never would be. He'd been trained to fight by the best of the best. He'd been trained to kill. If Kalturek were any other man, then he would be dead.

Catching his breath Kahner bent down before the woman.

"Angel?" he spoke gently. "Don't be afraid, I won't hurt you."

The woman moaned softly and shifted in her sleep. The mug slipped from her grasp and thudded softly on the floor.

"Three by three will set him free."

Turning suddenly at the unexpected voice Kahner bolted up from the floor. "What? Oh, it's you! Go away! I'm trying to take care of it. Can't you see?"

"Only through Angel will he be set free."

"I know, Kalabernus. Now go, I'm taking care of it." Seeing his brother turn to leave, Kahner gave a sigh of relief and returned his attention to the woman. "I'll take you to the study, Angel, and we can…talk there. It's a little crowded in here."

Without warning, Kalabernus lunged at Kahner unexpectedly. Grabbing him from behind, he forcefully wrenched Kahner backwards and away from the woman.

"What the... Kalabernus?"

"No, Kahner! Don't you see?"

Angry at being caught off guard, and from behind, Kahner pitched to his left, spun, and swung at his brother with an uppercut. Jabbing his fist into Kalabernus's face, he could see his brother's ferocious terrifying visage after having been hit. Realizing his mistake too late, he could feel the sharp pain in his shoulder as Kalabernus grabbed his other arm, hefted him, and yanked. Kahner howled in pain, the sound eliciting a groan from his twin on the floor.

Kalturek's vision was clearing slowly as he lay in his prone state on the rug. Slowly regaining consciousness, he tensed at the horrifying sounds he heard around him. He could see Kahner was fighting with Kalabernus, and it sounded about as brutal as the fight he had moments before with him. Only he realized with increasing concern that Kalabernus was pummeling the crap out of his twin brother. Hearing Kahner cry out in pain, Kalturek sprang into action, his inherent instinct to protect his identical twin outweighing his reason. Kalabernus's back was to him, and he was within arm's reach. Reaching out, Kalturek swiped at his feet, forcing him to his knees with a resounding thud. The second he heard Kalabernus's howl of rage, he knew instantly he'd made a mistake.

"Kalabernus? Man, I'm sorry. I really am. But what are you doing here?"

"I could ask you the same question, Kalturek," Kalabernus growled angrily. Then he punched

Kalturek, swift and hard enough to knock him back down.

Kalturek blinked, his vision blurring again for the second time that night, and it was pissing him off something fierce. He shook it off and struggled back up from the floor at the same time Kalabernus slugged Kahner as well, forcing him down.

"And what about you, Kahner? What do you think you're doing?" Kalabernus snarled.

"At the moment defending myself," Kahner snapped. "And what are you hitting on me for? He's the one…"

"No!" Kalabernus hollered, pointing at both of them in turn. "You're both wrong."

Panting, chest heaving, all three men took up fighting stances. Standing in a triangle in the middle of the movie room, their matching crystal blue eyes fairly gleamed at one another, as they all scowled in frustration and anger.

"I'm trying to help you," Kahner shouted.

Kalturek scoffed. "No, you're trying to help yourself to what belongs to me. You got your triplets, now leave me to mine," he yelled.

A low rumble rose from the depth of Kalabernus's throat putting both men at unease. Their brother was dangerous enough on his best day. But when the wolf sounds began to emit from within him that was when he was at his most lethal, and nigh onto impossible, to put down.

"You, Kalturek! Do you think having babies with Angel is going to fix your marriage? Man, you can't fix what's already broken."

"Kalabernus, listen… if you just…"

"No!" Kalabernus let out a strangled cry. "Don't you see? Both Stephanie and the shadows have got you all twisted up. Kalturek, you're a RavenCroft, you're a Sheriff, and you're a married man. Those three things alone would normally ground you in a second. Why do you think seducing Angel is going to give you what you want? No good ever comes from a wrong!"

Kalabernus's gaze was fierce upon his brother, forcing him eventually to look away in shame.

"And you, Kahner! What's the matter with you? You of all people…"

"Listen, Kalabernus, you don't understand what's happening here," Kahner urged, still trying to regain his breath. The battle he'd waged between the two brothers so far had seriously weakened him.

"No, I understand perfectly. After Nathan's call, Ariana and I, we worked it out. You're thinking another set of triplets sired within our line will somehow correct the balance and allow me to finally see the light."

Utterly confused Kalturek hollered at them both in exasperation. "What are you guys talking about?"

"That's what I've been trying to tell you, you idiot!" Kahner yelled back. "This is about so much more than just you and Stephanie having children. And the babies could never be Stephanie's anyway because they'd belong to Angel. Don't you get it?" Dismissing his brother in disgust with a wave of his hand, he attempted to argue his case. "Why are you fighting me, Kalabernus? I'm trying to help you! Stop fighting me and let me help you," Kahner implored, becoming desperate at the sight of him shaking his head.

"No."

"Why?"

"Because you have to ask why. You're married and you love your wife. Why would you risk losing that?"

"Because you're my brother. Forty years is long enough for one man to be tortured by those demons!"

"Then I'll go another forty years more," Kalabernus roared. "Don't you get it? A wrong won't make a right. And the shadows, Kahner, they're screwing with you just as much as they are with him."

The shock at the possible truth of his statement gave Kahner a moment's pause. He hesitated.

The slight hesitation was just what Kalabernus had been waiting for. As his identical twin brothers locked gazes with each other, he charged them. Leaping forward between the two he reached out with his vast arms, took them each by their heads with a hand, and slammed them together. The move rendered both men unconscious, dropping them to the floor in a heap.

Landing in a crouch Kalabernus stood, flexed, then turned to look at the two men he'd left on the movie room floor. Chest heaving, he groaned, knowing he'd have to drag them both to a secure location or they might wake and possibly go after Angel again. He expected Kahner had likely come to his senses, for he'd seen the look of understanding in his eyes, but he wasn't as sure about Kalturek.

"You know what? You're both a couple of idiots," he declared. Casting a quick glance toward the woman in the chair Kalabernus became worried. They'd made a lot of noise during their fighting and she hadn't stirred at all. Strolling quickly toward her, he bent down and gave her an appraising once-over. She was breathing and there was color in her cheeks. Taking two fingers to her wrist he timed her pulse just to be sure.

Thinking it odd that she'd managed to sleep through it all Kalabernus shrugged it off.

"Must be an awful sound sleeper," he stated softly.

Not wanting to disturb her any more than necessary, he began dragging Kahner from the movie room and down the hall, past the bathroom, and into the dining room. Hauling him next to the wall which shared the closets, he dropped Kahner roughly than began inspecting the wall.

"Now where is it? I saw it. Just the other day, the notch was there, I know it." Catching sight of what looked like a tiny notch in a knot of the wooden paneling, he attempted to grab it with his fingers. Unfortunately, his fingers were too thick and big to slide into the notch.

"Blasted oafish hands," Kalabernus swore.

Taking out the pocketknife he always carried, he slid it into the notch in the knot and gently pushed, then pulled forward. A soft swooshing noise came from behind the wall, and he realized what it meant. Pulling on the paneling slightly, a section of the wall swung open to reveal a hidden metal room the size of an elevator shaft. The floor was solid wooden oak but the walls were a sleek metal as was, it turned out, the door he held. In the little light coming in from the hallway, he could see it was void of anything, including light, with the exception of a small metal box in the very corner of the room.

Dragging Kahner into the room, he dumped him on the floor. Taking a brief moment to investigate the box, he noted it contained water and bags of snack foods. Smiling with satisfaction, he exited the room and lumbered back toward the movie room for Kalturek. Hefting him up, Kalabernus headed back to the dining room. While on the way he stopped and grabbed a couple of large glow stick batons from the hall closet. Bending the sticks, he heard a soft crack as the glass ampoule within broke. Then giving them a good shake, the sticks became luminescent.

Once he had both of his brothers safely ensconced within, what he could only presume had been meant as a panic room, he tossed the glow sticks in the room and closed them both inside. The door slid easily back into place making it impossible to see that there was ever even an opening. He shook his head, staring at the wall, wondering at the timing of having discovered his father's secret room before moving out with Ariana to his cabin. He was never more grateful than what he was now that his cabin was only a few minutes away.

After taking care of them, he swung back around to the laundry room where he'd last seen Nathan on his way in. His brother-in-law was still hunched over on the floor where he'd been knocked out cold by one of his brothers. Kalabernus lifted him up off the floor. Nathan groaned as he moved him, and he realized he was finally coming to.

"Which one got you?"

"Kalturek," Nathan moaned softly while holding his head. "I tried to stop him, Kala...Kalaber...you know, you have a really long name?"

Chuckling, Kalabernus couldn't help but grin. "I know, and I know you did. You know you can just call me Shadowman if it's any easier."

"But that's long too," he complained, wincing at the pain in his head. "Besides it's our code word. No one's supposed to know it."

"That it is," Kalabernus responded. Hefting him up from the floor, he pulled Nathan's arm around his shoulder and lifted him the rest of the way.

"How 'bout Kalab? I'll...oof...I'll call you Kalab. That's shorter."

Kalabernus laughed. "That'll do." Dragging his brother-in-law to his sister's door, he knocked three times.

Synedra's worried voice called out to him. "Kalabernus, is that you?"

"Yes. Open up."

After letting him in, Kalabernus helped Nathan to bed then moved to leave.

"Where are you going?" Synedra asked anxiously.

"Home."

"But Angel…"

"Is safe now."

"But how do you know that? What happens if they wake up again before morning?"

Kalabernus paused, realizing his sister had figured out what had been going on and became agitated for it.

"Let's just say I put them somewhere they won't be able to get out."

"Are you sure?"

He halted briefly by the bedroom door, casting a tired look her way. "I'll make sure she's safe before I leave." He was quickly growing tired and wanted nothing more than to head home and crawl back into bed with Ariana.

"Good." Mollified, for the time being, she turned her attention to her husband who sat groaning on the bed as he held his head. Bruises were already swelling around his eye, and he had a cut on his cheek. "Nathan, which one of my brothers did this to you?" Kalabernus could hear her asking as he left.

"That's not important right now. We've done what we can. Now it's up to Angel."

Gasping audibly Synedra whirled on him suddenly. "Is this why you had us out searching the mountains for that root?"

Jerking his head toward the doorway in alarm, he shushed her. "I'll explain in the morning. I'm afraid it's not over yet," he whispered back, hoping Kalabernus hadn't overheard.

Closing the door quietly behind him Kalabernus peered down the empty hallway uneasily, wondering what Nathan had meant, for he'd heard everything. It wasn't midnight yet. It occurred to him that if one of his brothers woke up and managed to find their way out of the panic room before then, that Angel would be an easy target where she was at. He'd only just discovered the room himself recently and was unclear as to exactly how it worked and whether his brothers had known it was there. Deciding he'd better move her, he headed down the hallway and back to the movie room once more.

For a moment he simply stood and stared at Angel's peaceful sleeping form as did his brother's before him. The way the moonlight caught her face as she slept, she almost looked like what she'd been named for.

An angel.

The possibility that one of his brothers might seduce her simply to gain what they wanted just didn't sit right with him. Right now she was vulnerable, especially because of the loss of her husband, and could likely be easily swayed as a result. Even if one of his brothers had been trying to help him gain some blessed peace from the shadows and the 'troublesome three,' he would have never wanted that freedom to come at the potential harm of another.

Even when he'd first saw her upon her arrival at the house, Angel had seemed like such an innocent to him, and he didn't quite know why. Maybe it had been the tears streaking her cheeks as she'd cried when she stood all covered in blood in the entrance of his father's home as if searching for someone. But he thought it much more likely the almost child-like hopeful look she'd had upon her face when she'd asked him if there was a pool in the house. He'd never forget that. The way she'd stared up at him in that terrible state. Tattered, torn, and all twisted up inside over her loss and the wonder of discovering that both her fantasy and her abilities had been real.

As he understood it, the books she'd been writing were deemed romances. He wondered briefly if she'd been hoping to find true love when she'd been writing them. Or maybe she had been seeking a protective guardian to champion her and her son's safety.

Kalabernus could feel a mixture of confusing emotions welling within his chest that he simply didn't understand. And the shadows he could see flitting about the room weren't making it any easier for him to figure it out.

"So beautiful," the demon called Zalman crooned. His slick, oily vaporous mass pulsed before him.

Clearing his voice Kalabernus agreed. "Yes, she is. Even with the bruises on her face."

"She's here, she's alone and ready for you," the shadow called Veranke said, taking up his favored form; that of a wispy dark faceless man.

"Take her," Fallon cajoled, joining his cohort.

"Love her," Zalman wheezed, attempting to sound gentle and breathy only to cough and hack at the unnatural tone.

"No one will know," Veranke urged. The demon hovered before him, his soulless hollowed out pockets for eyes gaped grotesquely, making Kalabernus sick to his stomach.

"I'll know," he insisted harshly, jerking his head toward them. Eyes narrowing upon the frightening creatures he'd come to know so well as 'The Troublesome Three,' he gave them a suspicious stare. "What are you playing at anyway?"

"Only through Angel shall you be set free?" the monstrous being cackled, "You'll get what you want through her."

"You'll get what is owed to you."

"What you crave the most."

The 'troublesome three' spoke one after the other in quick succession, writhing closer, ensnaring Kalabernus with their tentacle-like arms. They held him fast, inching him closer to the woman.

"Yeah? And what's that, pray tell?" he asked, trying with difficulty to stay grounded and not get pulled into their trap, for he was sure there was a trap.

"Why...love Shadowman, of course," Veranke replied as if the answer were obvious.

"And freedom." The demon Fallon hissed near his ear.

The shiver of excitement which zinged within his body at the mere thought, the mere notion of the combination of those two things made him euphoric with need. He inhaled sharply.

The 'troublesome three' were always at their best when they were together. Their taunts were coming quicker and fiercer as they whirled about him, forcing him forward, ever closer to the woman lying on the chair, oblivious to their presence.

It would be so easy, he thought. She slept through their fighting. Would she sleep through that too?

Reaching up toward his face, Kalabernus suddenly realized there were tears streaming down from his eyes. He couldn't deny her silent mesmerizing pull, so sweet, so pure. Had this been what his brothers had been fighting with all day? And what would it be like, he wondered, to have a little piece of heaven? An Angel?

In agony, Kalabernus closed his eyes to the shadows, struggling for control. The battle he'd waged with his brothers had weakened him and the demons knew it. They were playing upon his most basic desire.

The need for love and to be loved.

Eyes opening to mere slits, he peered over at Angel through his tears. The sight before him changed suddenly, like a ghost image hovering over the woman, and all he could see was Ariana.

"No!" Kalabernus roared. His fists balled at his sides, and his body was rigid and tense. He was angry that the shadows had managed to convince him to even consider such a horrendous thing, for he was married and deeply in love with his wife.

"I have all the love I need. It is Ariana that I love, and she loves me!"

In that split second between the thin shreds of hopelessness and hope, Kalabernus knew the greatest truth. Love was his answer and one day it would bring him the peace he sought so desperately, of that he was certain.

His body shook as he bent down and lifted her from the chair. "Let's get you somewhere that I know you'll be a little safer," he said softly. Ignoring the wailing angry cries of the shadows, he carried Angel easily from the room, up the stairs, and punched a code into the keypad on his father's bedroom door. Letting himself in, he then gently laid her on the bed, pulled back the covers on the other side, then placed her under the covers, tucking her in as though she were a little girl.

Before he left, he took one last glance at her before tightly shutting the bedroom door. "There now, you should be safe here until the morning, Angel. No one else knows Dad's code but me."

At least, that's what he thought. He had no way of knowing that all the RavenCrofts had access to their father's room.

Chapter 17

Angel awoke slowly.

Her body felt loose and languid and everything was dark.

She could hear soft crackling and popping sounds and smell the smoldering aroma of a fire burning.

Lying motionless for the moment, allowing her mind to slowly process the new sensory information she was receiving, she tried to figure out what was going on. Her eyes were open, she was sure of it, but somehow all she could see was pitch black.

Angel blinked several times, hoping her vision would clear but there was nothing.

Nothing but the blackness before her eyes.

Moving her head ever so slightly, she managed to discern the truth without any further exertion. She was not only blindfolded but naked, and there was a presence within the room. She could hear them breathing.

"Is someone there?"

Her voice shook, as she called out to the room and then reached up to remove the blindfold from her eyes.

"Don't move."

The deep mellow voice came from the other side of the room. That's when she realized what had happened and where she was; she had fallen asleep in the chair in the movie room, having been slipped a drug in her drink by Stephanie, and she now lay unburdened by clothes in someone's bed. What was just as noteworthy was that there was a man in the room with her.

A RavenCroft man.

He'd been waiting for her.

Angel froze, her hand in mid-air. Her first instinct was to cover herself, but then she figured what was the point? Whoever it was had likely been the one to undress her, and they'd seen her already.

"Who's there? Who are you?"

"Who I am is unimportant."

"On the contrary. It's very important to me."

"Why?"

Angel reached around the back of her head.

"Ah, ah, ah," the man tisked softly. "The blindfold stays or I leave. Now answer my question."

"I just...I need to know if you're the one I had hoped you'd be," she answered honestly. Her voice sounded small and meek even to herself and she hated that.

She received no response.

Should she be worried? If it wasn't who she hoped, then she was trapped and likely had no escape. Plus, her ankle was badly sprained so she couldn't run even if she wanted to.

Angel adjusted in the bed, her movements causing her to come to an instant conclusion. She was most definitely without clothes and the notion made her feel a little self-conscious. Oddly enough she wasn't cold. The air around her was warm, free of its normal nighttime chill, and it had a light almost sweet floral scent to it, in addition to the smell of wood burning.

Roses.

And chocolates?

She couldn't help but wonder if they were Alabaster Roses.

The man's silence was maddening. After a short while, her anxiety got the better of her.

"Are...are you still there?" Angel was sitting up in the bed now, her head turning about the room as if seeking him out. Would he really leave her if she took the blindfold off? And who was he? Was the man in the room with her now the one she wanted it to be?

"Are you afraid?"

"No."

Her response was too quick.

A soft rumbling chuckle wafted across the room.

"Liar."

She swore internally. Did that mean it was Kalturek? Could he see her aura turn black at her deception? But then again it could be Kahner, she realized, for he could have simply read her mind.

"Okay, maybe a little. If I could only take off the blindfold…"

"No."

"Please."

"Okay...but then I'll leave," he warned.

She heard movement but it was slight. Had he come closer? Or was he leaving?

"If…if you're truly the one I have loved for so long, would you really?" she asked quickly, attempting to stay his movements until she learned his identity. There was a brief pause then the voice spoke again, sounding softer than before

"That's right."

"Okay then," she agreed finally, in distress. She was so confused. Her breathing was becoming ragged as her anxiety grew. And yet somehow she was no longer afraid. Angel realized suddenly that her anxious state wasn't from fear but from the sensual tension within the room. It was cloyingly thick and charged with unnatural energy.

"Are you willing?" the man asked quietly, sounding hopeful.

His voice was like a caress against her skin. Goosebumps rose along her arms and raised the tiny hairs at the nape of her neck.

"Willing to what exactly?" she asked nervously. Her voice shook slightly and she disliked that it made her sound vulnerable. "Under the circumstances maybe we should make some kind of an agreement here. That is if we're gonna…"

"Angel."

"Yes?"

"Are you willing?" he asked again, more urgently this time. There was a note of impatience in his voice.

Her breathing became increasingly erratic. She knew full well what the man was asking of her.

Faith.

Faith that it was truly him without seeing.

She knew if she didn't give it, then she'd never be able to convince him one day when she'd need to ask the same of him. Her first instinct was to refuse him unless he allowed her to see who he was. But then she realized that if it was the man she wanted that he'd be true to his word. He'd leave.

If it was him, she didn't want him to leave. She'd been waiting for him for fifteen years. Thinking quickly, she tried another angle in an attempt to get her answer.

"Are you the raven?"

"The Raven."

"The black raven, from the notes?"

More chuckling. "Maybe."

She groaned in frustration. This was maddening.

"Angel?"

"What?" she exclaimed irately.

"Are you willing?"

She could almost hear the smile when last he spoke. He was teasing her and they both knew it.

Licking her lips, she made a hasty decision and finally replied.

"Yes?" It came out sounding more like a question. The man chuckled. "Good."

She reached up to remove the blindfold.

"Don't."

She hesitated. "I'm…to leave it on?"

"Yes."

"I don't get to see you…or know for sure that it's you?"

"No."

"Why?" She couldn't help it. A little thrill of excitement caused her heart to race. The notion of not being able to see him but only feel him made her quiver.

"As I understand it, your life is sorely lacking in romance."

"Your point?" Angel inquired, becoming annoyed at the reminder. Why did that matter now? It never had before.

"This adds a certain amount of romantic flair. Wouldn't you say?"

Angel didn't know how to respond.

"Angel?"

"Yes?"

"Close your eyes…"

"Why bother? I'm wearing a blindfold?" she asked impatiently.

"Angel," he crooned making a soft noise with his tongue. "Close your eyes. Imagine the man you want."

"Oh, I see." Nervous, she did as she was told.

"Angel."

"Yes?"

"Are your eyes closed? Do you see him?"

"I do."

"Good."

Her heart lurched to her throat and she gasped. Angel wasn't sure how he did it. When last he spoke she could have sworn he was on the other side of the room. Somehow he'd managed to skirt across the room in an instant, in order to be next to her. The knowledge he was so close was exhilarating.

A shiver ran down Angel's spine. He was right next to her, speaking to her in her left ear. Her head tilted to her shoulder as she shivered again. She could feel his breath against her neck.

"Angel?"

"Yes?" her response was breathy and her head swiveled about her, trying to determine his exact location now.

He'd moved.

- - -

For shame, for shame!

As previously stated in book one, we may take off our clothes and dangle them out in front of you in this series but when we do, we do it behind a veil of privacy. I'm sure you can figure out what's happening right about now. As much fun as those details might be to hear, we won't be getting into them. Rest assured Angel was treated with as much respect and care as any woman would on their wedding night.

Whoops.

Well, crap. Guess I let the cat out of the bag there!

That's right, believe it or not, what you don't know is that Angel is married to the man next to her right now.

Ooooohhhhh, see now, you're probably wondering how that's possible. Or did you figure it out?

For those of you who haven't, you're probably sitting there going, "Whaaaat? Vortigern Black, how is that even possible? She's not even certain who it is in that room with her right now, so how in the world can she be married to him? Especially when all the RavenCroft triplets are married already. What the … what the…"

For the rest of you who have uncovered the truth, you're about to be proven right.

And before any of you get all riled up about how the man stripped her down while she slept without having her permission just calm down because, technically, he did have her consent. Remember one of the last notes her mystery man sent her? You know, the one where he'd asked what she liked and she was marking off the pictures? He managed to get ahold of those torn pieces by way of the hidden passage in the panic room and put it back together. When he saw her response to the need for lingerie he about dropped to his knees. You remember what that was, right?

"Why bother? You're going to take it off me anyway, right?"

275

Okay, okay so one could argue he intentionally read more consent into the statement then what there was but… As far as he was concerned Angel was meant to be his by the time he found her.

All right, all right. I concede it's sort of a gray area… That said, I think we all know men aren't very rational when they're about to … well … you know.

I'm sure there are some of you who are thinking Angel is nuts for allowing an intimate exchange to happen with a man when she's not for certain who he is. But just you wait because, first of all, it's not your place to judge, and second, you don't have the whole story yet, but you're about to.

Right now you should get your pencils ready because within these next few pages you're also about to get a hint as to who I, Vortigern Black, really am. Or, more accurately, am not. But you're going to need to pay close attention cause it's awfully subtle.

Or maybe not.

In fact, it's pretty in your face.

That's right, you may well get a chance to eliminate a name on your list of suspects at the back of this book which is going to help you determine who I really am. Think of it as a game of Clue. You know? Colonel Mustard did it in the Library with the candlestick? Only here, all you have to figure out is the 'who.' I'll tell all about the 'why' once all the RavenCroft and Blackthorne stories have been told.

- - -

"Do I have to keep this on all night?" Angel asked in annoyance. She could feel the man tense slightly, but he didn't respond. Instead, he held her to his side.

"Is … is it you?"

"It's me."

The man was maddening.

"B-Bastion?" she stammered anxiously, hope swelling in her chest. She was sure it had to be him. The man hadn't sounded like anyone else she'd met so far since she'd arrived. Though she supposed he could have disguised his voice.

His chest shook as the man chuckled, the deep rumble instilling within her a desperate need to see his face. Ripping the blindfold off, she blinked several times as her eyes adjusted to the unexpected amount of light within the room. There were candles everywhere and the red and blue flames of the firelight in the hearth burned brightly. Vases of Alabaster Roses sat on either side of the bed and a small bowl of dark chocolates, their scent hinting at amaretto within, sat next to each vase.

Leaning up on one elbow she turned towards the tall giant figure who had taken up a spot next to her, ever hopeful that it *was* really him.

And there he was.

He was real, he was virile, he was blatantly male, and he was a kind of stud-worthy eye-candy for the soul that could make a woman's toes curl.

Bastion RavenCroft.

Angel's mouth went dry, her jaw dropped, and her heart began fluttering wildly in her chest. She beamed happily while staring in awe and recognition at the man she'd somehow always known had been promised to her.

Chapter 18

Bastion RavenCroft was the man from the first, and the only vision Angel had ever had that she could remember. But most importantly, he was just as she had foreseen and even imagined.

His jet-black hair was dappled with white from age, and there was a salt and pepper coloring above his ears and at his temple. His eyes...those amazing, heart-stopping, electrifyingly beautiful crystal-clear blue eyes, indicative of a man from the Blackthorne line, had her hooked from the moment they locked gazes.

Relief washed over her at the sight of him, and she was sure he was able to see it in her expression, for her face practically glowed with joy back at him. Angel could see there was a self-satisfied light in his eyes as they danced merrily, and she could tell he was extremely pleased with himself.

So, she punched him.

The resounding whack packed more of a wallop than even she had anticipated.

"What was that for?" he growled, rubbing at his shoulder lightly. It hadn't really hurt that much, but she'd managed to bruise his ego a bit for he hadn't seen it coming at all.

"That's for not being here this morning," she exclaimed, her voice rising. "*And* for not coming to get me yourself. I *hate* being a foregone conclusion," she cried.

Taking hold of her about her waist and between her shoulder blades, Bastion pulled her gently back toward him, cradling her in his arms. He could see the tears welling at the corners of her eyes. "You weren't, and you aren't," he insisted warmly. "I had no expectations, only hopes. And Angel, I hope you know you have a choice and still do," he said while brushing a lock of her silver hair away from her face.

She wiped at her eyes with the back of her left hand. "I thought I already made my choice," she said, inclining her hand toward the bed. It was then, for the first time, that she noticed the ring on her finger.

It was big.

It was beautiful.

And it was a wedding set, not just an engagement ring.

"Bastion, what is…what is this?" she stammered.

"Your wedding ring," he supplied. "If it's not too presumptuous, that is."

"My wedding ring?"

"Yes, I have our marriage license already, and it's been notarized and signed by witnesses too."

"How did you manage…"

He waved a hand in the air dismissively. "I won't go into that. Suffice it to say, it involved a drunk judge and a Romanian with a mighty strong sucker punch." He paused, then took a deep breath. "I know this is sort of backwards and all, but Angela Sparks, will you be my wife?"

"Angela what?" she blinked through her damp lashes, looking thoroughly perplexed. An instant later her eyes registered what he was saying. "That's my new name, is it?" she said excitedly. "Angela Sparks?"

Bastion chuckled. Her face appeared even more youthful to him than what the doctors had determined. Was it possible she was younger than forty-five years?

"Yes, it's your new name. Or at least, your new maiden name. Technically your already Angela RavenCroft." An easy smile played at the corners of his lips. Her responses tickled him. One minute she was feisty and refusing to accept crap from people. The next she reacted with child-like innocence. Right now he could see her face screwing into a frown.

"What's the matter?"

"Sparks. Do I look like I would have been a sparky kind of woman to you?"

Bastion couldn't help himself. He laughed, the sound rich and inviting. It sent a little thrill down her spine upon hearing it, not that she'd admit to it.

"More than you could possibly know."

She glared at him. "No, seriously. You couldn't find a better name than Angela Sparks?" Her nose crinkled, her face registering a look of distaste.

He shook his head adamantly. "There is no better name than Angela."

"But why?"

"Because I can still call you, Angel, and no one will ever think to question it."

"Because it's so similar to my name," she said, then smacked his bare leg with her hand playfully. "That's why you addressed your notes with the tiny angel, isn't it?"

"Exactly," Bastion confirmed. "Because you're *my* Angel," he insisted, glad to know she had received all his notes. He'd found them all carefully tucked into her sweatpants pocket when he'd removed her clothes, along with the one from one of his sons.

She inhaled sharply, touched by his words. "I'm your angel?"

"Oh, yes. You will always be *my* Angel, no matter your name; just as I will always be your black raven."

"Why the white raven in flight? That *was* you, right?" she asked suddenly.

"I was trying to let you know I was ready and that I understood, but that I was traveling. I had to leave in order to get what I needed for tonight."

"Oh, okay," Angel rolled her eyes to the ceiling in comprehension. "That makes *so* much more sense now. The song you were playing with it... That was one of Yanni's songs called 'Until the Last Moment' wasn't it? You were trying to tell me you wouldn't be back until..."

"-The very last moment," he finished for her. "I am truly sorry it took me so long to return to you. I assure you, at no time were you ever truly in danger, for as I'm sure you already figured out, I've been watching over you all day and only been a few feet away at any given moment in my war room in the basement of the house. Plus, I charged Nathan to look out for you as well, in order to assure no harm would come to you."

Pleased to hear her suspicions were true, she snuggled up next to him. It occurred to her then, that he had likely been the one to remove the miniature model by way of the trap door in the wall of the closet. Reading her thoughts, Bastion gave her a reproachful look, though she noted it didn't really reach his eyes.

"Yes, I managed to procure and hide away that blasted miniature model of my house you made, though barely in time."

"So you're the one who took the three notebooks, drawing pad, and flash drive case from my bag?"

Bastion grimaced, his face taking on a troubled expression. "Kahner nearly caught me in the living room when I attempted to grab the drawing pad from your bag. I tripped over the carpet and found myself hiding behind my own couch until he disappeared back in the kitchen with your bag." Angel giggled at the imagery. He playfully squeezed her hip and she stifled her giggles with one hand over her mouth. "But the stuff wasn't there, Angel. It was already gone. I checked the floor, under the furniture, and in the seat cushions but it's as if it vanished. That's why he nearly caught me. I'd hoped maybe you had hidden it somewhere but the fact that you're asking me... That leads me to believe someone took it."

"Did you check the footage of the living room?" she asked, alarmed at the thought that her blueprints, drawings, flash drives, and notes were missing.

"You know, I did, but the stuff must have disappeared about the time the system was in update mode. There's a window of about five minutes there where the frame freezes just before everyone left earlier this morning and when Kahner went in to grab the bag."

"So you don't know who..."

"-Took them? I have no idea, Angel, which is troubling. Do you know for sure everything was still in there all morning?"

Angel shook her head. "No, I haven't had my hands on it since even before we arrived at the house. Kahner brought it in, I think. Or wait, maybe it was, Drayke? I think I remember someone saying that he, Kalturek, and Kalabernus brought everything in along with my son. So, wait...you have no clue? No vision, or whisper, or..."

"Nothing."

"Then...then I guess we're not meant to know."

"Whoever has them could cause some serious..."

"-Trouble. I know, depending on who has them. But just as you asked me to have faith that it was you a little bit ago, then I guess we need to have faith that it didn't fall into the wrong hands."

Bastion harrumphed softly, his breath gently caressing the side of her face. She sighed, tucking her head against his shoulder. "I wish you had been here first thing this morning," she said softly. She felt safe and at home in his arms which felt really good after the last twenty-four hours she'd been through.

"I truly wanted to be here for you when you arrived," he assured her. "But I received that blasted call last minute, which tipped me off that I was about to get the offer for that job. I had to be ready. If I hadn't been then I might never have known…"

"I do understand the chaotic nature of the life you juggle," Angel insisted. Turning in his arms she reached up toward him, cupping his face with her hand. "I'm sorry about your friend," she said tenderly, her blue eyes shimmering with a silver sheen.

His body tensed, and then he spoke with a thick voice. "So am I." Bastion covered the hand at his cheek. It occurred to him Angel was the only person who had ever truly known him for who he really was. Not even his late wife Inara had known.

Her left hand interlocked with his and she noted he had a matching silver wedding band on his hand.

"Just curious, but why silver?" she asked, shaking their hands in the air.

"I'd think that would be obvious." Her inquisitive nature was making him nuts, but he humored her. "Because of your silver hair," he chided.

"It's natural you know," she said earnestly, her face was alight with a happy glow. He reveled in it, enjoying having her by his side. "I've tried dying it but it won't let me."

"What do you mean?"

"Every time I try, the color bleeds out within a few days, and it's back to silver," she said with a sigh.

"I like it fine the way it is," he assured her, and he truly did. It was unique and beautiful, a rare thing indeed; just as rare as a white raven, which was the other reason he'd picked that image for his last message.

Bastion knew he hadn't always been good. He'd done a lot of truly evil things in his life because of the kind of work he did outside of the ranch, much of which he'd never be able to atone for. He would argue, whether rationally or not, that he had done so because of the darkness which had plagued his life since the age of three.

But Angel on the other hand.

She was all things good and pure. An innocent who was still learning the ways of the world.

He knew now, that when she had been found fifteen years ago, she had no memory of anything or anyone; including the simple basics of life. She'd had to relearn everything all over again, just as a baby would from birth. Her body might well be of a near forty-five-year-old. But her mind was that of a teenager.

"Angel?"

"What's up?"

"If you need more time to think about your answer, I'll understand. Wilton's passing was very recent after all."

Angel blinked. "Bastion, what in the world are you talking about?"

"My proposal."

"Proposal?"

"Of marriage, Angel." He'd been pretty patient, but now he was simply getting annoyed.

Feeling mischievous, Angel giggled. "I'll give you my answer now if you want, but what the answer ends up being will depend on your answer to my next question."

"What's the question?" This time, *he* was confused. What in the world was she up to?

Angel gave him a sheepish grin and covered her mouth, giving what he could only describe as an almost girlish giggle.

"Can we do it again?" she whispered hopefully between her fingers.

Bastion barked out laughing. Crawling back over her, he slid his arms under her back and ran his hands up over her shoulders, causing her to shiver as he held her close.

"Oh, yeah," he grinned devilishly. "Again, and again and again…"

"Then, yes!"

Chapter 19

Wow...

Is your mind blown yet?

Did you see that one coming?

If you didn't it's okay because, frankly, I didn't either. Not until after the fact anyway. I hadn't gotten a chance to read that far yet into Angel's files and notes. But after hastily skimming through some of her flash drive files when I finally got a chance the morning after, it turns out that it was never meant to be any of the RavenCroft children. Angel was never there for them. Which makes sense because...

Hello!!!

They're all married!

And...did you forget? Regardless of whether or not Bastion RavenCroft had any contact with his two brothers, Rafe and Rourke Blackthorne, he was still, in fact, a triplet. He may have been taken in and adopted by the RavenCrofts but he was a Blackthorne at birth.

Yes, I know there is a fifteen-year age difference between them, but I've heard of worse and that shouldn't matter anyway. They're consenting adults. Besides, Angel's been in love with Bastion for fifteen years.

You're probably sitting there right now thinking, "Vortigern, that doesn't make any sense. How could she possibly have been in love with a man for that long when she'd never met him?"

I wondered that too. After we learned about them...you know...getting married, I found myself snooping a little more thoroughly through her spiral notebooks and I happened to discover the answer to that. Apparently, Angel had toyed with the notion of writing her own story of when she was found wandering through the Rocky Mountains. It would seem her first memory was of the ethereal image of a man she saw when she first woke up or became aware. So she knew what Bastion looked like even before she met him in person for the first time.

Shoot, she had a drawing of him in her drawing pad.

She's actually quite good at drawing too. The portrait is very detailed.

Angel eventually came to know what his name was and where he lived. The knowledge came to her out of the blue one day. She'd just never imagined her daydreams were real. Her late husband, Wilton had always told her she was imagining things and that her dreams were just that – dreams. That such a man couldn't be real and to wipe his image from her mind. But she never could. Over the span of fifteen years, more and more information about Bastion and his family would pop into her head at completely random times, as if being placed there. Once she had thought she might have met him before. That maybe he'd been someone from her past she was trying to remember. Somehow she knew that wasn't the case. The more she learned of him the more she found herself wanting to be with this 'imaginary' man. Which tore her up inside for two reasons.

One, because she had agreed to marry and had married Wilton before she even understood what marriage actually meant and what intimacy was.

And two, because about five years after being found, she was invited to attend a church service, much to Wilton's annoyance. It was there that she finally found answers to at least a few of the questions she'd be struggling with. It was also where she…

-Wait for it…

-Found God and became a born-again Christian.

You didn't see that coming either, did you?

No doubt some of you won't like learning this and will even be offended by the notion of Angel being a Christian woman. Particularly after reading what you've read so far. Because if she's a woman of faith then why on earth would she allow herself to be subjected to the…shall we call it…foreplay Bastion put her through? Some might call it sweet and even a little romantic, others would call it twisted and disturbing. Personally, I think the man was trying to make the night special for her, particularly after what she'd been through and after learning how long she'd been waiting for him.

Not to mention, Bastion may have seen to it that they were married by the standards of man's law –

well, at least as legal as it could be under the circumstances – but what about God's? Most people of faith marry in a church before a priest and, by extension, the eyes of their Lord near an altar.

So everybody's probably crying hypocrite right about now, right?

I'm not going to sit here and try to justify her actions. Christian or not, she is human. Angel had a desire within her heart something fierce and though a forty-five-year-old woman, her mind is that of a fifteen-year-old girl. Where was your head when you were fifteen? For those of you who believe, did you have a full grasp and understanding of the consequences of your actions at such an age? How many poor choices did you make that were against God's will?

And honestly, if Bastion and Angel are meant to be together for some reason – say because God ordained it – then would people of faith still call it a sin? Or, is it simply that His plan is finally coming to fruition, but maybe not necessarily as God would have liked because mankind deviated from His grand plan?

Something to think about.

Personally, I, Vortigern Black can't speak with any authority on Christianity. I never grew up with it myself, though I read some of the Bible as the result of college literature courses that were required. I know I mentioned this before in the second volume, Kayos Effect, but for those who aren't reading the inspirational stories, I'll mention it again.

For the most part, I've always considered myself agnostic, you know? Not really believing and yet, not disbelieving there was a God either way. But I must admit, finding Angel's notes and reading through her thoughts, desires, dreams, and wishes have made me start to ponder on the subject a bit more. I can't help but wonder, what with everything that has been going on in the past couple of months, if there might actually be something to the notion of an Almighty power.

Kalabernus does see demonic shadowy creatures. It stands to reason there could be angels if there are demons. If there isn't a God, then where does Bastion's and Angel's prophetic information come from?

Hhhhmmm. And if there are angels, is it possible that is what Drayke, and now Ariana, are seeing when the bright, white shining light appears?

It makes a body wonder.

Speaking of bodies... I believe there are two still stuck in a panic room.

What?

Did you really think we were done?

Nope. Not yet.

- - -

"When do you think he'll let us out?"

"Don't know, don't care."

Kahner sighed, resting his head against the wall. "I bet Sable has been wondering where I've been all night."

Kalturek glared. He was sure his own wife, Stephanie, thought she knew exactly where he was. She'd be wrong. "This is all your fault; you know? You should have stayed out of it. I could have fathered children by now."

Swearing, Kahner flung a large pretzel twist across the small space between them and hit his brother square in the face with it. Grabbing hold of it angrily Kalturek threw it back, missing his twin by half a foot. The pretzel broke against the wall near Kahner's head.

Kahner snorted. "You always did have lousy aim. And I think we both know full well it wasn't meant to be, Kal." For the first time since they were teenagers, he used his brother's childhood nickname. He only ever seemed to use it when they fought. "Kalabernus isn't wrong, you know," he finished on a softer note

Huffing angrily, Kalturek shoved a chip in his mouth and turned his head away. The determined set to his jaw gave away his unwillingness to believe that yet.

"You're a Sheriff, Kal. *A Sheriff.* You took an oath a long time ago to protect and serve the people of this community. Besides, it's never been in your nature to do such a thing."

Kahner could see his brother's eyes glisten in the darkened room. There was no light but for the soft luminescence of the glow sticks Kalabernus had broken and tossed in the panic room with them before he shut them in. "You would have never considered such a thing if the shadows hadn't been badgering you. And if they were trying to get you to do this then it can't mean any good would come of it."

Staring back at his brother, Kalturek slumped against the cool smooth solid metal wall, knowing both his brothers were right and not liking it. His eyes grew sad, gazing hopelessly down at the bag of chips in his lap. They'd found the snacks a little bit ago when they both awoke. They'd been stashed in the metal chest in the corner of the small room where they'd been trapped for most of the night.

Expelling a heavy breath Kalturek's gaze found his brother's. "Stephanie is going to leave me, isn't she?"

Kahner froze mid-bite. He dropped the pretzel back in the bag then set the bag on the floor next to him. "Yeah, I think so."

"When?"

"I'm not sure but I suspect it will be soon."

Kalturek nodded, struggling to reign in his tumultuous emotions. "I just love her so much..." His voice broke.

"I know. The fact you were willing to go this far tells me as much. But, Kal? Are you sure she feels the same? Would Stephanie do for you, what you tried to do for her?"

Kalturek's jaw trembled, his troubled expression proof that he was having the very same concern.

"Here's the thing I don't understand," Kahner said without warning. "If it was never meant to be you, and if it couldn't be me either like Kalabernus said, then who?"

Both men exchanged thoughtful looks.

"Kalabernus maybe?" Kalturek ventured.

Immediately they both shook their heads.

"Nah," they said in unison.

"Drayke," Kahner supplied.

"What? You think?"

"It's the only thing that makes sense. Sable's expecting triplets, so I already have my three. Kalabernus and Ariana are having triplets too. The shadows were bedeviling you guys so…"

Groaning low in his throat Kalturek angrily thumped at the wooden floor below him in despair.

"If it's any consolation… I wanted it to be you. I know how much you wanted kids of your own."

Exhaling, Kalturek ran his hands through his hair in agitation. "Yeah, well. I guess I'm not having any," he snapped. Pausing, he peered over at his brother worriedly. "What do you think this means for Kalabernus?"

Kahner sighed. "I don't know, Kal. I don't know. There's no way Drayke could have reached her last night. He and Laynie decided to go into Columbia Springs for the night. Besides, he's got no clue what's going on. Unless… Do you think maybe he and Laynie might have gotten pregnant last night?"

"No." Kalturek shook his head. "Somehow I doubt it. I have the feeling Angel was meant to be the mother of them for some reason. And Drayke's a twin, not a triplet, which is why this doesn't make any sense. It almost feels like the shadows have been messing with everyone. Including Angel."

A soft swishing noise had both their heads turning in the direction of the sudden flash of light spilling forth into the dark room. Covering their eyes from the unexpected assault of light, they both found themselves staring up at their brother's hulking frame.

Kalabernus stared back at them, his face one of shock and bewilderment. He just stood there before them, unmoving and seemingly unable to speak.

"Kalabernus? What's the matter?" Kahner asked uneasily.

"You have to see it to believe it." Stepping away from the doorway, concealed by the wall of the dining room, he allowed them room to exit.

The twin brothers exchanged confused and worried glances. What could possibly be up now? Grabbing up their respective snack bags, they gingerly came up off the floor. They each groaned from their injuries and padded barefoot from the panic room. Both men peered back inside briefly as Kalabernus closed the wall over the opening.

"When do you suppose Dad put that in?" Kalturek wondered aloud.

Initially, Kahner shook his head. Then a thought came to him, and his eyes lit up. "You know; I'm betting he did it when he renovated the house."

"You may be right about that," Kalturek responded.

"That would be because he is right," said a familiar male voice from the kitchen.

Stepping from the dining room, the twins gaped openly from the hallway at the sight before them in the kitchen. Their father stood at the stove pulling eggs and bacon from a pan and dividing it between two plates. The menial task he was performing wasn't what had them staring in shock. What had garnered their dumbstruck state of being was seeing their father wearing nothing but pajama bottoms as he cooked for and tended to the woman sitting next to him on a bar stool. She wore nothing but their father's pajama shirt. It was buttoned awfully low, and cascaded down her front, barely covering her to the middle of her legs.

Bastion spoke quietly, his tone cool, almost menacing. "Morning, boys. I understand we had some trouble last night?" He quirked an eyebrow at them in question at their silence then handed one of the plates to Angel who sat silently next to him. "Here you go, Honey, eat up. You're gonna need the energy today."

Angel giggled, a soft smile playing at her lips. Her eyes sparkled back at him. "Thank you," she said shyly. "I sure hope so."

Bastion smiled down at her, bent low, and kissed her gently on the lips.

"Uh, Kalturek? The note we caught her with, in the dining room... Please tell me that was from you," Kahner said suddenly, sounding stricken. It occurred to him then, that if his father had constructed a panic room they hadn't known about, then there might well be other secrets in the house as well. It would explain Angel's fear of him looking at the small model she'd made and how his father was now present within the home when he had supposedly been in Washington.

Kalturek's head spun toward his brother. "I thought it was from you."

Kahner swore, realizing what that meant. Both men looked at each other, exclaiming at the same time in horror.

"Oh, geez!"

"He's been here the whole time?" Kalturek's voice was strained and incredulous.

"The question is where?" Kahner was just as thunderstruck as his brother. He wondered briefly if their dad had any idea what had been going on yesterday. From the look of him, he had a bad feeling he did.

"Where indeed? Wouldn't you like to know?" Bastion gloated with a devilish air. "This should serve as a lesson to you all." His tone became stern. He whacked the spatula in his hand against the counter unexpectedly, causing both men to jump slightly. "I know all and see all in this house," he continued while gesturing around the ceiling, toward the hall, and into the living room.

At that very moment, a very sleepy-eyed Synedra strode into the kitchen, fully dressed and with bags in hand. Following not far behind her was Nathan, sporting a slightly blackened eye and a cut on his chin. Kalturek grimaced.

"We're heading out," Nathan said, giving a slight knowing nod toward Angel. "Congratulations to you both. Let me know if you need help with the celebratory dinner."

"What dinner?" Kalabernus inquired, suspecting he already knew what the celebration would be for.

He'd seen the flash of light glinting from the enormous ring on Angel's left hand.

"You don't know yet, but Synedra and Nathan do. They saw us before you all arrived," Bastion explained with a glint in his eye. Sidling up next to Angel he gazed down at her proudly and took hold of her gently by the waist. "I'd like to introduce you boys to Angela RavenCroft; my new bride and now mother of your half-brothers and or sisters soon to come."

The RavenCroft triplets gaped open-mouthed at the couple, appearing thunderstruck.

"What?"

"How…how…how…?"

"When did this…? *How* did this…? I mean, I know *how*… I just thought…"

"Close your mouth, Kalabernus. And it's impolite to stare everyone." Bastion glanced down at his new bride, noting one of the buttons of her shirt had come undone. He reached over and re-buttoned it for her, a silly grin plastered on his face as he did it. Angel beamed up at him happily.

Becoming slightly awkward at the sight of her father swooning over Angel in her scantily clad state, Synedra hastily walked toward them. Reaching out she gave her father a quick hug, placed a reassuring hand on Angel's shoulder, and then followed her husband as he headed out of the kitchen.

"And Nathan," Bastion called suddenly, causing him to stop near the kitchen doors.

"Yeah?"

"Thanks for trying, Son." Bastion cast an appreciative look towards Kalabernus. "You both did well."

The couple left shortly afterwards, leaving the RavenCroft triplets standing aimlessly and awkwardly in the hallway for varying reasons.

"I'd better find Sable," Kahner spoke first, realizing he had some amends to make with her for not coming to bed last night. He only hoped she'd understand.

"She is upstairs with your kids and Kal," Bastion offered. "You might want to give her some time, though. She's quite upset with you right now. I explained to her the situation, what you were thinking, and what you were trying to do for Kalabernus, but she's still upset and rightfully so."

"And Stephanie?" Kalturek asked, peering around the kitchen hopefully. "Where is…"

"Stephanie is gone," Bastion said shortly.

"Gone. What do you mean gone? Where did she…"

"You know what? I don't know, and I don't really care," Bastion bellowed, his voice rising exponentially as he spoke. Grabbing up his mug, the one Angel had been using the night before, he flung it towards his son in a rage. Kalturek ducked just in time, sending the mug smashing to the hallway floor behind him. "What the hell were you two thinking?" he roared. "Now, I get why you went after her, Kahner. You were trying to help your brother. That was admirable, very admirable indeed. But it wasn't the answer and it was still wrong! I *know* I taught you better than that. The question I have for you, is whether you would have stopped if she told you no?"

"Yes," Kahner responded promptly, somewhat affronted by his father's insinuation. "Angel, rest assured I'd never have forced myself on you."

"I know." She met his gaze, then peered away shyly.

"But you, Kalturek, and that woman of yours," Bastion fumed. "What Stephanie did was not only immoral and dangerous but illegal."

"What is Dad talking about?" Kahner asked his brother, giving him a strange look. Interestingly, Kalturek appeared just as confused

"The tea I was given last night was drugged," Angel explained. "If Nathan hadn't slipped into my mug that powder he made from the root he found in the woods yesterday, then I would have been complacent and compliant to any whim that any of you men would have had."

"That's absurd," Kalturek said quickly. "Stephanie would never…"

"Wouldn't she?" Kalabernus prompted. His haunted, knowing eyes caught Kalturek off guard.

"What do you know?"

"The 'troublesome three' often speak the truth as well as lies. We all know that, especially if it will give them cause to watch someone squirm," Kalabernus responded.

A lead weight dropped in Kalturek's stomach, making him question if what they were saying might actually be true. She wasn't here. Stephanie had left without him. Was she even concerned about where he'd been?

The sound of a fork clattering to the floor drew their attention to the woman sitting with her leg propped on the bar stool. Her face had become visibly pale and her other hand reached for their father, gripping his arm as if for support.

"Oh, no! There was so much more I needed to tell you all before this happened."

The unexpected sound of the doorbell ringing through the house prompted Kahner to escape his father's angry presence, in order to answer the front door.

"Angel?" Bastion said, looking worried.

"I wonder if Synedra and Nathan saw them on the way out," she continued, appearing thoughtful. Her expression was vague and her eyes had dulled.

"Saw who, Honey? Are you okay?"

"Get ready, Bastion. You're really not going like who has come to call."

"Why? Who is it?"

The sound of the door opening and voices speaking in the entrance drew Bastion's attention.

"Eliza?" Kahner could be heard exclaiming in astonishment.

Bastion's eyes flew open in surprise.

"Wait, Kahner, please! Don't shut me out!" the vaguely familiar panicked voice of a woman cried. Her voice carried into the kitchen. She sounded desperate and scared.

"What do you think you're doing here?" Kahner roared angrily in response. The twinge of pain in his voice was unmistakable.

"Don't you…"

"Talk to our…"

"Mother that way!"

Three teenage male voices, carried through the house, shouting down Kahner, as Sable came racing down the front stairs in order to see what all the commotion was about.

Bastion's face registered understanding the instant he gazed into Angel's beseeching eyes. "Oh, no!"

"Yes, I'm sorry. I'd hoped to have more time to talk to you in order to lessen the blow. And I'm afraid…Eliza is also here to stay," Angel said, startling everyone. She turned toward Kalturek then. "It could never have been Kahner either. He's already had his triplets. Eliza never aborted them, she carried them to full term. You thought she had because she was coming out of the procedure room in a gown when you found her. She'd decided at the last minute she couldn't do it."

"I have more grandchildren?" Bastion was stunned. How could he have not known this for all these years?

"Yes," Angel confirmed. "Kahner has spent fourteen years believing he'd lost his children because of your mistake, Kalturek. Twin brother or not, he's liable to kill you, so you better run."

Epilogue

Did I tell you this here twisted tale was messed up or what?

Everyone thought it would be either, Kalturek, Kahner, or Kalabernus. In the end, they were all trumped by Bastion, their own father.

Who knew?

Angel ... that's who.

Life, love, and our choice of faith, or lack thereof, can make things pretty messy.

Period.

There's no getting around it folks.

A person cannot expect to grow up and go through life without a little chaos finding its way within. I know for a fact the author of this here unfortunate lineage had more than a bit of chaotic circumstance occurring within her own life at one point or another. More often than she'd probably care to admit. It's probably why she leans toward stories filled with chaos. As Ms. Christine puts it, we're not meant to slide through existence without some kind of difficulty or hardship. If we think we are or have thus far, then we're either sadly mistaken or due for a bump in the road. No one is able to skate by without experiencing some kind of loss, whether it be family, friends, or a love we believe we cannot live without.

Angel? Or Angela as Bastion has renamed her – though I'll likely continue calling her Angel. It just fits her better; you understand?

Well … she lost thirty years of her life and still has no answers as to why that happened to her. She will likely never get those answers either, for the one man who might have been able to answer them for her, no longer has connections needed in order to gain that knowledge. Not all hope is lost though, for she has at least found the love she thought she might never find.

Does that mean she never loved her late husband?

Nope.

She loved him very much, though it might not seem like it from this story. Angel took the loss much harder than you might imagine for he was the father of her son. He was her hero during a time when she desperately needed a guardian and protector. Their relationship may have held hardships and struggles but that was what made it most worthwhile because amidst all that difficulty they managed to find joy.

And they had a son, little Kal.

What you don't know, and for that matter, not even the RavenCroft patriarch knows, is that Bastion was the one who was supposed to have found Angel on those mountains that night, not her late husband Wilton. Somehow Angel knew that even way back then. What she doesn't know yet, is why he didn't show.

But that's for another story.

And Kahner?

Weeellll, as you may have picked up on so far, it sounds like he's about to hit a boulder on the road, not just a little bump. I imagine it's liable to shatter his world in a mighty bad way.

Love lives on within us, regardless of whether or not we believe we've let it go. I suppose if you believe in that sort of thing…

-Then only God knows why we can't let it go.

The REAL Epilogue

According to the Author
Delaine Christine

As *well-meaning as Vortigern Black is – or at times isn't really – that was not the only shocking cliffhanger to the RavenCroft's and Blackthorne's story as the mysterious individual seems to think. The Real Epilogue, shifts out and back in time, taking place initially in Edinburgh, Scotland not far from where the Blackthorne line originated. It is also where you may pick up on another hidden truth. Dig deep and you shall see it within.*

- - -

The tremor coursed through Rathbourne Blackthorne, putting an abrupt halt to the argument he'd been having with his son, rendering him speechless and immobile at the most inconvenient of times.

-And places.

"Da... Da, are you listening to me or not?"

"Not!" Answering him had been a struggle but was effective in its intent for it made Rourke aware of his duress. The hoarse ragged response drew his son up short, abruptly ending his cantankerous tirade.

Pivoting on the heels of his custom-made size sixteen Oxfords, Rourke twisted about so he could see behind to the elderly man who, but moments before, had been chasing him from the Edinburgh restaurant in his tailored suit. He noted Rathbourne's sharp all-knowing eyes were becoming cloudy and vacant. His aging jowl slackened, and his thinning mouth dropped into a perfect O as he leaned heavily against the blackthorn wood cane he'd had the need to use since his knee surgery.

The thread thin creases in the corners of Rourke's piercing crystal blue irises instantly smoothed with the rapid widening of his eyes when he recognized what was happening to his father. The sudden expressive change likely confused passersby as to his actual age of fifty years for in his current state he now appeared ten years younger.

"Quick, take hold of my shoulder."

Reaching out Rathbourne attempted to do just that with his son's aid. He gratefully allowed his weight to shift into him rather than finding himself dropping to the pavement in humiliation. He was vaguely aware of the protective stance Rourke had taken with him, as the repetitive vision he'd been having replayed within his mind for the sixth time in the past seven days. It was becoming a nuisance

A thin haze outlined the movie-like images he was viewing. Once again he could see the very same intersection with a car waiting at a stoplight in heavy traffic. Within were three children bickering quietly in the back seat while attempting to eavesdrop on the woman in the driver's seat. Her dark head turned suddenly in shock and horror toward the man sitting next to her as she pulled into the intersection when the light turned green. The impact of the on-coming tanker as it ran through a red light and t-boned the car caused the vehicle to flip, pinning the family within.

Leaping from a nearby truck a man with black hair and a goatee in a construction uniform raced toward the vehicle, managing to pull the unconscious woman from the wreckage and dragged her to safety. Hastily moving to head back toward the mangled vehicle his progression was halted when the car exploded. Confusion muddled Rathbourne's mind when the image suddenly appeared to rapidly shift as though time was moving backwards. Another tremor surged throughout his body in the same instant, causing him to shake involuntarily, and his balance to become unsteady. His alarming state and his sons attractive and well-to-do appearance gained the unfortunate attention of a pleasant looking red-headed woman walking to her car. Pulling a cell phone from her purse she quickly stopped at their side in the hopes of being a Good Samaritan to them.

"Is the gent alright? Does he need assistance? I can call someone if you'd like."

Head bowed with one hand clasped on his

father's shoulder as another covered his hand on the cane for support, Rourke barely spared a glance her way.

"Concern yourself not, he overate is all." He indicated the well-touted establishment from which they'd exited. "Be on your way then, *Lass*."

Put off by his dismissive and snobbish response the woman curled her lip in distaste as her eyes flared. His intentional rib had hit its mark for most women of Scotland disliked the so-called endearment. Shoving her phone back into her purse, she stormed off, muttering about aristocratic arses.

Caught up in the unexpected and alarming change in his vision, Rathbourne was unaware of the exchange. He was still seeing an intersection but the scenery around it was different. Where once was a car there was now an older model black Chevy truck with a man sitting in the driver's seat. Next to him were two young boys and in the extended cab were three girls only a couple of years older than them who did not appear happy in the slightest. A similar series of events began to repeat but as the truck pulled into the intersection the vision abruptly ended, causing Rathbourne to blink several times in surprise, and to wonder if they too met the same fate.

"What is it? Was it not the same one as before?" Rourke asked, suspecting something was amiss.

Rathbourne had no doubt his son could sense his distress, for concern was evident in both his tone as well as the features so similar to his own. But for the whitened, thinning hairline, clean-shaven face and twenty-four years age difference, they could have been brothers.

"We must return to the Estate with haste. I must know if he's seen the change too." Hollering at the nearby valet who was looking at them oddly, he demanded his driver and car once again. Before he could chastise him further, Averill, his driver, pulled up in their Mercedes.

"About bloody time," Rourke grumbled.

For once Rathbourne agreed with him.

Forty minutes later they were greeted in the foyer of the Blackthorne Estate upon their return by, Curtis, his long-time butler and Chef.

"I thought to try and call you when it happened, Master Blackthorne, but felt since you would be arriving home soon that you'd prefer receiving the news in person."

Handing his cane off to Rourke briefly, he shrugged out of his jacket and loosened his tie, then hesitated at his butler's words. "Did you just call me Master Blackthorne?"

"Yes." The butler's pause was ever so brief. "I regret to have to inform you, Master Blackthorne, that he passed-on about forty-five minutes ago."

Taken aback by the unexpected news and coincidental timing, Rathbourne hovered briefly where he stood then sat on the settee near the closet doors. At a hundred years of age, his father, Alestair Wilhelm Blackthorne was dead. The man had outlived most of their line by easily over twenty years. He took a moment to allow that to sink in.

Kicking off his shoes his hooded eyes shifted up toward his son who towered over him with an unreadable expression on his face.

"It would seem the bastard finally went to his maker."

"About bloody time," Rourke groused.

Incensed, Rathbourne grabbed for his cane with the intent of smacking him with it. Shifting it out of his reach, Rourke narrowed his gaze upon his father, fully aware of his plan.

"Have some respect, boy!"

"Says the man who just called his own recently deceased father a bastard."

"That's because he *was* a bastard, you idiot. He was born before his parents were wed."

Curtis attempted to intervene, knowing full well where this argument would end for he was well aware they were forever arguing. "If I may, Master Blackthorne..."

"Sir," Rathbourne insisted while shoving his feet into his leather fur-lined slippers. He appeared more agitated than usual.

"Pardon?" Curtis was perplexed by the singular gruff response.

"I much prefer the term, Sir, for I am not now, nor will I ever be anyone's master but *his*." Rathbourne thumbed his finger in the opposite direction of the butler.

Seeing his father had indicated him, Rourke rolled his eyes heavenward with an exasperated sigh. His father had been about as difficult as ever all day.

He wondered briefly if he'd foreseen this was coming then quickly dismissed the notion. Rathbourne had appeared just as surprised as he had been over the news.

"As you wish, Sir." Curtis acquiesced happily, glad to be free of having to ingratiate himself more than necessary. Having to call Alistair 'master' for so many years had always been more than a little bothersome to him. He suspected Rathbourne had always known that. "Before ... Alestair passed, he asked me to pass on a message. He was quite insistent about it, Sir, though I daresay it doesn't make much sense."

"Knowing him, it was likely his last-ditch effort at having a go at me." He knew he sounded grouchy but didn't care. His father had probably died knowing full well he'd be leaving him with more questions than answers. For all he knew it was likely what had 'tickled him to death' as they say, in the first place.

"Uh, Sir?"

"Oh, out with it already."

"Yes, Sir. He wished for me to tell you that it should be a car, *not* a truck. He was very insistent upon that point. He said that a poor choice shattered chaos and that *he* must mend the balance. Not sure quite what he meant by that last part or any of it for that matter, but it seemed awfully important to him, Sir. So much so he made me write it down so I didn't, as he put it, blunder it up." Handing off the scrap of paper with the message to his employer, Curtis assured him that he'd made the necessary calls to arrange for Alestair's removal and imminent burial in the family plot, then excused himself and headed back to the kitchen.

Rathbourne noted the man hadn't bothered with condolences and appreciated him greatly for not prattling on about his loss. The man knew him too well.

Exchanging knowing looks with his son he opened the scrap of paper and re-read his father's last words once again.

"It should be a car, *not* a truck. A poor choice shattered chaos and <u>he</u> must mend the balance." The word 'He' had been underlined several times. "How interesting. Your grandfather said *He*, for once, and not *You*." Rathbourne's eyes suddenly blazed angrily with understanding. Snatching the cane he'd mistakenly left in Rourke's care before he could step too far away this time, he whirled about and cracked it against his son's leg. He didn't care that he was aggravating his own knee after the surgery he'd had the week before. "What the bloody hell did you two do this time? And why was your twin brother wearing a construction workers uniform anyways? Did he sink the horse ranch to nothing in my absence?"

Ripping the cane from his father's grasp Rourke brandished it in the air angrily with one hand while staggering to the settee to sit for the pain in his leg. "*I* didn't do *anything*," he yelled back. "And you're wrongly presuming the construction worker in the vision was Rafe."

Completely flummoxed, and irritated that his son had bested him in getting his cane, Rathbourne straightened his stooped shoulders to his full six-foot, three-inch height and scowled down at him. He'd shrunk an inch over the years which meant Rourke was now taller. He hated that. As a whole, he hated aging in general.

"The man looks just like you," Rathbourne roared. "Who else could it possibly be?"

Rourke fixed his father with a furious glare of his own, wondering at how long it would take him to figure it out. He'd sussed it out the first time he'd had the same vision his father and grandfather had been having. Only he had yet to experience the changes his father spoke of in the car.

"Gee, if it's not me and it's not Rafe but he looks just like us, who else do you *think* it could possibly be, you *idiot*?" He knew he was pushing it, throwing the man's own words back at him like he was, but he was a right tyrant; not much better than his grandfather who had just died. Rourke was quickly becoming fed up for having to live among such hypocrites for so long.

Rourke watched his father intently as the knowledge of his late wife's betrayal finally found its way into his thick skull. The strangled sound that escaped his lips upon realizing what that must mean had Rathbourne clutching at his chest. An excruciating look of horror and pain engulfed his face twisting it up in anguish as he dropped to the floor.

That was unexpected, Rourke mused silently as

one eyebrow rose. He quickly hobbled over to his father to check on him. He appeared to be having a heart attack.

"He's alive? Randulf's alive?" his father choked out, going into shock.

"So it would seem."

"How... how could she? Saphire..." Rathbourne's eyes rolled back into his head.

Rourke growled at the sight of him, heaving a sigh of great frustration. "Oh, *fine!* I'll do for *you* what you never in your life ever bothered doing for *me*." Taking one last look at the man who seemed to have aged twenty years in the last five minutes, he hollered for Curtis and Alestair's nurse to call for an ambulance and promptly disappeared to the study. He knew full well it was best to stay out of their way so they could do what they needed to.

Taking a seat in his father's chair he laid the paper on the desk and stared at it. His expression suddenly softened from its normally hardened shell the more he thought about what his mother, Saphire had done. He should have known this would break him. The man was an arse but he still had a heart. Learning that his so-called loving wife had kept his third son from him and left him to believe he was dead for so many years had to have shattered him.

Shattered chaos.

Could that be what the message meant?

Through the doors of the study he'd left propped open, he could hear Curtis tending to his father along with the live-in nurse that had been hired to tend to his grandfather. They were both exceptionally good at what they did so he wasn't too concerned. Somehow he knew Rathbourne wouldn't go before seeing his son Randulf for the first time in forty-seven years which meant it was time for Rourke to find him. Though after another glance at the paper he suspected he had so much more to tend to than that.

He must amend the balance.

Bloody hell.

Where would his duplicitous conniving mother have taken his 'long lost brother,' and what could Randulf have brought on them all, to have adversely affected the course of time?

A Note From the Author

Thank you for taking the time to read my story. I truly hope you enjoyed it. And if you wouldn't mind... Please be sure to leave a review of Deadly Karisma at amazon.com. I'd love to hear from you! I'd also like to welcome you to experience...

Kayos Know
An Unfortunate Lineage
Volume VI

OR, if you're disinclined toward reading faith-based fiction or are just plain ready to skip to the finale then feel free to skip over everything and go straight to it.

Karisma Kayos: Out of Time
An Unfortunate Lineage Finale
Volume VII
By Delaine Christine

Either way, I hope you're enjoying the series so far!

Delaine Christine

Character List Of Suspects

Vortigern Black - Narrator of the RavenCroft story and a character within. But which one of the following characters lays claim to the pseudonym?

Angel Stryfe (?) – The heroine of this story and an author with the gift of 'knowing' which surpasses Bastions. She is married to Wilton Stryfe and is the mother of little Kal Stryfe (10) who is also gifted with the ability to have dreams of both present and future events.

Kal Stryfe (?) – (Capable of having prophetic dreams) He is ten years old and the only son of Angel Stryfe. His father is Wilton Stryfe.

Wilton Stryfe – He is married to Angel Stryfe and is the father of Kal Stryfe (10).

Bastion RavenCroft – (Can discern a person's thoughts, receives visions of future events, knows things without knowing how or why) Patriarch of the RavenCroft clan and father of the following from eldest to youngest. Triplets: Kahner, Kalturek, Kalabernus. Fraternal twins: Drayke and Mackenzie. And last but not least, the baby of the family, Synedra. He was married once before to the love of his life, the late Inara RavenCroft.

Kahner RavenCroft aka Toni Starck – (Can discern a person's thoughts) Firstborn of triplets, he is now married to Sable RavenCroft and helps his father with the family horse ranch. He will one day inherit the RavenCroft home though at one time he worked undercover for the CIA.

Sable RavenCroft aka Kalysta Radford – (Can discern a person's thoughts, knows things without knowing why) New wife of Kahner RavenCroft. She was formerly married to drug kingpin Lionel Radford for over ten years. She is the mother of Lisa (10), and fraternal twins Adam (7), and Jordon Radford (7).

Eliza RavenCroft - Former wife of Kahner RavenCroft from fourteen years' prior who had presumably aborted Kahner's child.

Kalturek RavenCroft – (Can discern a person's thoughts) The Second-born of triplets, he is married to Stephanie RavenCroft and he is the Sheriff of Loveland County, Colorado

Stephanie RavenCroft - Wife of Sheriff Kalturek RavenCroft, she desperately wants to have and raise a gifted child. She is a Sales Representative at a high-end woman's clothing store.

Kalabernus RavenCroft – (Can see shadowy demonic creatures) Third born of triplets, he is recently married to Ariana Davis and is expecting his first child. Though an artist by trade he is an excellent singer

CHARACTER LIST OF SUSPECTS

Ariana Davis aka Sareena Davis – (Capable of seeing the shadows and the light, knows things without knowing why, receives visions of past events) Recently married to Kalabernus RavenCroft, she originally came from Dalton, Massachusetts posing as her deceased sister Sareena in order to escape a violent and murderous stalker who is now out of the picture.

Drayke RavenCroft – (Can see a bright warm comforting light, Capable of discerning the truth) Mackenzie's fraternal twin and fourth born, he is married to Laynie RavenCroft.

Laynie RavenCroft - Wife of Drayke RavenCroft, she also wants children but it doesn't matter whether they are gifted or not. She owns and runs Laynie's Pizza Emporium.

Mackenzie Funnie (RavenCroft) – (Capable of discerning another person's emotions, occasionally has prophetic dreams) Drayke's fraternal twin and fifth born, she is married to Dr. S.T. Funnie.

Dr. S.T. Funnie - He is the husband of Mackenzie Funnie (RavenCroft) and is an ER doctor at the local Loveland County Hospital.

Synedra Kayme (RavenCroft) – (Capable of discerning ailments in people, can sense when a woman is pregnant.) Sixth born and the baby of the family, she is married to Nathan Kayme.

CHARACTER LIST OF SUSPECTS

Nathan Kayme - He is the husband of Synedra Kayme (RavenCroft), and he is a licensed and practicing private investigator who is co-owns a PI business with his partner.

Angela Powers - Old college roommate and good friend of Ariana Blackthorne aka Sareena Davis. She has a, on-again-off-again boyfriend by the name of Heaton Jones.

Heaton Jones - On again, off again boyfriend of Angela Powers. He's kind of a dead-beat where employment is concerned as he's always in-between one job or another.

Avery Shenanigan - Bartender at Shenanigans and little-known owner of said business. But now *you* know. Can you keep a secret?

Agent Ricardo Pegueros - He works for the Central Intelligence Agency (CIA) in undercover operations, specializing in information retrieval.

Lionel Radford - Younger brother to Kobi Radford, he and his brother are drug cartel kingpins with brutal tempers. Lionel is the former husband of Kalysta Radford aka Sable RavenCroft and is the father of Lisa (10), Adam (7), and Jordan Radford (7).

Kobi Radford - Older brother of Lionel Radford. He heads the drug cartel left to them by their father Di'ktrah Radford.

Troublesome Three – Encompasses three shadowy demonic creatures, or fallen angels, by the names, Zalman, Fallen, Veranke.

Author Delaine Christine

Who is this lady,
who writes what she knows?
And what part of this warped story
is her, do you suppose?

For sure she's an author
much like Angel, one can see
With a spouse who did serve
in a North American country.

And though her eyes change color
dependent upon her mood,
she'll skip the hot toddies
for a dark coffee, hot and brewed.

But add some amaretto
and she'll be doing just fine
while writing one of her books
In the evening way past nine.

For more about the series
and the author

vortigernblack.com

Or to Contact the Author:
delainechristine15@gmail.com